LALLAN SWEETS

Srishti Chaudhary was born and raised in Delhi, and studied English literature at Lady Shri Ram College and creative writing at the University of Edinburgh. The author of *Once upon a Curfew*, she also has a series of short stories to her credit. She has written for BBC Travel and *National Geographic*, among other publications. She wishes she had a cool signature, the apparent prerequisite to being a writer. For more about her, you can visit www.srishtichaudhary.com.

PRAISE FOR *ONCE UPON A CURFEW*

'Simple story, crisp language and powerful narration'—*India Today*

'An engaging, light-hearted read packed with strong characters that keeps the reader hooked to the story'—*Hindustan Times*

'Srishti Chaudhary does something altogether novel. The book is quite compelling'—Ajoy Bose, author

'A love story that simmers just below the surface until it erupts into a tangled mess of confusion and fear'—Women's Web

Lallan Sweets

Srishti Chaudhary

An imprint of Penguin Random House

EBURY PRESS

USA | Canada | UK | Ireland | Australia
New Zealand | India | South Africa | China | Singapore

Ebury Press is part of the Penguin Random House group of companies
whose addresses can be found at global.penguinrandomhouse.com

Published by Penguin Random House India Pvt. Ltd
4th Floor, Capital Tower 1, MG Road,
Gurugram 122 002, Haryana, India

First published in Ebury Press by Penguin Random House India 2020

Copyright © Srishti Chaudhary 2020

All rights reserved

10 9 8 7 6 5 4 3 2

This is a work of fiction. Names, characters, places and incidents are either the
product of the author's imagination or are used fictitiously and any resemblance
to any actual person, living or dead, events or locales is entirely coincidental.

ISBN 9780143450290

Typeset in Adobe Garamond Pro by Manipal Technologies Limited, Manipal

Printed at Repro India Limited

This book is sold subject to the condition that it shall not, by way of trade
or otherwise, be lent, resold, hired out, or otherwise circulated without the
publisher's prior consent in any form of binding or cover other than that in
which it is published and without a similar condition including this condition
being imposed on the subsequent purchaser.

www.penguin.co.in

This is a legitimate digitally printed version of the book and therefore might not
have certain extra finishing on the cover.

For my father, who bought me books and showered on me the kind of love and encouragement most people can only dream of

Preface

A huge crowd waited outside Lallan Sweets, cheering and yelling, 'Lalaji ke laddoo! Lalaji ke laddoo!'

Lalaji walked into the shop, a huge smile on his face, raising his hand as if he were a superstar. He held a bag in which was hidden the secret of Siyaka, the reason why all the people had gathered, as they did almost every weekend. He went into the room and locked it from the inside, even as people's eyes brimmed with fascination.

They muttered about the secret of the magic ingredient, their faces aglow with curiosity. Seconds turned to minutes and, after a while, Lalaji emerged from inside, sweat on his face, and continued his performance, folding his hands in a big thank you. The crowd broke into applause and the chants grew louder: 'Lalaji ke laddoo, Lalaji ke laddoo . . .'

Chapter 1

'Sale, sale, sale!' I yelled over the din as children rushed out of a school the moment it was two and the school bell rang. 'Sale only till tonight, at Ultimate Mathematics Tuition Centre! Twelve classes for the price of ten!'

I forcibly handed out pamphlets to the children hurrying out, my arms moving left and right mechanically. Most of them took it, happy that school was over, while the others pulled faces until I glared at them.

'Math classes, tuition classes!' I yelled out. '*Dus ke* rate *mein baara*, math *ka darr gaya saara*!'

'I don't want this, Didi,' a bespectacled boy said. 'I don't need math tuitions.'

'*Abbe o*,' I sized him up and said, 'everyone needs math tuitions. Do you know what a tough paper they are setting this year? Where are you doing your practice papers from, huh? I read every question from R.D. Sharma, R.S. Agarwal and previous year papers, and use them to set model papers. Now go and show this to your mummy!'

Once all the pamphlets were given out and the last of the children had waved goodbye from their rickshaws, I put my bag around my shoulders and kick-started my Kinetic, riding over the bumpy road, speeding towards Batti Chowk. As I parked right outside Lallan Sweets, the smell of hot kachoris wafted towards me. I walked through the glass doors which still gleamed, although it had been fifteen months since they were installed, and went to my mother who sat tallying the receipts behind the counter.

'Mumma, I am still at twenty-two registrations,' I said, 'but if I just get seven or eight more, we will be done for the year.'

I was happy to note that she looked pleased, although she hadn't looked up from the receipts. I sat on the stool next to her but got up almost immediately as a customer walked in and asked for a kilo of laddoos.

'Which laddoo do you want?'

'Which else,' the man said raising his hands in a come-on gesture, 'your famous ones, Lallan ke laddoo.' I could see him eyeing the inviting, round sweets.

'Lallan ke laddoo, yes,' I said impatiently, 'but boondi or besan?'

'There is an option between boondi and besan?'

'Yes.'

'Whichever one has the magic ingredient!'

'*Arre*, both have the magic ingredient. Just tell me if you want besan or boondi.'

'I don't know, my sahab just said Lallan ke laddoo. Let me go back and check.'

I sat back down to observe my mother. She looked tired today, the greys in her hair looking even greyer, the wrinkles on her face running deeper. But the smirk lines at the end of her lips, I was glad to notice, were still twitching.

'Boondi,' the man said decisively when he came back, and I got up to enter his order and cut him a receipt, yelling out to Pyaare Lal to pack the laddoos.

'Kachoris smell nice,' he said. 'Can I have one of those too?'

I cut him another receipt without answering and told Pyaare Lal to pack a kachori as well.

'Is there place here to sit and eat?' the man asked and I shook my head, to which he bowed politely and left after collecting his order. I put the cash into the drawer.

'So,' my mother said, 'something important is to be discussed tonight, I was told. Make sure Taru is home too, I was told.'

I looked at her blankly. 'What? If Pappu Uncle tries to suggest one more time that I get married, I will—'

'I don't think it's about that,' my mother replied coolly. 'It's something important.'

I wasn't sure whether to be happy or sad about the fact that my mother didn't consider my marriage an important issue. I didn't have issues with getting married, but I absolutely wouldn't leave it to Pappu Uncle, who would definitely take on the responsibility of arranging a match for me in the absence of my own father. My mother had told me to bring home a suitable boyfriend before Pappu Uncle started parading boys in front of me. 'Even if you don't really marry him later,' she had added slyly.

Of course I would love to bring home a boyfriend to keep Pappu Uncle away from this marriage business once and for all. But how? I couldn't even call Sahil my boyfriend yet, let alone bring him home to ward off marriage proposals.

Sahil, I was quite proud to say, was known to have the most fashionable haircuts in town; after Beckham and Zidane, people would say, it was Sahil who sported the trend. But that was not all Sahil wanted to be known for: I will not rest in life, he had been repeating for the past few months, until people know me only as DJ Buddy.

Struggling to keep the contempt out of my tone, I had asked him as sweetly as it is possible to ask a man obsessed with being a DJ, why.

'So I can play at a music festival in Europe one day, Tara,' he had replied with a far-off look on his face. 'I will be a DJ in Europe and the world will know my name.'

If you ask me, it had all started when Sahil had shifted to Delhi for his post-graduate course. One year of the capital city's fancy parties and nightclubs had turned his head, and instead of studying for the service exams, as his parents wanted him to, Sahil was convinced that he'd make the greatest DJ alive. This posed a huge problem in my plan. How was it possible to bring him home to my family when all he wanted to do was press some buttons and play music that made people drink and dance? I could already imagine Pappu Uncle saying with a derisive, hurt look, 'We'd rather you marry a *band-wallah* . . .'

Not that Sahil was any more eager to meet my family. He had told me straight up, his chin held high and eyes shut, 'Tara, I am sorry, but I have a duty to myself to follow my dream. Before that, I cannot make any promises to you or someone else.' This even though we had already spent many nights in his car parked in a dark corner by the stream, on the other side of which was Jay Mangla Dhaba. And while I appreciated his stance, it was extremely impractical for me. Who was going to help me run Ultimate Mathematics Tuition Centre and expand Lallan Sweets? Definitely not a man who wanted to change his name to Buddy.

I had opened Ultimate Mathematics Tuition Centre three years ago. I had seen how many schoolchildren needed help with solving even simple equations. What I had in mind was a thriving centre with multiple classes at the same time, running practice tests and holding activities. And then there was my vision for Lallan Sweets, which had far more hurdles. I wasn't even sure if I would ever be told what the magic ingredient was.

That night at dinner, the conversation came around to the magic ingredient. We were eating rajma-chawal at Pappu Uncle's, which Aunty had made. I sat next to Lalaji, my grandfather, who always sat at the head of the table, while my cousins Mohit and Rohit sat on either side of their mother. Aunty turned to her sons often to check if they wanted anything more to eat. I often glared at Rohit and Mohit, just to rile them up and see the frenzy in their eyes behind their glasses. My mother sat next to Pappu Uncle, slightly stiff.

'I had to go to the doctor again today,' Pappu Uncle remarked, crunching on cucumber as he spoke, 'difficult situation, quite difficult. Cholesterol very high again. He suggested a check-up immediately, to see how much blockage.'

Aunty nodded sympathetically as he spoke.

'But you're always having laddoos, Uncle,' I said. 'I've caught you so many times, stuffing them into your mouth.'

Pappu Uncle made a pitiful face and picked at the vegetables on his plate. 'What should I do, you tell me, Beta?

Even I feel like eating good things, like you all! How much of this *ghas-fus* should I eat?'

I spooned rajma-chawal into my mouth to stop myself from replying. Lalaji merely took a gulp of water and so Pappu Uncle went on.

'Very hard, life these days. Not like old times, Lalaji. In those times, all these problems were not there—just eat your roti with some achaar, sattoo and lassi, and sleep in peace! Not like these days, always worrying about one thing or the other. Who will sit at the shop today? Are all the bills adding up? Arre, that scooter must not park in front of the shop. So many troubles this modern life brings with itself.'

I thought it was rich of Pappu Uncle to mention these issues; he had his own job and wasn't involved in taking care of Lallan Sweets. Lalaji was nodding now though, and I saw Pappu Uncle, now encouraged, continuing more excitedly.

'Take care of children, their education, their marriage, their houses . . . yes, life is very complicated these days. I have so many duties on my head, actually both Lalaji and I. Of course, I became a clerk, got a secure government job, but for everyone it's not like that. My brother was able to take care of the shop until . . . God bless his soul. Point being, I was secure. Now I've to set Rohit and Mohit, get our Taru married . . .'

I looked up, my eyes narrowed. 'Pappu Uncle, please. How many times have I told you? Worry about Rohit and Mohit, not about me.'

'Arre, it's not like that. I am the elder one, I have to think about all your futures, make sure you find a good husband—'

'No, you don't have to find me a husband. I will find one myself!'

To Pappu Uncle, it seemed as if I hadn't even spoken. He went on, 'Lalaji, I think it's time we settle some matters. I don't know how long I will hang on, you know.'

He looked perfectly robust to me.

Lalaji was now picking at his raita and I could see that he was going over what Pappu Uncle had said. My mother apparently had noticed it too, as she suddenly spoke up.

'What do you have in mind, Bhaisahab, *Bhabhiji*?'

Aunty shook her head innocently, acting as if it was Pappu Uncle who took a call in these matters.

'What can I have in mind, Bhabhiji?' Pappu Uncle said, looking upwards. 'Whatever happens in the end will be by the will of God. But I do think, Lalaji, it is time to settle the matter of Lallan Sweets.'

I immediately looked towards Lalaji. He was still moodily picking at his food and had obviously expected this suggestion. I opened my mouth to say something but my mother widened her eyes at me and gave the slightest shake of her head. I stopped.

'*Dekhiye*, Lalaji,' Pappu Uncle went on. 'Lallan Sweets is the most traditional and popular mithai shop in all of Siyaka, and by God's grace, we will keep on doing the good work. But those who don't grow get left behind. It's the rule of business. We need to grow, make Lallan Sweets larger than ever, and for that reason I would like to suggest that we buy the shop next door. And when the time calls for it, we expand.'

It was now time for me to widen my eyes, but Pappu Uncle, in the flow, refused to stop. 'So I ask you now, Lalaji, to leave the fate of these children up to me. The best way to settle everything is that Lallan Sweets be left to Rohit and Mohit. And for Taru, I will find a very good home for her.'

A babble erupted as soon as Pappu Uncle finished. Everyone had something to say. Everyone except Rohit and Mohit, who simply looked at each other and went on eating rajma-chawal. Aunty broke into hysterical justifications for Pappu Uncle's propositions, Pappu Uncle sought to further strengthen his stand, my mother demanded reasoning and clarifications, and I of course could stand none of it.

'How can you talk of my marriage without asking me? How can you plan to send me off so that I have nothing to do with Lallan Sweets? I have as many plans for it as you. I am as good at selling the laddoos as anybody else! And I already have twenty-two registrations for Ultimate Mathematics Tuition Centre. I am fully capable of standing on my own two feet, Lalaji! I want to know the magic ingredient!'

As soon as I mentioned the magic ingredient, everything else was forgotten. Every member of the family went on to elucidate why they should know the magic ingredient.

After a few minutes of this bickering, Lalaji got up from the table and simply walked back to his room, leaving his dinner on the table. We called out to him but each of us was too busy fighting to actually convince him to come back. I realized this and fell silent. All of this was so unfair, every single thing about it. Just because my father died a long time ago didn't mean that his brother could claim that my mother and I had played no part in setting up Lallan Sweets. We had toiled as much, if not more, to sell Lallan ke laddoo in Siyaka, spreading the word about a magic ingredient, telling everyone that nobody knew what it was, except of course Lalaji.

But what was even more infuriating was that Pappu Uncle didn't want me to play any role in the future of Lallan Sweets because I was a girl. How could I bear it quietly that Pappu Uncle wanted to cut me and my mother out of it and hand over the reins to Rohit and Mohit so that he and his family could live happily ever after? Well, I had news for him: I was ten times more capable than Rohit or Mohit at managing Lallan Sweets, and I would prove it by convincing Lalaji to tell me the magic ingredient. I mean, did I not laugh off their attempts at bullying me all their lives? Did I not beat them in every Maths exam ever, much to the chagrin of their parents? Did I not puncture their bicycle tyres whenever they got out of line? Sitting there arguing at the table would do nothing. I needed to speak with Lalaji, alone.

'Lalaji?' I called out, knocking softly at his door. 'Can I come in?'

'I'll speak to you tomorrow, Taru,' he said. I bowed my head and walked away. I felt bad for the way we had behaved—all of us pouncing on Lallan Sweets when Lalaji had spent his whole life building it. I didn't know what else to do.

Lalaji always started the story the same way. 'At that time, Siyaka was still a town and not a city,' he would begin, 'when there was nothing to do but sit outside our houses and stare at the stars in the night. We could see them clearly then, you know, there was no electricity. The Raj had just ended and we had made the terrible journey from Pakistan, having to leave behind our shop in Anarkali Bazaar.'

This was the point where he would excitedly reveal why it was called Lallan Sweets. 'My nickname was Lallan, because I was such a *lallu*, such a dunce. Everyone would say, "Arre o, Lallan", and so the shop was named Lallan Sweets. My father died soon after we moved here. It was up to me to make sure that his dream of the mithai shop came true, the dream that we had left behind in Anarkali Bazaar. I set up Lallan Sweets and the rest, as they say, is history.'

It really was one of the important moments in Siyaka's history. From a small little *halwai* to the glass-panelled shop it was today, the key reason for Lallan Sweets' propelling to success was the magic ingredient. And in my opinion, the real magic was that while the whole city knew that Lallan ke laddoo had the magic ingredient, nobody except Lalaji knew what it actually was. Not his son. Not his grandsons. Not even his beloved granddaughter.

Shops had mushroomed around Lallan Sweets because that was where most of the town spent its evenings. Lallan ke laddoos were the most delicious laddoos in town and still are.

How could Pappu Uncle then expect me to bow out of such a legacy? Marry some idiot who neither knew nor cared about Lallan Sweets or Ultimate Mathematics Tuition Centre, and forever pave the way for Rohit and Mohit to live their lives out as kings of Siyaka once the magic ingredient was finally revealed to them?

I sometimes wondered if my father knew what it was. My mother told me that he was always kind and patient, very invested in the shop, and Lalaji's right hand. Lalaji trusted him with everything related to the shop. When he died, it was twice a blow to Lalaji, as he had not just lost a son but also his business confidante.

I didn't remember much of him though. There were, however, some childhood memories that I always carried—walking with him by Dima Lake, holding his hand, going to eat an ice cream, buying a toy car from the shop in the town. Yet, every time I think of him, it's like trying to catch sand through open fingers.

I wanted to talk to Lalaji about all this but was too apprehensive to approach him then. In the past couple of years he had grown quieter, receding into his own thoughts in the presence of too many people. It often seemed like he might be falling asleep in the middle of all those people. At moments like these, I felt sorry for him.

I decided to take a walk. There were many things I liked about Siyaka, but the summer breeze was my favourite, what I thought of when I thought of home and Siyaka. The gruelling heat of the sun was made far more bearable by the light wind. In the evenings, chairs and charpoys would be put out in the verandah and the kulfi-wallah would have a roaring business. Soft murmurs could be heard from within houses as everyone sat together after dinner to talk about their day. 'It's always a good time in Siyaka,' the line from a tourism campaign for the city always seemed true at that time of the day.

In the recent years, more and more tourists had started coming to Siyaka, but they would generally gather in the city, concentrated in the centre, watching the well-maintained Victorian buildings in fascination, starkly different from the other towns and cities in the region. In school, we had always laughed at such people, remarking that they did not know the real Siyaka, that there was more to it than the centre, the fort and Dima Lake. The real Siyaka lay in the hearts of the people who lived on the edges of the city, taking walks at night, in their gentle nature and easy manner of talking and, of course, in Lallan ke laddoo.

Surbhi Didi, from whom I had been getting a haircut for the past seven years, lived at the end of my street. Each time she would tell me the style was the latest from Dilli, but my hair would end up looking the same. Yet, it was agreed that all the modern beauty parlours paled in front of hers. Beside her lived Dua-*waali* Aunty from whom my mother got all her suits stitched, almost as if it were a way of life. On the other side of the city's centre was Jay Mangla Dhaba where all of us would go to eat once a year, sit right by the river and order the same food each time: tadka chicken, fresh fish fry, black dal and tandoori naan.

I thought about walking to Sahil's house to see what he was up to, but then I remembered that he'd most likely be practising how to be DJ Buddy, which I couldn't deal with right now. I walked past the big field where the kho-kho championship took place every year. By mid-April, it would be the season for it. I relished the thought of watching some amazing matches. I had been one of the best players in my time, and the team I was in had won the cup five times.

I turned around and headed home. It was quieter now. Most of the people sitting in their verandahs had gone back inside and the lights had been switched off. I slowed down as the peach walls of my home came into view. My feet dragged against the road as I focused on the crickets buzzing.

I noticed the silhouette of a man standing outside our gate and was about to call out in alarm, before he turned around. Even in the darkness, I recognized him.

'Nikku!' I yelled.

Chapter 2

His ears still stuck out.
When we were in school, Nikku's ears were an easy target for every teacher. In fact, they pulled his ears so much that Nikku spread the story that his ears had got so big because they were pulled by aggressive teachers. But floppy as they were, I always found his ears adorable.

The rest of him was different though. He was taller than when I had last seen him, and had a bigger built. He wore a loose T-shirt and shorts that revealed lean legs. His calf muscles were taut and his knees looked slightly scraped.

Why was I thinking about his legs at all? I was glad that my own legs were hidden beneath my pants and kurta. I was aware of my too-loose ponytail, random strands of hair ducking out.

'Taru Taneja *moti hai*,' he said in a sing-song voice, walking towards me. My smile turned into narrowed eyes. He pretended to clear his throat and began again:

Taru Taneja *moti hai*
Uski naak choti hai
Naak mein kuch kaala hai
Uske dada lala hai!

'I will kill you,' I said as Nikku stood right in front of me, playfully mocking my nose and calling me fat. It was hard to look serious about my threat with the grin that wouldn't stop spreading across my face. We were nine again, standing outside my house, measuring with footsteps how far his home was from mine. It turned out to be 153 steps from mine to his and 157 from his to mine—how was it possible? The mystery remains to this day. Now he was smiling as widely as he always did, especially like the phase where his milk teeth came loose and people called him cute. He smiled wider as he looked into my eyes and I suddenly remembered how strikingly brown they were. Sometimes, after looking into them, I felt like I had eaten orange-flavoured Poppins.

'How are you?' I asked, suddenly breathless. He bent down to give me a hug. I put my arms around him, and now it definitely wasn't like we were nine again. At nine, we were skittish if even our fingers brushed against each other.

'Taru Taneja,' he repeated, and I remembered how he loved saying that, calling me Taru instead of Tara. All through school, the teachers who would be fed up of us would yell 'Taru Taneja' in exasperation.

'Nikku Sabharwal.'

'I hoped to find you wandering outside.'

I couldn't think of anything clever to say in return, so I just asked him, 'When did you arrive?'

'Just this evening.'

'And you're coming straight from—'

'Bangalore.'

'Can't believe I met you, just like this.'

Nikku shook his head, his eyes shining. 'I knew it. I knew I would find you roaming outside.'

'You would always come after me when I would go out for a walk with Lalaji.'

Nikku raised his eyebrows, pouting. 'Wouldn't you say it was the other way round, Taru? I could almost see you struggling to ask Lalaji if you could join me instead of walking with him.'

I giggled. It was true. Whenever I'd go out with Lalaji for a walk and see Nikku, I'd be itching to run to him. But I couldn't let Nikku know. It was time for revenge.

In a dramatic gesture, I clapped my hand over my mouth. He stopped in his tracks and asked me what had happened.

I took a nice long pause before answering, making fun of his ears.

Doodh mein paani ghol raha hai,
Saara Siyaka bol raha hai
Nikku bada beimaan hai,
Uske haathi jaise kaan hai!

Nikku burst out laughing and I felt happiness bubbling up inside me. He asked if I was still good at math and I asked him if he was still that bad. We sat together on a bench and I told him all about how Ultimate Mathematics Tuition Centre had grown from three girls sitting in the drawing room of my house to a tuition centre where a new batch began every July. His eyes twinkled as he listened to me. The twinkle used to be my favourite thing.

When the crickets grew louder, we knew it was time to say goodbye.

'What are we doing tomorrow though?' Nikku asked, grinning.

I looked at him in surprise, but then smiled. 'The usual?'
'The school one, you mean?'
'Ganne ka juice, aloo patty, then orange ice cream.'

Nikku laughed in delight and I wondered if he still felt the same way about these things.

'Can you still break a ganna?' I asked him curiously, surprised that he would doubt my ability to deal with a sugar cane.

'Of course I can. I will show you tomorrow, Taru Taneja. You think just because you've been here longer you are the queen of Siyaka?'

I leant closer to him and had he been a little shorter we would have been face to face, but he bent his head, his arm around the bench. I remembered how he would bend his head like that each time he lost a badminton match.

'Nothing *makes* me the queen of Siyaka,' I said. 'I was *born* the queen. You seem to have forgotten a lot, Nikku-Tikku.'

He suppressed a snigger. 'We will see about that.'

I woke up the next day thinking about Nikku. How long would he stay? Memories of him flooded my mind. It was a while before I remembered the dinner table conversation and how Lalaji had retired to his room. I hurried towards the bathroom to get ready. When I went out, Mumma was reading the newspaper on the divan, her morning tea done and dusted.

'Do you know Nikku is back in town?' I asked her before I could stop myself.

My mother looked up in astonishment. 'What? Seriously? Your Nikku-Tikku? Sabharwal's son?'

'Yes.' I was pleased to see the smile on her face.

'Oh, how he used to trouble me, that Nikku,' my mother started off. 'You and Nikku both. Chucking golgappas at people going past, teachers always calling and complaining from school, Pappu Uncle always catching you up to some mischief and giving me an earful about it.'

'Yet you never made me stop,' I said, peeling a banana.

'Of course not! Stop children from being children! Thank God Nikku was around to turn you into a smart kid, otherwise you too would have ended up like Mohit–Rohit; these Taneja genes are like this. What are children without their mischief and sparkle? Pappu Uncle would always interfere and say things like, "Is this right for a girl of her age to run around with a boy", "What will the neighbours say?" I never cared though, I like Nikku . . .'

I ate the banana slowly as my mother spoke. If I really were to take a walk down memory lane right now, I wouldn't know where to begin. I was slightly nervous at the prospect of seeing him again, and I think my mother guessed as much. But she didn't say anything and went back to her newspaper, asking me to invite him home later. My real concern right now was Lalaji, and if he was willing to talk to us.

Our house was connected to Pappu Uncle's, where Lalaji also lived, by one verandah—where I had spent many summer afternoons fighting Mohit and Rohit. Back when my father was still alive, my mother would tell me, he had campaigned hard for the comfort of a separate home. 'One of the smartest things your father did,' my mother would say. 'Pity it didn't happen with Lallan Sweets.'

When I went to Lalaji's room, he was not there. I looked around, hoping to find a clue about his whereabouts, but his room was the same—the old divan in the corner, some books on the bookshelf behind, his rocking chair on the side and a steel almirah. I noticed that the diary he kept by his bed was gone too, and the hookah behind his bed was unlit. I gave his room one last look and came out to see Mohit and Rohit stuffing their faces with aloo-poori at the dining table.

I nodded at them, asking if they knew where Lalaji was, but they just shook their heads.

'Arre, Taru,' Aunty said, gesturing for me to sit, 'come and sit, have some aloo-poori. You're becoming so thin.'

'I'm fine, Aunty. I already had breakfast,' I said.

'You and your mother's breakfasts! Who will look at you and say you're a girl from the Lallan Sweets family? The daughter of a family that owns a sweet shop and standing lanky and thin like a hanger!'

'She's trying to get thin for her boyfriend,' Mohit snorted. I ignored him and shook my head at Aunty, smiling, and quickly waved goodbye lest I run into Pappu Uncle. I didn't bother saying bye to Mohit and Rohit, but I did glare at them. There was a time when we had been close, but years of rivalry and petty competition had made us mildly hostile and suspicious of each other.

I looked at my Kinetic parked outside and wondered if I should take it out or go back inside and wait for Nikku to turn up and act cool about it. Before I could decide, I heard him walk up behind me. His face broke into a smile, but before the situation of an awkward greeting arose, I turned around.

He was wearing jeans and a white T-shirt. It looked as if he had just taken a bath because the T-shirt was slightly wet around his neck.

'So,' he said, 'are you ready to show me around? I bet I still know more than you about the city, even though I've barely been here for years.'

'What do you even think of yourself, *Mister?*'

'You've got yourself a really sweet ride there, though,' he said, eyeing my Kinetic Honda that was gleaming under the sun. I beamed proudly. 'But are you sure you can handle it?'

I started walking away in a huff, but he caught me by the wrist. 'I'm kidding! Come on, Taru, you're already losing . . .'

I narrowed my eyes at him again and wordlessly started up the Kinetic. He sat behind me, still sniggering, and placed his hands on my waist, lightly at first, and asked, 'Do you mind if I hold on tight? It's just that I'm not sure if I can trust your driv—'

I accelerated at that point, making sure to hit a bump on the road.

We munched on the aloo patty. When Nikku got some crumbs down the front of his white T-shirt, I brushed them off laughing.

'I did it on purpose,' he laughed and I told him that I didn't believe him. Sadly, we couldn't find the man selling ganne ka juice, although Nikku did suggest that we head over to Nathu's farm and get a few out, to which I shook my head. I didn't know if Nikku would actually be able to break the ganna; his long years in Bangalore might have made him forget the ways of Siyaka.

'And do you remember there used to be the place where we would play *pithu*?' I asked. 'That one time when we were playing after school and you threw the ball so hard at the stones, straight at Mohit's face, breaking one of his teeth!'

'How your aunty ran after me that day,' Nikku said darkly, 'with the *jhaadu* in her hands . . . I was sure she would hit me with that broom.'

Taru giggled. 'I distracted her as best as I could.'

We finished our patty and walked further ahead, stopping at the empty park where a few boys were playing cricket in the dust.

I saw him smiling as he watched, his arms behind his back. For a while, neither of us said anything. The clouds were beginning to clear up and very soon I was sweating. I tied my hair up into a tight knot and readjusted the strap of my bag.

'22*va* Vishal Jai Maa Bhagwati Jagaran,' I read from the great hoarding in the maidan.

Nikku laughed loudly this time, throwing his head back. 'Those were my favourite, Taru. My favourite nights with you.'

I looked down and smiled, not knowing what to say. We were the stars of the annual *jagaran*, where we would stay awake the whole night as bhajans and prayers went on. When we were younger, they would always dress us up in costumes, and mostly Nikku and I would be Krishna and Radha. But once we were old enough to get out of it, Nikku and I would sneak up on unsuspecting people in the jagaran and trouble them. Before even half the jagaran was over, people would start to get sleepy and start taking naps whenever they got a chance.

It was amazing, being given so much more time with friends than the usual two hours in the evening. We would hop from one point of the jagaran pandal to another, gorging on golgappas and jalebis all night.

'And look, there is Manchanda, the new sweet shop. They are trying to give competition to Lallan Sweets . . .' I pointed out to Nikku.

We walked back to the Kinetic and he sat behind me again. I decided to take him to Dima Lake. But before I could start my scooter, someone on the road recognized him and he got off to greet them. Little, sweet Nikku, everyone used to call him. I could see he was still like that, laughing and polite. They used to say he was soft, keeping me company all the time instead of the boys who spent their evenings beating the cows and bullying younger boys.

Later, we rode off to Dima Lake and I noticed how his hands no longer held me by the side of my waist, instead they were locked around it. I straightened up, ignoring the pang in my stomach. He seemed completely at ease though and looked around at the city, as if trying to take it all in.

We now sat at the edge of Dima Lake, under the shade of a tree, with Nikku throwing stones into the water—the flat ones like a Frisbee, so that they would flip over the lake, and the others as far as he could.

'How long are you here for? You didn't answer me last night,' I asked him.

He looked at me once and threw a couple of more stones into the water.

'I don't know, Taru. I knew everyone would be asking me this question, but I don't know. I quit my job. I had been working every single day after finishing engineering, and suddenly I realized that I didn't know why. I didn't understand the point of any of it.'

'What do you mean?'

He shrugged. 'I guess I just feel a little disoriented, a little faithless.'

I watched quietly as a couple of ducks swam along the edge of the lake. The leaves rustled and I felt a light breeze on my face.

'Should have stuck to Sabharwal Stationers, huh?' I asked.

Nikku laughed again. 'Stay here in Siyaka and I will build you the best stationery shop in the city,' he imitated his father, his hands on his waist. 'You will live out the rest of your life a happy man.'

I laughed along too as I remembered this phase, and then later when Nikku's father was convinced that photography was the future and nothing was more lucrative than a photo studio.

'Can you imagine how things would have turned out if I had stayed here in Siyaka? I would have remained stupid, not knowing anything of the world outside.'

Affronted, I raised my eyebrows. It was classic Nikku to say something like that. 'What do you mean? You think just because I never went away from Siyaka I am stupid?'

'No, that's not what I meant at all. I meant, for me, I needed to go out, I couldn't have stayed here, I knew that I had to go out and see the world.'

I nodded at him and looked away, trying to fight off the wave of indignation that came over me. He always spoke about going out there as if the rest of us were lazy idiots to not want to do the same as him, as if our minds were smaller.

'You turned out completely fine, Taru Taneja,' he said, almost as if reading my thoughts. 'It's a battle I had, or still have, with myself. I'm so proud of what you have done, building a name for yourself, Ultimate Mathematics Tuition Centre. But my mother always wanted me to go, she told me to go and make a big man out of myself, in Delhi or Bombay.'

I still didn't look at him, continuing to stare at the lake instead. It was that time in the afternoon when everything fell quiet. He looked towards me once more.

'I'm sorry I didn't keep in touch,' he spoke abruptly.

I swallowed my tears. 'You said you would call every week, but you even stopped writing nice letters after a point.'

Out of the corner of my eyes I saw him hang his head. 'I'm really sorry.'

Of course I wasn't going to forgive him. Years and years of broken promises. I simply got up and ignored whatever he said, putting on a bright smile and walking towards the Kinetic. 'Come on now, we are yet to have the orange ice cream.'

He looked like he was going to say something, but then thought the better of it and sat behind me.

I met Nikku's mother when we got back. She gushed over me excitedly, although we did occasionally see each other around. She was happy to see Nikku and me together like old times. I think she half expected me to start playing *stapu* in her backyard, probably forgetting that we were past the age of playing hopscotch.

'Now stay for chai and pakoras,' she said, settling the matter. 'Nikku always gobbled up the paneer pakoras. You better let her eat them now, Nikku!'

Nikku laughed and sat back in the jute chair while I settled on the charpoy. His mother seemed very excited to have him back. As the tea simmered, she mentioned the word marriage about five times. Nikku just shook his head and laughed, telling me that she thought he had come back because he wanted to get married.

When we were younger, we would connect the water pipe to a tap in the verandah and drench each other. When the others decided that it was inappropriate for a boy and girl our age to do so, we continued our game at the handpump on the street corner and waited till we were dry before going home.

'Taru Taneja,' Nikku interrupted my thoughts. I looked at him with raised eyebrows. 'You don't make the braids any more. Two little braids with red ribbons at the end. Why not?'

I pursed my lips at him and shook my head.

He grinned, spread out lazily in his chair. I reached out for a pakora from the plate that his mom had brought in. But before I could bite into it, I heard Mohit yelling outside. I couldn't be sure, but I thought he called out for Rohit and mentioned Lalaji. It was a good thing that I heard him. I hurriedly got up and told Nikku I would see him later.

I went straight to Lalaji's room. He was sitting on the divan, his feet touching the floor, his hands by his side, gazing at the floor.

'Where were you, Lalaji?' I asked immediately. 'I've been looking for you since last evening.'

He looked up, gave me a cryptic smile and then went back to staring at the floor. I looked quizzically at Rohit who had just entered the room. He shrugged.

'Lalaji, err . . . what happened? Lalaji? Lalaji?'

When he still didn't respond, I shook him gently by the shoulder. He finally looked at me and said, 'I will talk when all my family is here.'

Rohit and I turned to each other, even more confused. We went around the house, telling the others that Lalaji wanted to talk. My mother immediately put on her dupatta, almost as if she had been expecting something like this. Aunty looked puzzled. I asked Mohit about Pappu Uncle and he said that he would be there in a couple of minutes.

Lalaji, meanwhile, came outside and sat at the head of the table, crossing his arms and not looking at any one of us. Aunty awkwardly asked if he wanted tea. When Lalaji didn't answer, she soothed herself by bringing water and putting some biscuits and namkeen on the table. Just as I was wondering how long all of us were supposed to remain silent, Pappu Uncle arrived, placing his bag at the side of the table.

'What's going on?' he asked. When all he got was silence as an answer, Aunty got up to give him a glass of water, also asking him if he wanted some tea. Pappu Uncle didn't reply, instead he looked around at each one of us, sitting right next to Lalaji. Aunty took her seat again. We all looked pointedly at Lalaji now, who cleared his throat.

'It was in 1947 when we undertook that perilous journey, the nightmares of which haunt us to this day,' he began. I was surprised to see that he had a whole talk prepared. What was going on in his mind?

'We had a thriving business in Lahore, doing very well, in Anarkali Bazaar. Children, do you even know of Anarkali Bazaar?'

We nodded. Lalaji often spoke about his life on the other side of the border, still affronted that his family had to pack their bags and leave from what was always their home.

'How Anarkali Bazaar would come alive during the day, especially when it was festival time. Rows and rows of shops and vendors selling everything, and amongst those were we too. My father worked very hard to buy one of those shops, and we finally managed to do so. We owned a small shop, and the future never looked better. Two years later, however, we had to leave it all. It was the most devastating moment of our lives. We made that journey in complete shock, not knowing what would happen, not knowing what we would do, camping at one place, then another. We finally reached Ludhiana and stayed there for some time, until we were finally allotted this place in Siyaka.

'It was not too bad, mind you,' he continued, 'we got enough land for a house and a shop. It was quite enough. But a small shop in Anarkali Bazaar was still worth ten shops in Siyaka—this town was nothing! There were hardly a few families living here, most of it was farmland. What would I do selling our famous Lahori sweets here? It seemed like we had lost everything, for some time.

'But with my father urging us on, asking us not to lose hope, we began again. We built it all up, brick by brick. Even this house, we made it on our own. Siyaka too became a thriving town—we got lucky there—and after a few years Lallan Sweets was running.'

I glanced at Pappu Uncle. While he might have known more of this than us, we still didn't know why Lalaji had decided to bring it up now.

'Some things helped us, of course. Our magic ingredient being one! Our location, the fact that people here were much more supportive, the local government not so corrupt; we did well. The pinch of salt we always add to our laddoos, not everyone thinks of doing that you know, is always appreciated. Lallan Sweets is the labour of love of not one generation but two, an effort at trying to rebuild all that we had lost due to the cruelties of fate. I don't want to see it crumble again.'

Pappu Uncle put his hands on the table and pushed his chair back. 'I see what this is about. About our talk yesterday, isn't it? You don't trust my sons to handle it, do you? What? You want Taru to take it on—or perhaps her mother?'

Aunty looked at Pappu Uncle in horror. We too were shocked at this sudden hostility. There was always some jealousy and rivalry between us, but it was always concealed beneath a veneer of friendliness. Nothing was spelt out in this manner.

'What about us then?' Pappu Uncle continued. 'My two sons? They will have sons and wives too, children they have to feed, families to take care of—you want to give Lallan Sweets to Taru who has no credibility at all, who might run off with the next DJ she finds, dishonouring the family name!'

'Pappuji!' my mother stood up, indignant. 'Please mind what you are saying, I will not hear my child being spoken ill of like this!'

'Pappu, enough!' Lalaji said, putting his hand up. 'I'm not finished yet and you're not so wise yet to be able to interrupt your father.'

Pappu Uncle went as red as it was possible to, his bald head looking like it would explode.

'The time has come to settle the matter,' Lalaji went on. I bent forward.

'I will not bear to see any injustice happening to my grandchildren, be it my grandsons or granddaughter. There might have been a time when girls were not considered important-enough members of the family, but, Pappu, I am not barbaric, and I hope to God you are the same. No, and now I will tell you how it will work, something that my own father did for me: Lallan Sweets will not be inherited at all.'

'Not inherited?' Pappu Uncle asked blankly.

'It will not be inherited. It will be earned.'

Silence followed: not because it was a shocking statement, but because it was incomprehensible in this scenario. How do you earn your inheritance?

'And what,' I asked, clearing my throat, 'exactly will we have to do to earn it?'

Lalaji looked at me, a wide smile on his face. 'You'll have to find out the magic ingredient, of course.'

Chapter 3

'A quest,' Lalaji continued, grinning widely, his broken incisor more apparent now.

When none of us replied, he looked a little let-down. 'What! Don't you want to know what the magic ingredient is? Haven't you been asking me forever? How many times did I catch you sneaking around to find it, huh, Pappu?'

Pappu Uncle had nothing to say now.

'What kind of quest?' I asked him.

'The quest to find the magic ingredient, and like all great quests it will span multiple locations. There will be hurdles to cross, clues to find, riddles to solve and stages to complete, so you may finally reach the magic ingredient. Whoever gets to it first will earn Lallan Sweets.'

'What do you mean whoever?' Pappu Uncle was quick to ask.

'Well,' Lalaji began, glancing at his grandchildren and their mothers, 'since the entire debate here is about who should oversee the upkeep and running of Lallan Sweets in the future, I believe the competition should be between Tara, Mohit and Rohit.'

'My sons will never compete against each other,' Aunty said, moving towards them as if to cover their ears. I looked at them, but their expressions were inscrutable. They must already have known what Pappu Uncle was going to suggest, but they probably hadn't expected this from Lalaji.

Lalaji shrugged. 'They can do it together then.'

I instinctively looked at my mother. We knew how this would turn out, Pappu Uncle pitting both his sons against me. No sooner were the words out of Lalaji's mouth that all of us were already planning it in our heads. Classic Taneja.

'Is this really happening?' Aunty interjected. 'A trap route will be set up for our children, so they can fight each other?'

My mother lowered her head with what I thought was guilt. It sounded completely crazy to me as well that such a plot would be thought of, the stuff of Shah Rukh Khan movies, but I was excited too. I could, of course, beat Mohit and Rohit, even though the odds were against me. And if I beat them, if I really could solve this 'trap route' on my own, that would be it. That would shut Pappu Uncle up forever. Never again would he think of fixing my marriage with any *anadi*, any random fellow he chose. Never again would he doubt my business acumen. And Lallan Sweets? It could be a restaurant, a large shop—the possibilities were endless.

'How do you expect Tara to do it alone?' Aunty asked and I shot her a look of annoyance. I knew she meant well, but if she hadn't figured out by now that I was smarter than both her sons, then she never would.

'Taru will do what she has to do,' Lalaji said, shrugging once again, 'like the rest of us.'

Aunty looked doubtful, and that's when Pappu Uncle stomped his foot.

'No, I will not allow it,' he said. 'Does this trap route involve going to do things alone?'

'This quest,' Lalaji re-emphasized, 'involves travelling far and wide to get to the root, because only when the future generation understands their roots will they be able to—'

'Travel far and wide, alone! Our little girl? Have you lost your mind, Lalaji? You know what the whole of Siyaka will say? Letting our daughter run wild like that, alone?'

'I'm perfectly capable of managing myself—' I began fiercely.

'I will NOT allow it!'

Lalaji sighed. 'This is my word. Lallan Sweets has to be earned, and to earn it the children must embark on this quest. Lallan Sweets is neither some corner *panwaadi* that is to be passed around, nor is the magic ingredient some common ghee or shakar that everybody should know its secrets. It has been in our family for decades and I intend it to stay that way. Tell a person the secret to a business and they will never value it, but make them work hard to earn it and they will take it to their grave. This is a traditional family secret that I shared not even with my wife! My decision is final: to inherit Lallan Sweets, the children must embark on this quest.'

He ignored the rest of Pappu Uncle's spluttering and walked towards his room, looking suddenly frail. I too found no merit in staying back to hear what Pappu Uncle thought was wrong about the concept, because though he may have tried to convince everyone that his concern lay in my safety and reputation, it was obvious that it was a lot more about his fear that I would beat his sons.

My mother followed me. Neither of us knew what to say to each other. My mind was racing, trying to imagine the possibilities that suddenly lay open. A quest—a quest! I tried to imagine what Lalaji might have been thinking when he came up with this, and the more I thought about it, the more it seemed like something he would do. Wasn't he the one who had insisted that all of us take on equal shifts at Lallan Sweets, even Mumma and Aunty, so we all could respect and appreciate what made our life? Of course, he wanted to give all of his own time to managing the magic ingredient, which he didn't reveal to anyone, not even Pappu Uncle.

And then I realized that if this did happen, I would finally know the magic ingredient. The ingredient that I and the whole of Siyaka had grown up hearing about, the elusive ingredient all the way from what was now Pakistan. Merely heard of, and of course tasted, in the ever-special Lallan ke laddoo. If I knew the magic ingredient, I would use it everywhere, in all the sweets, expand the business beyond all that we had ever seen . . .

We barely looked at each other, my mother and I, as we made our beds. I knew that she too was lost in her thoughts. Was she thinking about my father? I wondered what he would think about me knowing the magic ingredient, what he would think about me going on that quest. I was sure he was a logical and understanding man.

I slept, turning Lalaji's words over in my mind. I woke up still thinking about them, refusing to move out of bed until I heard a shout of '*Aye*, Taru'. Straightening my kurti, I looked down from the window to find Nikku, his hand over his head to block the sun. 'Will you wake up or should I sing the song?'

I had almost forgotten about Nikku. I grinned as memories of him calling out to me for school, yelling my name for the whole street to hear, came back.

'What do you want?' I yelled back, hoping he couldn't see how pleased I was at being called in the old, familiar way.

'I thought I'd come hang around with you at Lallan today,' he said. When I didn't reply, he added, a little uncertain, 'Is it okay if I do?'

I nodded and asked him to wait while I got ready.

There was a time when most days I would wake up to Nikku's shrill call. I caught myself going back many years, trying to remember how we became friends. It had happened when I used to play pithu with Mohit and Rohit, and Nikku used to watch us, swinging on the iron gate of his house. I had hazy memories of him peering at us, his expression giving away how badly he wanted to be a part of our group but too ashamed to ask if he could. I can divide my entire life into 'Before Nikku' and 'After Nikku', also because it marked a clear division between me being close to Mohit and Rohit, and later drifting apart.

What really sealed the deal with Nikku was when one late evening I wanted to return home from the other end of the street and there were two dogs running around. I didn't have enough courage to cross them. Nikku, seeing this, ran into his house and got his grandfather's walking stick. He walked towards me, banging the stick on the ground to make sure the dogs wouldn't get near him. His own hands were shaking with fear, but we got back to the house safely. This marked the beginning of how I grew apart from Mohit and Rohit. They were always scared of Nikku and didn't like it that an older boy wanted to be friends with me and not them. And so they stopped talking to both of us, no doubt encouraged by Uncle and Aunty.

I got my Kinetic out from the back and wheeled it towards Nikku who was smiling with his hands folded behind his back. He was wearing a white T-shirt and blue jeans again, his hair combed, his eyes warm and happy.

'What?' I asked him.

'What?'

'Why do you look like Diwali came early?'

'Just the sight of you,' he said. When I looked up, he added, 'And your pudgy little nose.'

I handed him the helmet with a little more force than necessary. He laughed.

'So you're going to just sit there all day, troubling me?' I asked.

'Basically. I might also have some of those laddoos. Do you still make the kachoris?'

'Yes! No place like Lallan Sweets.'

Behind the glass counter lay trays of sweets spread out on shelves: diamonds upon diamonds of kaju katli topped with shining silver, melt-in-the-mouth doodh ki burfi, crystalline cubes of chewy Agra petha, gleaming orange boondi laddoos and grainy balls of besan ke laddoo, all ready to be bitten into. There was also the rugged and pale red gajar ki barfi, mewa bites packed in glistening wrappers, anjeer burfi in all their brown glory and badam halwa with a taut little almond on top. Nikku stared at the sweets in fascination and then turned to me, his mouth shaped in a curious 'o'. 'How do you not eat all of these while they sit in front of you?'

'It's easier than it sounds. Growing up with sweets all around you, they are just not that special any more, you know.'

Nikku shook his head like he didn't believe me. I, in turn, told him to take the chair behind the counter and asked which sweet he would like to eat first.

'The magic one,' he said happily. I took out two besan Lallan ke laddoo for him and placed them on a small paper plate. I then went around the back, taking a round as Pyaare Lal and the two boys, Monu and Shyam, set up the frying kadais. Since everything seemed to be in order, I nodded at them and headed inside. Nikku was still munching on the laddoos. I opened the sales book and went through the previous day's sales, comparing those with the figures from last Friday. After that I turned to Nikku to ask him what he wanted to sample next, but he had already started on the boondi laddoos.

Before I could say anything, the glass door opened. Rohit and Mohit walked in, their hands behind their backs, eyes narrowed behind their glasses as they stared at Nikku whose head was bent over the laddoos.

'Why are *you* here?' I asked. Nikku too looked up to see Rohit and Mohit glaring at him from behind the glass counter.

'As much our shop as yours,' Rohit replied, his glasses slightly askew.

'Who is this . . . ?' Mohit began, but Nikku had recognized them and got up to shake hands. 'Hello!' he exclaimed as they also seemed to recognize him. Though Rohit and Mohit looked tensed, Nikku went on, oblivious.

After a couple of minutes, Rohit and Mohit started peeking around, staring at the walls, opening cupboards and tasting the laddoos as if it was the first time they had ever had them.

'I know what it is!' I slapped the sales book on the counter. 'You are already looking for the magic ingredient!'

Rohit shrugged at Mohit. Neither of them was very tall so I could barely see their noses above the glass counter, but

I knew from their expressions that I was right. Their round faces weren't very good at hiding their feelings, hardly the veneer for scheming masterminds.

'Are you serious! You really think you will find the magic ingredient here? These laddoos come in all ready from Bulla's, you know that, so why are you wasting your time?'

Neither of them replied and I saw Nikku open his mouth to ask what was going on when Rohit spoke, his voice barely a whisper. 'Taru, I know that all your life you've thought you're better than us. Smarter, better at math, whatever . . . but this is our thing. This is what we have been trained for. We will win this quest.'

'In your dreams will you win this quest.' I was livid.

'No, we are already two steps ahead of you. You don't know how long we have been talking about this and how close we are to finding the—'

'Shhh!' Mohit said, pulling his brother back. Rohit seemed to have realized what he was doing.

'I don't care what tricks you use, but I—'

'Madam, is the shop open or should I come later?' a man standing at the door asked and we all straightened up. I ignored Nikku's stares. Rohit and Mohit went out while I served the customer. When he left, I put the radio on, annoyed at my cousins. For a long time, almost till the clock showed it was afternoon, I yelled orders at Pyaare Lal while customers lined up, all the while feeling Nikku's gaze upon me. My thoughts flitted between the tuition centre and the magic ingredient, wondering how in the world I would solve this quest when Rohit and Mohit were apparently 'two steps ahead' of me.

But they could have been bluffing as well. Did they really have the brains to embark on this adventure of all adventures, to actually solve the mystery of the magic ingredient? In all the years I had known them, they had been so indifferent about everything in general. They hung out with other boys, failed exams, stayed out on their cycles till late and demanded motorbikes when they were older. They didn't bother to engage with me much, especially since I became friends with Nikku. It was always Pappu Uncle putting things in their heads that resulted in our spats. I was sure he was helping them this time too. But who would help me?

'What is this quest thing you're talking about?' Nikku asked.

I sighed and was about to explain when the door chimed again and Sahil walked in. A quick glance at Nikku showed me that his eyebrows were raised so high that they almost disappeared into his hair.

'Yo, Tara,' Sahil said, his arms resting on the counter. I could see he had razored in a new pattern on his head, one that seemed to match the tattoos on his bulging biceps. He had the most black, intense eyes that I could not stop looking into, not unless he interrupted my staring with his music, because then I had to focus all my energy on not grimacing. At least he hadn't tied that dumb ribbon around his head today.

'Sahil,' I said slowly, fighting the urge to glance at Nikku again.

'*Tara mere yaara, maine dhoondha jag saara, par tere jaisa koi mujhe mile na dobaara,*' Sahil rapped, apparently singing praises about our bond, slapping the counter in a beat only he could understand. I heard what seemed to be Nikku choking on the barfi, almost struggling for air. Regaining control, he brushed the crumbs off his hands and got up to face Sahil, looking very eager to be introduced.

'Sahil,' I said, 'this is my neighbour, Nikku, I mean, Nikhil Sabharwal. For the past few years he has been making computers in Bangalore.'

'Not making computers, Taru, working on them.'

'Oh, you don't make them?'

'No someone else does.'

'Then what do you do?'

'Well, we make other stuff on the computers, you know, with the language of the computer—'

'Can you also teach me how to use the computer? I hear all great DJs use them. To do what, I don't know.'

I refrained from rolling my eyes at Sahil, and before Nikku could answer I spoke up. 'And Nikku, this is Sahil, a . . . musician. Also known as DJ Buddy.'

'But not your study buddy, yo!' Sahil said, holding up his hands and laughing while Nikku tried to join in. I smiled tightly, hoping Sahil would get the hint.

Nikku was now staring at us both, amused. 'So! How do you two know each other?'

'Know each other?' Sahil laughed, looking at me. 'She's my girlfriend, Brother!'

Nikku suddenly looked like he was entitled to free mithai from Lallan Sweets for the rest of his life. 'Really? Taru, you never told me! Amazing! Did you know that she too writes great songs?'

Sahil furrowed his eyebrows, perplexed. 'What? Tara, do you mean? She writes songs?'

'Yes! Haven't you heard her song about the little, fat girl with the pudgy nose?'

'Shut up, Nikku,' I said before Sahil could reply. He laughed, holding up his hands in mock apology.

'Anyway, you were saying something?' I turned to Sahil.

'I wanted to check whether you will come to that party, yo. The one at Ishaan's house. He has the biggest cassette collection, all the way from Delhi, so you can be sure that it will be one of my best performances ever!'

'Uh, I'll try.'

'What do you mean? You have to come, Tara!'

'I told you I'll try, Sahil. There's been some trouble at home.'

'Come to the party and you'll forget all about it! And you can come as well,' he said, turning to Nikku. 'I know Siyaka is a small place, but in a few years we'll be just like Delhi. Parties, beer, girls . . . of course, by that time I'll be long gone, you know.'

Nikku nodded, his eyebrows still raised, a smirk on his lips. 'Yes, sure. I'd love to, if Taru comes.'

'Taru? Oh Tara!' Sahil turned to me and leant forward. 'I'll wait for you tonight, Baby,' he said, and I almost died. Blood rushed up to my cheeks and my underarms began to sweat as I felt Nikku's gaze on me. I knew he was longing to laugh and so I kept looking at the sales book as Sahil exited. I refused to look up until Pyaare Lal came in. 'Madam, only a few kachoris left now,' he said. I nodded. I chanced a glance at Nikku whose face was now solemn. In fact, he was looking at me very seriously. 'Do you cut his hair? I too want that hairstyle, Tara.' With that, he finally allowed himself to chuckle.

I decided to go to the party, for the following reasons: one, I wanted to wear my disco shirt that my friend Simmi had got from Delhi. It was white with sequins all over and had to be tied in a knot at the navel. Two, I wanted Nikku to see that Sahil was considered a cool guy in Siyaka. He was invited to all the parties, and he and his friends were always the ones dancing the most. I wanted to make sure that Nikku knew that I had many more people in this town, that I hadn't been 'left behind' as he obviously seemed to think.

When I told my mother that I would be going to the party with Nikku, she merely nodded and told me to have fun. Tousling my hair, I wore big hoops and sneaked out my mother's red lipstick, putting it on once I was out of the house, using the Kinetic's mirror for help. When I heard Nikku approach, I put the lipstick into my purse. His eyes seemed to lose focus for a few seconds.

'Wow,' he said, giving his head a little shake as he stared at me. I waved my hand dismissively, as if I did this every day and wasn't surprised to see his reaction. He was dressed in a regular T-shirt and jeans, but somehow he made it look fancy. Maybe it was the fact that his T-shirt wasn't tucked inside, or the style, but he looked nothing like Sahil's friends. His hair was longish, but it still fell neatly on the side, making his floppy ears less so. When he smiled, I noticed a new dimple. Where did that come from?

'So,' I cleared my throat, 'shall we go then?'

He nodded. Enjoying the cool breeze, I cruised along slowly, taking the longer route through the Victorian part of the city so that Nikku would have a nice view and appreciate it in the darkness.

'So, what do you do on the weekends?' he asked, bending closer to my ear to make sure I heard.

'Well, there's lots to do, especially in this area,' I said loudly, flitting my gaze between the rear-view mirror and the front. 'Without golgappas, it isn't a weekend though. The Sunday market still goes on, all the children play outside—cricket, kho-kho, football. When you walk around the city, it's even more fun: you can eat kulfi, tikki, popcorn . . .'

'I don't like popcorn,' Nikku said. Almost as if in shock, I stopped the Kinetic dead in its tracks and turned around.

'So how do you watch movies?'

'I appreciate the story and the actors.'

'Even I appreciate the actors. I don't think there is anyone who appreciates Shah Rukh Khan more than me.'

He snorted and urged me to get a move on.

'Seriously,' I said, starting the Kinetic again, 'once there was Rajesh Khanna, then came Amitabh Bachchan, and now it's Shah Rukh Khan. The next superstar of Bollywood.'

'You have to be joking. He's a good actor and all, but there's no way he can take Bachchan Sir's place. He just doesn't have it in him.'

'He does! You mark my words, Nikku Sabharwal, Shah Rukh Khan will be the next superstar. And I am not a new fan, like all the other girls who started swooning after *Karan Arjun*. I knew about him from the start, when I used to watch *Fauji* and *Circus* at Dua Aunty's home, you know, until we got a small TV.'

'We'll see. Which movie of his is coming out next?'

'*Dilwale Dulhaniya Le Jayenge*! Have you heard about it? It's with Kajol again—'

'Watch out!'

'We're fine. Relax!'

A few minutes later, we were at Ishaan's house. It was lit up and loud music blared. Only he could play the music so loud because his house was a little way off from the others, and also because his father was the MLA.

'Let's bet,' I said.

'On Shah Rukh Khan being a superstar?'

'On Shah Rukh Khan being *the* superstar.'

'You're on,' Nikku laughed. 'Shall we write it?' He produced a notebook and wrote: *Taru v/s Nikku. Bet made: 17 April 1995. Shah Rukh Khan to be the next superstar—Tara's claim. Opposition: Nikku.*

'We need a time period though,' Nikku said, 'it can't be a lifetime. You have to say when you think he will become a superstar.'

'As soon as *Dilwale Dulhaniya Le Jayenge* releases!'

He shook his head, laughing again. 'I'm going to break your heart.'

I stared at him. 'Let's go in.'

'Wait. We haven't decided what we stand to win.'

'We'll decide later.'

The music got louder as we went into the house, multicoloured lights flashing in every direction. There were balloons bunched up here and there, and a great disco ball that shone silver hung from the ceiling. There was a wall at the back where the name 'Ishaan' was spelt out with buntings. Everyone blew party horns in time with the beat. I realized that we had walked in right when 'Ice Ice Baby' had started playing. Everyone seemed to have gone mad. The whistles blew in unison and everyone had their hands in the air. I looked at Nikku. He was nodding and smiling, his hands in his pockets, staring around.

I walked on, making sure that Nikku followed me, looking for Sahil. I spotted him behind the music player, dancing and singing.

'Ice Ice Baby!' he yelled at us. 'Vanilla, Ice Ice Baby!'

Nikku gave him a high five. I realized that I was the only one who didn't seem into the music and proceeded to arrange my face like I was singing along, but sadly I didn't know the lyrics. We stayed like that until the song ended. Sahil came down to give me a hug as everyone clapped.

'Cool party, Bro!' Nikku said. I was happy that he was impressed.

'Sahil knows the entire rap,' I told Nikku proudly.

'Cool,' Nikku said as Sahil wandered off to set the music again.

'I don't understand much of it though,' I admitted to Nikku, 'except "Ice Ice Baby".'

He smiled and spoke loudly as the next song picked up. 'What do you like to listen to?'

'Well, I like to dance to Daler Mehndi.'

'Because the song has your name in it? "Bolo ta ra ra ra"?'

I couldn't help but giggle. 'Yes, exactly! It's like the song was written just for me. But I also like all of Bollywood music. I tell Sahil to model himself after Daler Mehndi and Bally Sagoo—that's what works here, you know. But he keeps running after English music.'

'Oh, but he just mixes music, right? Or does he play as well?'

I stared at him, confused. 'What's the difference?'

Before he could answer, Sahil came back and asked us to grab a cola, leading me to meet his friends.

'Tara!' Ishaan, who was wearing a birthday cap and a garland of buntings, yelled.

'Happy birthday,' I almost screamed, trying to make my voice heard above the music.

'Saturday night, I like the way you move! Pretty baby!' Sahil and Ishaan sang in unison. I tried to follow them, but it was hard. I tried to catch the eye of the others around them, but they were all singing. I gazed around at the outfits and was glad to see that I fit in. All the girls wore a tie-up shirt, and some of them, God save them, had even tied them just under their breasts. It was going to be the biggest night of the year in Siyaka. Only Ishaan could have a party like this without people objecting.

Nikku came over and handed me a cola, which I accepted gratefully but almost spat out after the first gulp. 'Why didn't you tell me it's mixed with alcohol?'

He raised his eyebrows. 'I thought you knew. A guy over there told me there is no plain cola, just these mixed drinks.'

'I knew, I mean, but it was unexpected . . .' I took a sip again. It tasted terrible.

I tried to catch Sahil's attention but he was behind the music player again, going through the cassettes, so I walked over to him.

'What's going on?' I asked him.

'I'm trying to find this one song . . . but.'

'Why don't you play some Bollywood? What about "Yeh Kaali Kaali Aankhein"?'

'What? No, of course not,' he said, looking scandalized.

I shrugged. 'Well, anyway. You want to go out for a walk in some time? Things have been really insane at home. I haven't even got a chance to tell you. You know what Lalaji said? He said we must go on a race, like a quest, to find out the—'

'I found it!' Sahil said excitedly, holding up a cassette. 'What is love! Baby don't hurt me, don't hurt me, no more!'

'Sahil! I was talking! I need to go find the magic—'

'And you'll win it for sure. You're great at races, Tara! Now let me put on this track.'

I wandered around aimlessly for a while, watching people groove on the dance floor, drinking the spiked cola under the disco ball. I wondered whether Ishaan had that smoky mist apparatus as well, the one which let smoke loose in the middle of a song. No sooner had I thought about it than half the people were blurred out with the mist. All I heard was shrieks of 'Baby don't hurt me!'

'What's up?' Nikku asked, coming up from the back. 'You want to head out for a while? It's so loud.'

'Yes, please,' I said, and we left through the front door. I stashed the unfinished cola on a table on the way out.

We sat quietly on the steps for a while. My mind kept going back to Rohit and Mohit, and their warning.

'I didn't know Siyaka was so cool,' Nikku laughed.

'It is. You've been gone far too long.'

We were quiet for some more time before Nikku spoke again. 'I should have been a better friend.'

I looked at him; his eyes were full of sincerity. I wondered what would have happened had Nikku not left. There was so much that could have happened between us, but it seemed to be so long ago that I hadn't thought about it for really long. 'It's not entirely your fault. I think I didn't keep in touch because I was mad at you, for so many things,' I said. 'Do you remember when you came to visit three years ago? We were talking and I said "didn't came" instead of "didn't come" and you laughed at me so much.'

Nikku put his right hand over his mouth, looking genuinely shocked. 'I am really sorry.'

'Nah, it's okay. It was such a small thing, but I held a grudge for so long. And, of course, you were gone for too long.'

'I'm sorry, Taru,' he said, patting my back, 'if it helps, I have said "didn't came" many times.'

We sat there for some more time and I ended up telling him all about Lalaji's crazy plan. He found it fascinating, excited that at the end of the quest lay the answer to the magic ingredient. I told him that Rohit and Mohit already had a headstart, and a lot of help from Pappu Uncle to boot.

'What do you have to do first?' he asked curiously.

'Lalaji will tell us later, when we are ready to leave. But I am sure I have to go somewhere. I've hardly ever spent a night outside Siyaka, you know. Just a few days in Delhi when I was very young. I don't even remember it.'

'How will you do it then? I mean, you'd have to go on this journey or whatever for at least two to three weeks, I'm guessing.'

'Yeah, but I'll have to. I mean, that's the challenge.'

Nikku spoke after a short pause. 'I can come with you. I mean, if you want. And if Buddy Sahil is okay with it.'

I scanned his face carefully. 'I'm capable of doing it by myself.'

'I'm sure you are, but it's always more fun to have someone for the journey, isn't it? Plus, I was actually thinking of taking a holiday as well. I haven't had a vacation in years, you know. This sounds like a fun idea. It will be just like old times.'

I considered it for a moment, wondering if I should play it cool and tell him that I would think about it. But who was I kidding? We would have an absolute blast, and with our brains put together, we would easily beat Mohit and Rohit. *Easily.* I would have to tell my mother, but since she loved Nikku she would most likely agree.

I beamed at him and extended my hand, which he shook excitedly.

Chapter 4

'*Ravivar, ravivar, bhandara ravivar, aloo khao, poori khao, laddoo khao chaar!*'

I looked at Keshavji, the organizer of the bhandara, in annoyance and said, 'I told you. We sponsor this bhandara to promote LALLAN ke laddoo. Not laddoos in general. You have to include the words "Lallan ke laddoo" in your rhyme!'

He nodded nervously, mechanically pouring aloo ki sabzi into leafy bowls. 'We say Lallan ke laddoo in the next rhyme, Madamji. Parathe, aloo ke! Bihar ke vote, Lalu ke! Magar meethe mein laddoo, Lallan ke, Lallan ke!'

'No, no, no. This one is not as nice. It makes the customers' attention go in too many directions—aloo parathe, Lalu Prasad Yadav, and by the time our name comes up, they've already gone off with the aloo-poori. Is this how you expect us to beat Manchanda? Change this rhyme.'

Later, as people lined up for the monthly Sunday bhandara, clutching their plates and bowls, I couldn't help but be proud of my genius marketing idea: to sponsor the Sunday bhandara and remain a step above Manchanda for our laddoos. Since we started this three months ago, our dip in sales because of the Manchanda store being renovated had shot right back up. The Taneja marketing genes had only improved over the generations.

Pappu Uncle likes to say that the reason we even have Manchanda as competition is because I rejected their shaadi ki inquiry. A few years ago, they had sent a marriage proposal of their eldest son to Lalaji—for me! I had obviously laughed it away. Out of revenge, Pappu Uncle says, they try to compete with Lallan Sweets. Which is bullshit I say: had I married that Manchanda, there might not even have been a Lallan Sweets left.

I lingered on, waiting as the rhyme was tweaked and the bhandara kicked off in full force. Once I was sure it was going well, I headed home to let Lalaji know that I was ready for the quest, and that Nikku would be joining me. I had no idea how he would take it, but it was one of those things that had to be done. I swung my leg over my Kinetic and set off.

Lalaji lay on the divan, reading the newspaper as I entered, the coal in his hookah still sizzling. It took him a few seconds before he realized that I was there. He gave me his broken-incisor grin and I sat on the rocking chair next to his hookah.

'I'm ready, Lalaji. I'm ready to go for the quest.'

He nodded, his eyes still on the newspaper. 'Alone?'

'No, I have found a partner,' I said, my stomach feeling squeamish. 'I need a partner. You used to say, *ek aur ek gyaara baraabar*. And . . . and Nikku said he would go with me. You remember Nikku?'

Now Lalaji stared right at me. 'Of course I remember Nikku. So he will go with you? Is he in Siyaka?'

'Yes, he has come back for some time.'

He paused for a while, his eyes on me the whole time. 'Do you want to marry him?'

'What? No, Lalaji! We will go as friends! He is my friend.'

'Friend?' he snorted. 'Sure! *Dhoop mein baal safed nahi kare maine.* I have seen enough of life to see what that is! You like that boy.'

'Lalaji! Please! How can you say that? I have a boyfriend, you know!'

'That DJ?'

'Oh god, Lalaji! Please just tell me what we have to do now. Tell us how to start.'

Lalaji finally got up and rested against the back of the divan, still staring at me intensely. 'Bring Mohit and Rohit. I will give you the first hint.'

'Hint? A hint and we have to find out—ROHIT!' I yelled, jumping up from the chair and running into their house to fetch him. I ran right into Mohit and hurriedly brought him to Lalaji, with him muttering all the while that Rohit had stepped out.

'So one from each team,' Lalaji said. 'That's fair. Time for the hint. Are you ready?'

'Yes!' We yelled in unison.

He grinned again and then took his own sweet time fetching a little box from under the divan, one I had never seen before. It was bronze and ornate, and quite small. I could hardly contain my impatience as he opened it slowly and revealed a little piece of paper.

He cleared his throat. 'Ready?' he asked. We nodded.

'Four brothers we were: Buntu, Mithu, Lallan, Muraar. Where we grew up, in Dera Ghazi Khan, was a small town with big fields surrounding it. We ran around all day and everyone knew us to be the naughtiest boys around. Every year, we were made to play Krishna on Janmashtami. Sometimes me, sometimes Buntu. We were very handsome back then, you know. People were scared that we would start talking to the girls, make them run away with us. Our mother would laugh at that and had just one thing to ask of us: to take her to Mathura just once in her lifetime. But then Partition happened and she didn't survive that. When I started Lallan Sweets, I first went to Mathura, to seek the blessings that my mother wanted.'

'Oh,' Mohit said, 'you want us to do the same? Seek blessings from Mathura before we start off on the quest?'

'I want you to go to Mathura and seek out the Rasiya group. I met them when I went there.'

'And then?' I asked.

'Just seek them out and you will know what to do,' Lalaji replied cryptically. I exchanged a look with Mohit.

'What about the magic ingredient though?' I asked him urgently. 'How will we know when we have it? You have to tell us something about it. What does it look like?'

Lalaji's eyes seemed to lose focus as he looked for words to describe it. 'It is the most magical thing you will ever know. Your life will be different before and after you know it. It contains the light of the sun and the twinkle of the stars. When you hold it, it will stand out against anything else in its surrounding. It is a being in itself, a world in itself, and yet it is . . . just a little ingredient. Nothing else. You take a pinch of it, and that's that.'

We were absolutely enthralled.

'So that's it? Rasiya group in Mathura?' Mohit asked.

'Yes.'

Mohit dashed out, looking for Rohit. I knew that they would try to leave the same night. I gave Lalaji a long look.

'You sure we should—we can do this?' I asked him.

He didn't reply and instead prodded at the coal in his hookah. I ran outside too, rushing to tell my mother, and of course, Nikku.

'How should we go?'

'How will Rohit and Mohit?'

'They'll take Pappu Uncle's Zen,' I told Nikku.

His mouth fell open. 'He has a Zen? So lucky! I have been dreaming about that car ever since it came out!'

I nodded sympathetically. When Pappu Uncle had driven in the brand-new white Zen, a loud gasp had escaped my mouth. It was so beautiful, with its sleek steering wheel, seat covers, and boot. So beautiful that I couldn't help but say yes the moment he asked me if I wanted to go for a drive. I had decided that one day I would buy a car too, but not a Zen. I'd buy an Esteem. The real rich man's car.

'Well,' Nikku said, 'we could take a bus or train. But I think the best way is by car, which we don't have . . . yet.'

'Can you tell me something I don't know?'

'I was just getting to it. I spoke to the mechanic, Shambu. Do you know him?'

'Not really. My Kinetic never needs a mechanic.'

'Well, Shambu said we could take one of . . . his cars.'

'What do you mean one of his cars? He's a mechanic, not a car dealer.'

'Well, he kind of is.'

'What do you mean?'

'People sell him stolen cars, and he makes them new.'

'What? Nikku, that is stealing!'

'Yes, but it's actually not because he pays for the stolen cars.'

'Nikku!'

'I know it's not ideal, but it will get the job done. We can't win the race on buses, and this is the only way to get a car . . .'

I thought about it for a few seconds. 'And why would he just give us one of his cars?'

'Well, when a car is stolen, they don't want it in the area for some time. He said that he has a Siyaka car that he would be glad to get rid of for some time. We can take it as long as we maintain it.'

'What if the police catch us? Then what?'

'I thought about it too, but he'll change the registration plate. So really, what are the chances?'

A car was our best bet. And how unlucky could we get? If the registration plate was changed, there really was no way of anyone finding out it was a stolen car.

'Do we have to pay him?' I asked quietly. Nikku shrugged, and so we decided to speak to Shambu. Half an hour later, we had a car at our disposal as Shambu handed Nikku the keys, asking him to pick it up from his garage.

There was no other way, I decided, except for us to leave early the next day. I asked Nikku if that was okay with him. He said yes after a couple of minutes.

I felt butterflies in my stomach. Things had escalated quickly. I had barely spent more than two days away from Siyaka, and had never felt the need to either. My life was here. It felt like a big step, and despite the competition and ill will, I was excited. I had never heard of anyone taking a trip like this, and I hadn't even begun thinking of what lay at the end of it—inheriting Lallan Sweets.

However, what really made me nervous was spending all these days with Nikku. While I did see flashes of his old self, there was so much about him that felt like a completely new person. The way he put his hands in his trouser pockets, raised an eyebrow, or looked at me like he had moved on. Would he laugh at my ways? If the going got tough, would he stick it out or scoff at this strange race? For me it had been simple—he had offered to join me and I couldn't refuse. But I had never gone on a trip, let alone going with a man. What scared me was the possibility that I had probably lost the old Nikku forever. And then Lalaji's voice singing his favourite song rang in my ears. '*Waqt ne kiya, kya haseen sitam.*'

'You must leave very early, before anyone wakes up in the house,' my mother said, sitting at the edge of the bed, helping me pack. I rummaged through the almirah, its door squeaking, taking out anything that I deemed useful. It was strange packing for this. I had no idea where we would actually be heading. But I didn't worry much about the clothes as the summer was upon us. Now that we had a car, I could easily pack a bunch and still have enough space.

'I will pack some snacks for both of you,' my mother went on, 'if I knew, I would have had something ready, but—'

'Mumma, please! We don't need it. We're just going to Mathura! I'm sure we'll find enough food on the way.'

'Who knows where this trip will take you? I am happy though that Nikku is there to take care of you . . .'

'I can very well take care of myself,' I said, wondering if I should take my jeans and tie-up shirts. I doubted we'd be going to any discos, but I didn't want Nikku to see me only in baggy pants and kameez.

'Confidence is good, but not too much of it, remember that!' she said, lifting her finger as I rolled my eyes. She'd been watching too many movies and there was a story coming, I could feel it.

'You don't know,' she said, as I darted off to our common dressing, picking up the comb, wondering if I would need bindis. 'When we got married, your father and I, it was because of our confidence that we were able to run away. But we paid the price for it, I can tell you that much.'

'Yes, so I've heard,' I muttered, but she obviously pretended not to hear me and raised her voice as if she were talking to a room full of people.

'I was just nineteen,' she began, as I went around the room picking up things. If I forgot something essential, I'd definitely be blaming my mother. I wished there was something like a takeaway phone, so we wouldn't have to keep looking for a booth to call.

'There weren't so many love marriages as there are now, huh, Taru? Ever since this Shah Rukh has come, every second person wants a love marriage, but it was not so common back then and that's why we had to run away. Your father picked me up in the middle of the night, and quite frankly, we never looked back. Your Lalaji took us in, but my parents, they didn't speak to me until after you were born, you know. But I don't regret it, of course.'

I, meanwhile, packed my favourite pink and white suit, deciding to wear it on a nice day, probably when we finished the quest. I wanted Nikku to see me in it.

'We settled in and, quite honestly, became the coolest couple around. At least once in two months we would drive to Delhi and watch movies. There were not many theatres back then. There were your father's friends, we would regularly go to their houses for dinners and all. When you were born, he was so happy. I knew he wanted a son. Lalaji here was very understanding that way, you know. The moment he saw you, he loved you.'

I smiled at her and then continued packing.

'It was through one of these friends that he met the ashram people. At first, your father was very sceptical, but slowly they became friends, and pretty soon he was going to the ashram a lot! He wanted to put you in the ashram school. They don't have normal schooling, it's quite different. He would wear a mala every day, you know the ones these hippies who come to Siyaka wear? The one with the big, brown *moti*s?'

'Yes, I know which kind,' I said waving my hand.

'But the mala could not protect him that night when he was coming back from the ashram, could it? When that car hit him. Sometimes I think it would never have happened had he not started going to the ashram.'

I sneaked a look at her and was relieved to see that she wasn't crying. She didn't cry often, but when she did I never knew what to say. I didn't know how to pacify her because I only knew my father through what I had heard about him. I didn't have any memories, just photos and anecdotes to form a picture in my mind.

'I'll get the magic ingredient, Mumma,' I said, folding a towel and handing it to her. 'I will get it and make him proud. This shop, it is his legacy, he put all his life into it. I am going to inherit it and then take Lallan Sweets beyond what was ever dreamt for it.'

She held my hand. 'Yes, you will. But my point is that we were so confident about everything going our way. Life couldn't have been better. And then I lost it all. Don't make the same mistake.'

I wanted to tell her that what she said didn't really make sense in my situation, but I nodded all the same.

'Nikku!' I called out, trying to be loud and quiet at the same time, trying not to yell out to him from the street below and hoping my voice would carry to him but not to Rohit and Mohit. Where were they anyway? Would they really have left without even telling me? My stomach flipped at the thought. Of course, they would. If they had left already, they'd be many hours ahead of us.

'Nikku!' I called out again.

He appeared at the window after a few seconds. 'What's wrong?'

'We leave at four,' I whispered, holding up four of my fingers, but he obviously didn't get it and decided to come down. He was wearing tracks and a T-shirt, rubbing his floppy ears, reminding me of a puppy. I wanted to laugh.

'Your PJs look completely stupid, by the way,' he told me. I stared at him, indignation written all over my face, so he added, 'But not you!'

I narrowed my eyes at him. 'Don't try to be smart.'

'I don't have to try.'

'Whatever. I came to tell you that we'll leave at four tomorrow morning.'

'I like an early start to an adventure.'

'Where's the car?'

'It's at Shambu's garage. I have the key, but we'll have to walk till there in the morning.'

'Walk there with my luggage!'

'What the hell are you carrying?'

'Just essentials, but . . . why don't you get the car and then come here?'

Nikku raised an eyebrow. 'I could but . . . what will I get?'

'What do you want?'

'I want to make "Taru Taneja Moti Hai" a proper song. With a chorus and all, you know,' he said, grinning.

I glowered at him as he chuckled and left without saying goodbye.

I didn't get much sleep that night. It felt like one of those school days when we were going out for a trip. I'd be so excited that I wouldn't be able to fall asleep, and then I would be tired during the trip. Nikku would laugh at my groggy face and run off with his boy friends, until I woke up and went to find him. After a couple of hours of disturbed sleep, I finally got out of bed and decided to get ready.

It was while I was packing my toiletries that I heard someone creeping around the house. I had a pretty good idea who it was. I crossed the verandah and, sure enough, there was Pappu Uncle with a torch in his hand.

'Pappu Uncle,' I said suddenly and deliberately, startling him and making him drop the torch.

'Tara beta,' he said, bending to pick it up, 'what in the world are you doing up so late?'

I'm sure he knew perfectly well what I was doing. But I didn't mind telling him.

'No, Pappu Uncle. I wasn't up late. I woke up early and am about to leave.'

'For where?'

I smiled a dangerous smile, annoyed by his pretence. 'For Mathura.'

'What, Taru, you are going alone!'

'I'm not going alone. Nikku is going with me!'

'You are going with a man! Taru, you should think about what people will think of your family!'

'I know Rohit and Mohit have already left, and they didn't even tell me,' I said, ignoring him, 'but I am winning this.'

His lips quivered, but before he could say anything else I bid him a cheery goodbye.

My mother was up by now and I was ready to kiss her goodbye.

'Good luck,' she said, holding my free hand while I held a duffel bag in the other. I suddenly didn't feel like leaving, but with a loud heave swung the bag around my shoulder and made my way to the gate. My mother stood with me while I waited for Nikku.

The air was cool and breezy, and there was a stillness that was characteristic of that hour. No sound was to be heard except the distant swish of the wind, and even that was occasional. I peered at the end of the road, looking for a sign of the car. *It's always a good time in Siyaka,* the jingle ran in my head. I couldn't help but marvel at how little I actually knew of the world outside. Perhaps that's why Lalaji wanted to send us. I was aware that I hadn't said a proper goodbye to him, but I think that is what he wanted.

Just as my thoughts wandered off to where Rohit and Mohit might be, I saw two headlights turn around the corner and the grumble of a car. I eagerly craned my neck and was stunned to see that it was a Fiat . . . a sky-blue Fiat. Nikku stopped the car in front of us. My mother was smiling, talking to Nikku rapidly, squeezing in all the advice she could. I hurriedly got inside, put my luggage in the boot and waved goodbye. The Fiat jolted forward, and we were off.

'A Fiat!' I exclaimed as I noticed my mother's shape get smaller.

'What did you expect?'

'Something a little less . . . striking. A sky-blue stolen Fiat might be easier to track than a Maruti.'

'It's the best that was available. Achcha, check the dashboard. I think I saw a couple of cassettes there.'

I took one out and put it in the stereo. The beats to 'Made in India' rang out.

'Made in India . . .' I sang along, delighted, and looked at Nikku. He laughed in resignation and began singing along as we left Siyaka behind.

'God, Nikku, you are so out of tune . . .'

Chapter 5

I woke up to the sound of Nikku whistling lightly, the cassette player wasn't on. I rubbed my eyes, straightened up, and saw that we were on a highway.

'Good morning,' Nikku said as I retied my hair.

'Sorry, I slept off.' I was still groggy.

'Don't worry, I didn't mind the snoring,' he said, 'or the drooling.'

I immediately brought my hand up to my mouth, only to realize that he was joking. I hadn't been drooling, at least not yet. And my mother would have definitely told me if I snored.

'Oh, ha ha. If we are going to be together on this trip, then we should be nice and not try to embarrass each other all the time.'

'Where's the fun in that!' Nikku asked in exasperation. 'And also, a bit too late to negotiate the rules, don't you think? We are already a long way from home.'

'Really?' I asked, looking around. There wasn't much to see, except random houses and stores that passed by quickly, or a cow or two standing by the roadside. 'Where are we?'

'Somewhere in Haryana, not sure exactly where, but we have a long way to go.'

'How's the Fiat doing?' I said tapping the dashboard.

'Pretty well for a stolen car.'

'Nikku, you said it's not stolen!'

'A matter of perspective,' he grinned at me. I decided to drop it for now. I didn't even remember falling asleep. I was leaning against the window and the next second I was drifting in and out of sleep.

'Sorry, I should have stayed up to give you company.'

He laughed and put his arm around my shoulder. I felt my face heat up. I bent to take out the map from my bag. When I came up, his hand was on the gear again. I opened the map to locate Mathura and marked a big circle on it with a pen, marking a '1' on it, for the first stop.

'Are you excited?' Nikku asked. I nodded.

'What do you think we have to do with the Rasiya group?'

'I have no idea, really. It seems so strange that Lalaji set this up, but at the same time it is so . . . characteristic of him. He said he too inherited the shop in this manner. By completing some tasks as a test.'

Nikku nodded, seemingly impressed. 'And don't forget,' he added, 'we still have to place stakes on the Shah Rukh Khan bet.'

'I won't forget because I will win.'

He smiled and shook his head, his dimple peeking at me. I felt a pang of thrill when I realized that we had so much time to spend together. We were still in school when we spent entire days together. They had stretched out ahead of us, as long as the sun was out. We'd go home for dinner and then be out again for a quick walk once the breeze set in. I wanted to tell Nikku I was really excited that he had joined me but couldn't bring myself to say it, so I chose to look outside instead.

The sun was now high up in the sky and the car was beginning to get warmer. We mainly had fields to see as the road took us further and further south. There were many trucks and carriers too on the way and Nikku constantly had to change lanes in order for us to maintain speed. A lot of people we passed stared at our car; the Fiat wasn't discreet, that was for sure. I wondered where Mohit and Rohit were, and if they had already found the people we were supposed to look for in Mathura. What must be happening at home? I hoped Pappu Uncle wasn't giving my mother a hard time.

'I am thinking we should make a stop, get some strong tea and breakfast. The sun's starting to make me feel sleepy,' Nikku said, looking at me. I nodded in agreement.

A minute later, he got off the highway and stopped at a dhaba. I stepped out, stretching my arms and legs, and found a few people sitting around the tables, staring at us unabashedly. I looked at Nikku. He clapped his hands in anticipation and sat down, asking if we could be served *kadak* ginger chai.

The song 'Didi Tera Devar Deewana' was playing on the radio somewhere. I hummed the song in my head as we waited. A lanky boy came and asked us if we wanted to eat something as well.

'Aloo paratha?' Nikku asked me. When I nodded, Nikku asked him to bring four. On the road, cars and trucks dashed past at great speed. I couldn't believe that years later, years after I thought the time of Nikku and Taru was done and dusted, I was sitting with him, not exactly sure of where we were heading, and ordering aloo parathas.

When I looked at him, he simply smiled.

'Where you from?' A woman walked over to us, hobbling slightly, clutching her pallu in one hand, her old skin wrinkling. She sat next to us and smiled widely, revealing a broken front tooth. I was immediately reminded of Lalaji.

'We are from Siyaka,' I said, looking at Nikku.

She clapped her hands in delight. 'Siyaka!' Looking at the boy who served us, she yelled at him, 'Chotu, bring another chai!'

'Siyaka is a beautiful city,' she said.

'Yes, we grew up there,' Nikku added.

'Not like this rot here—the sun is too strong and a woman can't even go 200 metres away from her field, not even for natural business, without men jumping at her.'

Nikku hung his head, but I continued smiling at her. 'It's your dhaba, this one?'

'Yes, of course. My son does the hard work while I sit here and enjoy talking to people who stop by, especially those from Siyaka!'

The boy came with two steel plates, each holding a couple of brown, fat parathas with a huge wad of white butter in the centre and what looked like aam ka achaar on the side.

'You two married?' she asked, as I started eating. I shook my head vigorously while Nikku didn't react. The old woman shifted her gaze between us.

'Oh,' she said, her eyes widening, 'so *not* married. Boyfriend–girlfriend?'

I shook my head quickly again, to which she waved a hand. 'No need to lie. There were some in my time too. Boyfriends–girlfriends. I had one too.'

Nikku's eyebrows shot up. I couldn't help but ask, 'Really?'

She scoffed. 'No need to appear so shocked. I was the village beauty! In fact, let me tell you the story of my first love.'

We nodded meekly and I realized that 'Didi Tera Devar Deewana' had stopped playing. The beats of 'Aa Aa Eee, Oo Oo Ooo' rang out.

'He used to call me Kamal, you know, because there were a lot of lotuses in the ponds in our village. He said I was beautiful just like them. We never had a proper conversation, but we did see each other from afar. He worked really hard to convince my father to let him marry me. And finally it did happen. Everything was arranged: a mandap at my house, food for a hundred guests, my mother's wedding sari. I had never looked so beautiful and everyone was dying to see me. But you know what happened?'

'He never came?' I asked, and even before she answered, Nikku seemed impressed with my guess.

She nodded. 'So you're not so naive after all, huh? Men! Yes, he never came; the baraat never arrived. We waited until people began leaving early, and then it was clear to us that he wouldn't come. He had ruined my life in the worst possible way, and the sad part was that I still loved him. Even his betrayal couldn't make me hate him. Such is life. Sometimes you are dealt the worst possible hand and there are no reasons or explanations.'

I was prepared to offer my sympathy, presuming it to be the end of the story, but she was not finished.

'Yet everything passes, and bad time, no matter how long it may seem, goes away, ushering in the good. And a chance for revenge.'

Nikku's jaw dropped at this and I listened intently.

'I was sent off to stay with my *mamaji*. His village was located very far away, where no one would know of this unfortunate incident. Pretty soon, my mamaji received marriage proposals for me. I was then married off to my late husband. He was a farmer for some time but later decided that toiling in the heat was not his passion. So we moved here and opened this dhaba.'

'What was the revenge?' I asked.

She smiled again. 'I didn't expect to see him again, you know. But there he was one fine day, parking his truck by the side of the highway, sitting for dinner at our dhaba, ordering chai with his companions. I recognized him from afar. My heart froze for a second. Did I really care now, married with four children and running a successful dhaba alongside my husband, that a man had called me Kamal years ago and promised to marry me? When I saw him laughing with his friends, of course, I cared. What happened next was very simple. I took his order to him, my veil in front of my face. He didn't even bother looking up. Had he shown me even the slightest sign that I reminded him of someone, even if it was by the way I walked, I was so close to him at a point, I might have forgiven him. But he didn't.'

I put my hand over my mouth.

'I did what I had to next. At the back here, in our fields, used to grow these vines. Harmless to touch, but if consumed, poisonous. I plucked them, beat them into a paste and served them to him, in the chutney.'

I suddenly wished Nikku was sitting next to me rather than in front of me. His knee touched mine, assuring me, but I didn't dare to look at him. I didn't dare to look at our empty plates and tea cups, feeling the aloo parathas squirming inside me. I tried to look around without moving my head, wondering if I could still spot some of those vines. And then I heard Nikku gulp. I looked at him and as soon as we caught each other's eye the old woman burst out laughing.

Her voice cackled and I sighed in relief, my tense shoulders drooping. I tucked a strand of free hair behind my ear. Nikku shook his head, equally relieved.

'You believed me. I am glad. It means I still haven't lost my touch. Poisoning a guest! Who would ever do such a thing?'

I finally felt free enough to breathe loudly and had just begun smiling again when her face went sombre. 'I just made him a little sick.'

Nikku's smile was wiped right off his face.

'Tell me,' she said, obviously enjoying our discomfort, 'do you not put your life in someone else's hand every time you order tea and look away to gossip with your partner? Is our life not riding on this fragile code of trust, which if not respected will result in the breakdown of society? Never trust anyone! You are your only accomplice. I did not poison his food. Or did I? Only the gods are worthy of judging me. On our first night together, my husband came into our bedroom and started rolling a chillum, full of ganja. "Listen, Mister," I said to him, my voice in full command, "you cannot smoke ganja here—not without me,"' she added with another mischievous grin.

I looked down and saw that the menu had a lotus printed on top, which I had failed to notice until now. Nikku nodded at me and got up, asking where we could pay.

'Take care, you two!' the old woman said laughing and waving. 'My name is Kamal!'

We hurried back to the Fiat and locked the doors. Neither of us said a word until we were well back on the highway and a little way off from the dhaba.

'She was definitely crazy,' Nikku said. I nodded.

'What about the food?' I asked.

'What about it?'

'We ate it.'

'Come on, Taru, she didn't put anything in ours, I'm sure of it. I'm sure she didn't even put anything in that guy's food. I think she's a bored old woman who loves to have fun with all those who stop by.'

'She seemed crazy enough to do it though. "I said to my husband, listen, Mister, you can't smoke ganja in here, not without me."'

Nikku laughed. 'That was funny. I bet she saw that lotus on the menu and made it up on the spot.'

Her voice still rang in my ears. 'I didn't poison his food. Or did I?'

'What say you to another round of "Made in India"?' he asked chirpily, his hands fixed on the wheel.

'No,' I groaned, 'we've listened to it about fifty times now!'

'Or have we?' he asked cryptically, imitating the old woman.

I laughed.

'Well, it's only one of the two cassettes we have. Don't let the old woman get your spirits down! Come on, let's hit it—*Dekhi hai saari duniya . . .*'

We had been driving for quite a few hours now, and our initial excitement, fuelled by the old woman's story, had now faded. As the day progressed, it got hotter and the Fiat seemed to trudge on, also less enthusiastic because of the heat. I was hot, cranky and constantly thirsty. Siyaka also got quite warm in the day, but the breeze always helped cool things down. Here, in the car, we felt nothing except the bumps on the road and the relentless sun. We had decided to take a super-quick lunch break because we realized that we hadn't made great time, and if we didn't move quicker we wouldn't reach Mathura before late in the evening. Nikku had refused to drive on the highway after dark.

'Do you know how dangerous it is?' he had asked me.

I had abandoned all the aloofness I had decided to show. I sat cosily in the Fiat while he drove on. Though he had volunteered to come along, I was still extremely grateful that he had, for it gave me time to think about other stuff. My thoughts constantly harked back to Lalaji's cryptic smile when he talked about the magic ingredient and about us embarking on this quest. What did he want us to do?

At the same time, we had heard the term 'magic ingredient' so much in our lives that I never thought of questioning it: what exactly it might be, or contain. Could there be actual magic in it, something above the grasp of normal human beings? It couldn't be, I told myself, but what of it then? I swatted these thoughts away, it was premature to think of it.

'Are you tired?' I asked Nikku, my voice low while he sat attentive at the wheel. I felt a bit bad.

'Of you? Yes,' he said, shaking his head in exaggeration.

'I know you're not. I know you missed me a lot.'

He smiled before asking. 'Didn't you?'

I looked away. 'I was mad at you. You left to study and whatever you wanted, and you didn't look back . . . not even once.'

'I did!' he said earnestly, looking at me as much as the road permitted him, 'I did, I always thought of you and Siyaka, but I . . .'

He couldn't even finish his sentence, making me realize that he didn't even have a valid excuse. He wasn't able to say anything that would justify leaving, which was just as well: there really wasn't much to say. He had moved on to bigger things and I didn't seem to fit into those plans. In time with the rhythm of the car, with the sounds of the highway in the background, I wanted to say everything that was buried deep inside my heart.

But I held back, thinking back on the years and years of hurt which I considered betrayal.

'Come on, it's been years,' I said, a big, fake smile on my face, patting his hand that was on the gear. He looked at me, doubtful, perhaps realizing I didn't mean what I said.

'Taru . . .' he began, but I cut him off.

'God, how far are we, do you know? I could really stretch my legs.'

'I'm really—'

'Let's play Alisha Chinai again. But it's going to be the last time. We have to find some new cassettes in Mathura, Nikku. This damned radio never works on the highway!'

It was dark by the time we entered the city and though we were tired, we were still upbeat. I could feel Nikku's gaze on me more often now, perhaps waiting for me to decide the next step. Just the thought of that made my stomach curl up in nervousness. I didn't know anything more than what I had told him, and it suddenly seemed a little foolish to have driven all day and be completely without a plan. We had no place to stay, and moreover, nothing concrete to look for. The Rasiya group was our only vague hint. I made special effort to not catch his eye, looking outside in concentration, almost as if we would come across a signboard that would say, 'Rasiya Group this way!'

Soon, as the streets became narrower, it was harder and harder to drive. I could see that the stares we received were harder and more curious. Almost every inch of the streets was occupied by rickshaws and scooters, all of them honking continuously. The colour of our Fiat seemed to be even more prominent in the dark. We must have been in the centre of the city, for now the roads were choked. Markets bustled on both sides and someone often tapped on our car.

I looked at Nikku in frustration. 'Let's park a bit far from this *hulchul* and then decide our next course of action? The commotion won't allow for space to think.'

He nodded, honking patiently at the big group of boys who were now walking leisurely right in front of us. After ten or so minutes we came on to a wider street. Seeing some space in a corner, Nikku stopped the car there.

He turned to me and I suddenly felt nervous.

'Okay, why don't you stay here and I'll walk around a little to ask about the Rasiya group. Lalaji said that everyone would know them,' I said.

'What, no!' he said, looking around. 'Why would you go alone? It's late, Taru!'

'So what if it's late? We have to finish the task!'

'Yes, but wouldn't we be better off if we started in the morning? We don't even have a place to sleep. Shouldn't we find a room for ourselves?'

His answer made me forget what I was going to say next. A room for ourselves? Would we stay in the same room? Were we going to share the same bed? The thought made my face heat up.

'I think we should start now, Nikku,' I said. 'We'll figure out the sleeping part, but I wouldn't be able to wait until the morning to ask around.'

He took a couple of seconds, but then nodded and jumped out of the car. He locked the Fiat and said he'd come with me. We walked back to the main market, dodging scooters and puddles. I lifted my pants as my feet flopped in some dirty water. I felt dirty and tired. I looked at Nikku. Surely he must be more tired than me. He did seem a bit haggard, but he still smiled when he looked at me.

A loudspeaker blared out announcements or advertisements, I couldn't tell, and I wondered who to ask. A man sold chaat where we stood, expertly plating bhalle with dahi in oodles of imli ki chutney. I looked at Nikku and then approached him.

'Uh, *Bhaiya*,' I asked, as his hands moved swiftly and he nodded to indicate that he was listening, 'do you know where I can find the Rasiya group?'

He grinned at me, beads of sweat shining on his face, his hands still moving mechanically. 'Rasiya! Go there, to Mandir Chowk.'

'What is it?'

'What is what?'

'The Rasiya?'

'You just asked me for it!'

All I could do was stare at him, confused, unable to explain why I was there.

'You want chaat? Five rupees, one plate.'

Nikku, who was one step behind me with his hands in his pockets, raised his eyebrows on hearing the question.

'We can take one and share,' he said, and I nodded at the chaat-wallah. Within seconds, he had handed us a plate that had two bhallas and papdis. I realized it had been a while since we had lunch and the chaat was delicious, just the right amount of tangy. We ate slowly as we watched the street. Men and women walked about haggling at the stalls, crying babies in their arms, little girls holding their fathers' hands. Next to us, a man sold colourful wares and peacock feathers. Rickshaws lined the roads behind which hung T-shirts in rows, all claiming to be the latest style. There was a huge queue outside Shreeji Doodh and Petha Bhandar, and I wondered if we should also try the petha there.

'So what about this Rasiya?' I asked the chaat-wallah again, more confident now. 'What is it?'

'They do *naach-gaana*, what else,' he said, 'but the whole city comes to watch them perform. Young boys want to join this group, dance as Radha . . . it's very prestigious to be chosen as Rasiya.'

We nodded and quickly finished the chaat, handing him back the plate. As we walked towards Mandir Chowk, folk music flowed through the streets.

Soon, we could see the towering temple, lit up from the outside. It was easy to find the path leading up to it. With barely any space to walk, the streets were packed with sellers who had on offer everything from little white-beaded decorations to hampers of prasad, including cakes and nuts. Some booksellers sold literature on Krishna, or the book of *aartis*. The further we went, the more crowded it became. I felt Nikku standing close, his shoulder bumping against mine.

'Madam, buy some prasad, evening bhajans going on!' a seller called out to me. I smiled and walked on.

I looked around for Rohit and Mohit, expecting to see their round faces in the middle of the crowd, peering from behind their glasses. But there were strangers around me, laughing and heading towards the mandir. Where were the Rasiyas? Would there be a signboard? And how would I talk to them? How many of them would be there?

Almost as an answer to my volley of questions, we entered a courtyard and saw people around a group. We knew instantly it was them and walked over, pushing through people to get a clear look.

A few men sat in the middle, one playing the harmonium, another on the tabla, two more with manjeeras and another with a tambourine. Women danced around them, singing, clapping their hands in the air—they wore colourful lehengas with dupattas expertly placed into the skirts and around their heads. Their bangles jingled as they sang along to words I barely understood. I decided it must be proper Braj Bhasha which they were singing in and glanced at Nikku to ask if he understood anything. He was watching them curiously. I then tried to figure out who to talk to and gave Nikku a nudge when I saw an old man sitting at the very back, behind the dancing women.

'Are you part of the Rasiya?' I asked, walking up to him.

He had a large, thick beard and very expressive eyes. One look at me and then Nikku, and his face hardened.

'Yes, I am.'

'Well, do you know my grandfather, Lallan Taneja? Or do you know of someone who would know him, in your group maybe? We are from Siyaka.'

He made an expression that could only be called a grimace. I took a step back towards Nikku.

'Do you even know who we are, who are the Rasiyas? We are the direct descendants of Krishna! We don't remember the names of commoners, of people who come to learn from us!'

'So, he came to you to learn?'

He made an annoyed face and looked away, trying to ignore us.

'Sir, sorry, but you seem very learned. Wisdom shone on your face from across the courtyard and that's why we came to you. All we want to learn is some of, uh, Lord Krishna's teachings,' Nikku tried.

The man looked him up and down, and said after a pause. 'And why do you want to learn it?'

'To follow the path of righteousness. Her grandfather sent us here; he said we should learn from the best.'

I saw him raise his chin high and realized that Nikku had managed just the right amount of flattery.

'The ways of Krishna, how he teaches us to be and behave, are many and most nuanced and complicated. All these *bal gopal*, stealing the *makhan* tales are but for entertainment. The real Krishna is in the Gita, and we have been charged with the responsibility of spreading his word in this modern, blasphemous age. People from Australia to America follow us and here our own culture disrespects us!'

'We don't really,' Nikku said, sitting down beside him, 'tell us something about him. Something you recently read, or thought about.'

I suppressed a sigh. I didn't want to sit there, listening to the old man talking when we could be out there asking the other Rasiyas if they knew my grandfather. But the old man would get offended if I walked away now, so I too sat next to him.

'Very few have what it takes to follow the path carved out for them, without giving in to desires or follies. Every day the world becomes more materialistic, full of objects and people that tempt us to move away from the path of duty, the right duty. Very few have it in themselves today to detach from worldly pleasures and keep their eye only on the goal, to not stray. Can you remain equally unattached to failure and success, indifferent to desire and revulsion, in the throes of calm at the time of your greatest happiness and sorriest grief? It is only when you understand that this world is just a passing, a mere path in what is actually to come, that you start shedding these man-made emotions and creations.'

I stifled a yawn. Nikku probably sensed that and hurried with his question. 'Well, we do want to learn more about that. We would like to follow our grandfather's wishes and meet the person who taught him.'

The man shrugged. 'Why don't you go to the back of this courtyard and find a woman named Meenakshi? She's the big gossip, I'm sure she will be able to tell you more.'

I couldn't get out of there fast enough and ended up dragging Nikku by the hand. When we got there, I called out to strangers, asking if they knew Meenakshi.

She obviously was well known for a couple of other girls called out to her, soon after which she walked towards us. She had kohl-rimmed eyes and was barefoot, her dupatta trailing after her. She smiled widely, looking at Nikku curiously, but then turning her eyes to me.

'Are you Lallanji's granddaughter?' she asked. I nodded, almost breathless. 'Wonderful! Lallan told me to expect you. He said you wore these classic Siyaka pants and kameez. Next time, bring me a pair, okay! Now follow me inside.'

Chapter 6

I let Nikku lead this time, following close at his heel, as Meenakshi led us through dark and narrow lanes that were still abuzz. It seemed like there was some kind of festival going on, with *torans* hanging outside every door and people up that late. They looked on curiously as we walked by, the children making silly comments. It took all my strength to not hit back or reply. I was going to ask Meenakshi where in the world she was taking us when she finally stopped and pointed to a small door. When we walked through it, I couldn't believe my eyes.

The place was twice the size of the courtyard we had just seen and full of more Rasiya people. All the women and men there were dressed up—some looked as if they were ready to perform, the others just enough to practise. Little groups sat together, some singing, others chatting. There was a house at the back, with people rushing in and out. I glanced at Nikku who seemed as dumbfounded as me.

Where in the world were we, and what was this place? A dance troupe? A circus? A conglomeration of folk singers? I looked at Meenakshi for the answers, but she merely grinned at me. Before I could open my mouth, she led me to one corner and pointed to a charpoy. 'Sit and stretch, you've had a long journey. You want something?'

We shook our heads.

'The food is over, but there are drinks at the back,' she added lowering her voice, a giggle escaping her. 'But in a bit.'

'What is this? What are you?' I asked, making an effort to shut my mouth that hung agog.

'Look around. What do you see?'

Nikku nudged me towards another huddle close to where we were. They were practising with some puppets while another group behind them had one man standing in the middle, his dhoti neatly tied, his hair in a thin ponytail, reciting something that the others around him gasped and exclaimed at. Next to them, a woman walked with multiple clay pots on her head. I had just about managed to focus on her when another man interrupted my line of vision, a humongous peacock feather sticking out of his hair, dressed in a bright yellow dhoti.

I looked blankly at Nikku who asked Meenakshi, 'Do you do . . . *raslila*? That Krishna story performance?'

Meenakshi raised her eyebrows and scoffed. 'Raslila! A much abused word now, isn't it! We have gone a lot further than what traditional raslila groups have ever done—we have expanded into so many art forms, and that's why traditionally they never accepted us. But look at us now; do people come to see the Bhakti Sagar group? Do people come to see Sri Radha Shyamsundar Mandir? No, it's us they come after, because we change with the changing times!'

I was utterly confused by then. What was she talking about? What did any of it have to do with the task Lalaji had assigned to me? I tried to ask her, but she held up a hand and shut me off.

'He told us. Do *you* know who we are?'

'The Rasiya . . .' I said.

She narrowed her eyes. 'Huh, and I took you for the smart one!'

Nikku smiled at me smugly.

'We are the descendants of Krishna, girl! Our tradition, our living, our livelihood is his doing, his teachings!'

'The descendants of Krishna!' I exclaimed, finding it hard to keep the note of scepticism out of my voice.

'Well, it can't be that rare, can it,' Nikku snorted, 'if he had 16,000 wives?'

'Not descendants by blood, silly boy!' Meenakshi said. 'Do you not know the Yadava clan all killed each other? We are the descendants of his word. We make sure his word passes from generation to generation, never dying out!'

I nodded. 'And what does he say?'

Meenakshi folded her arms. 'Well, I can't tell you everything yet; it's something you learn slowly. I can tell you some things though.'

'Like what?'

Her eyes were like little beads by now, lights shining behind it. 'What is it that you want most in the world?'

The immediate answer in my head was Lallan Sweets. I was about to say it out loud when I caught Nikku staring at me. Meenakshi grinned.

'Really? The *most* in the world?' Nikku asked.

I swallowed my answer. Lallan Sweets couldn't be what I wanted the most in the world. Continuing the legacy of Lallan Sweets, along with Ultimate Mathematics Tuition

Centre? For my mother to be happy? For sure, my happy, smiling mother . . . Nikku looked at the sky, contemplating his own answer. I couldn't think of what he would want the most in the world.

'Okay, let me make it easier for you,' Meenakshi said, 'these things that you want, are they real?'

'What do you mean?' I asked.

'Most of what we want is not real, but an illusion. It will vanish in a second. We hardly ever know to want the right things.'

I pouted, looking at Nikku. So now this was going to be a life lesson. Did we have to pretend to learn and then she would tell us what we would have to do? Was this it, this quest, a series of life lessons that the inheritor of Lallan Sweets must learn? Nikku still looked sincere, so I tried not to roll my eyes.

'My things are real enough,' I replied.

'I'm not sure,' Nikku shrugged. I gave him a curious look.

'You *must* know,' Meenakshi said. 'You must know what you want the most in the world, and it must be real. This world is full of unreal things, of illusions that mean nothing, but we grow up to believe that they mean everything. Right as children, maya's *jaal*, its vicious net, is set up, which tells you to do one thing after the other. Go to school, study for this test, give your board exam, then go to college, get a job, marry someone, take care of your stupid children. This jaal teaches you to worry so much about everyday things. How must one go beyond it, to want what must really be wanted?'

'And what must really be wanted?' I asked. It was easy to say such things; it was hard to make them relevant.

'It's different for everyone,' she grinned.

'That's convenient.'

'Do you have it in you then, Tara Taneja, to want something beyond the material, beyond what will gratify you?'

I squinted, and before I could say anything, Nikku asked, 'But what must we do to want this—this real thing—if we are already trapped in maya's jaal?'

'You must do, stoically, your duty, which is whatever you are supposed to do. Every act of yours is karma. You being here is karma, you and I talking right now is karma. You must do your karma in accordance with what you should be doing. If you follow this path, you will soon find maya's jaal behind yourself, the lust of ordinary, everyday things, which in their core essence are meaningless.'

'But all those things are not meaningless,' I piped in. 'They have all the meaning in the world. What we are here for, it has meaning.'

'And what's that meaning?' Meenakshi asked. 'What meaning does it add to your life?'

I wanted to lash out and tell her what Lallan Sweets meant to me, and what it had meant to my father and Lalaji who spent all their lives at it. How could something like that be meaningless? I held my tongue though; I wasn't there to change her opinion, I was just there to finish my task and walk away.

'Right now, I'm here to do my *duty*,' I said, 'what I came here for. What is my task? What must I do? And did Rohit and Mohit already come to you?'

She paused for a few seconds and then Nikku spoke up. 'I don't want these things. These which you talked about? That's why I left what I was doing. But how do I know what's the right thing to want?'

Nikku was staring at Meenakshi now, transfixed, completely oblivious to the fact that we were there for something else. I tried to nudge him, but Meenakshi had leaned closer to him by then.

'I could tell you,' she said, 'but I suspect you'll know soon enough.'

I could see Nikku's mouth parting a little; this was absolutely ridiculous. Nothing she had said yet was so shocking that his mouth should fall open. I accidently-on-purpose pushed my elbow into his ribs.

'So,' I said, crossing my arms, 'are you going to tell me now or not?'

Meenakshi smiled again and then pointed to her right. 'You see that woman? In the yellow skirt?'

'Yes,' I said slowly. She was obviously a part of the troupe and practising right then, multiple pots on her head.

'You have to do that,' Meenakshi said, getting up and clapping her hands in finish.

I looked at her blankly. 'Wear a yellow lehenga?'

'I think she means balancing those pots on your head,' Nikku pointed out, staring at the woman.

'A woman who is able to cross the main mandir stage, during our evening show, with three pots on her head will have completed the first task and will get the hint for the next one,' Meenakshi said.

'Are you serious?' I looked at the woman in the yellow lehenga. 'How in the world will I do that?'

When I turned around Meenakshi had walked off. 'What are you—Nikku! How will I do that!'

He shook his head and asked if I wanted to go find some drinks at the back, where Meenakshi had pointed. He had already started walking before I could answer, and so I followed him in the direction Meenakshi had gone.

'Oh, I get it,' I hurried to walk in step with Nikku. 'I know what's happening here!'

'What?' he asked, looking straight ahead.

'You like her! Meenakshi!'

'What!' Nikku tried to look outraged but did a poor job of it.

'You do!' I almost yelled.

'Well, she's pretty and had interesting stuff to say!'

'I don't believe this,' I said and crossed my arms, walking straight into a backyard where some of the troupe drank from plastic cups in a corner. I tried to look away from Nikku but continued to watch him from the corner of my eyes. Someone offered him a glass and, after eyeing it suspiciously, he accepted it.

'I just think she's pretty,' he repeated lamely.

'Oh, I agree with you. She's very pretty. I'm sure it helps when she's trapping people in her maya jaal bullshit and then idiot guys like you end up joining this raslila! Or Rasiya, whatever!'

'I won't be joining this group, Taru,' he said taking a huge swig from the glass. 'She just . . . she looks a lot like—did I ever tell you the story of my first crush?'

Had I been holding a glass, it would have definitely fallen from my hands. The last few days of my life had been quick, surprising and full of unexpected twists. Yet this was the most shocking of all, so much so that I couldn't believe what he had just said. The story of his first *what exactly*?

'The story of your first crush?' I asked.

'Yeah! I'm sure I never told you. I mean, I was too shy to say it, especially to you . . .'

How could Nikku be saying all this? How was I not his first crush? He spent his every waking moment with me until he was eighteen and I fifteen. He was *my* first crush! Still is, I realized with a pang. The pleasant, nostalgic expression on his face made me want to punch him. How could he say all this so calmly? As if on cue, Meenakshi arrived, her *payal*s going *chan-chan*.

'In case you were wondering about your sleeping arrangements, I have a place for you,' she said.

I'm sure she had a place for Nikku—in her bed!

'And where is that?' I asked, smiling dangerously.

'Women's hall on the left, men's on the right.'

I nodded in response and throwing Nikku one last, dirty look, stalked off to the women's hall, leaving him to reminisce about how much Meenakshi reminded him of his first crush.

I sat on the courtyard steps in the light of the morning sun, watching the *matka*s in front of me. They were painted pink, white and green, a sheen over their curved walls. Bundled up, they sat atop each other, and I couldn't help but think how hard could it be.

I clutched the turban in my hands and put it on my head. I had got it from one of the women. Perhaps I should practise with something smaller first.

I kept the turban aside and picked up a smaller *kulhad*, one of the smaller clay cups, placing it on my head. I felt stupid doing it, but then I looked around to gain some confidence. Who wasn't looking stupid there, with the costumes and practices? The moment I took a step, the kulhad began shaking, toppling off the side of my head, ready to crash had I not caught it. At least that was a win.

I tried a few times again, finding it hard to balance the kulhad on my head, continuing until one finally fell and broke.

'About time that happened,' Nikku said, appearing from the back. I made a face at him.

He then came and sat next to me, making a whole show of observing me with his arms crossed. I ignored him and went for a steel glass. I wasn't sure they'd be very accommodating of us if I broke all their kulhads. And then I remembered!

'Nikku, the car! Is it still parked there? All my stuff's in there!'

'Of course. I already parked it safely once you went off to sleep,' he said, his face lighting up in amusement. 'It's funny how you thought of it just now.'

'I forgot. Had other things on my mind . . .'

Indeed I did. Who could possibly be Nikku's first crush besides me? Surbhi Didi who used to cut our hair? The kho-kho girl who came one summer to train us? Some tourist that he saw in Victorian town?

'Listen,' he said, coming closer and looking right at me. I leaned forward, wondering if he was going to tell me that he had meant me after all.

'I transferred our important stuff to the backpack,' he said, pointing to what he was carrying on his shoulders. 'Money, licence, our clues . . . remember that we always keep these with us, okay?'

I nodded in disappointment and went back to the steel glass. Guess it didn't matter, and perhaps I would never know if he even had a crush on me or not.

I tried a few times again with the steel glass, but it was even worse than the kulhad. Ultimately, we gave up and went looking for breakfast.

Nikku ordered two glasses of lassi along with aloo-poori, and it helped cheer me up a little. I didn't know what was bothering me more—the fact that I couldn't carry three pots on my head and walk across the stage or that I wasn't Nikku's first crush. When we had eaten, I asked him to wait while I went to the phone booth next door to call my mother. Her voice sounded anxious and distant, but I assured her that we had reached safely.

'How will you balance the pots on your head? You should have learnt yoga when I asked you to,' she said.

'Mumma, what does that have anything to do with this? Anyway, did anyone ask for me? Buddy?'

'Buddy who—Sahil? No, I don't think so . . .'

'Okay. Tell me something. Do you remember when we were young, when Nikku and I used to play, do you think that Nikku . . . liked me?'

'What do you mean?'

'I mean, do you think he had a crush on me? When we were kids?'

I could almost hear her scratching her head. 'Of course, he did. He was always running after you. A boy his age would only be friends with a girl if he had a big crush on her.'

That definitely made me feel a lot better, but there was the chance that she only said it because she knew I wanted to hear it. I hastily bid her goodbye and returned to our table.

'I'm still in two minds about having another poori,' he said.

I put my head on the table without answering, resting my cheek on the back of my palm. All the noise seemed to be blurred out and I shut my eyes, ashamed to be already feeling so dejected. This was just the start of this great adventure. What would Nikku think of me? While I sat there ruminating my fate, Rohit and Mohit were probably on to the next clue already. I saw Nikku place his chin on the table, asking me if I was okay.

'I need a bath,' I told him.

The kurta was wet around my shoulders as my hair dripped water, but I already felt much better. We had asked the kind-looking woman at the aloo-poori restaurant if I could bathe at her house. Apparently the Rasiya group went to communal bathing pools, which I told Nikku I couldn't handle. I had even slipped on a pair of earrings that the woman had insisted I take; she said that it went well with my peach kurta.

'You look like you're feeling better already . . . and pretty,' Nikku said, giving me a huge smile. He had been waiting outside. I smiled back at him, but only a small smile for I couldn't forget that I wasn't his first crush.

So engrossed was I in trying to ensure that I appeared cool that I bumped into a large, solid figure right in front of me.

'I am so sorry,' I said, holding up my hands. The tall guy turned around and waved off my apology, when suddenly his expression changed and he looked me up and down. Come on, I thought angrily, the kurta wasn't even that wet any more. I looked at Nikku, ready to take him by the hand and walk off, when I saw that he was equally mystified by the stranger.

'Tara Taneja!' the man yelled. I took a step back, wondering how he knew my name. I stared at him. It took me a few seconds to realize that I knew him, but how! And then something clicked as soon as he said his name.

'Vijay Mathur! You don't remember?'

I looked at Nikku, who seemed to have recognized the man standing before me. I smiled, still unable to place him though. 'Our senior, Taru, do you not remember him?' he said and I looked at the man again who then took note of Nikku's presence.

His smile tightened. 'Nikhil Sabharwal! Still together you two, huh? I see . . .' his face turned red.

And then I remembered—the boy with the tomato face. The senior from our school with the big, red face. What was that rhyme Nikku had made for him? I couldn't stop myself from turning to Nikku and mouthing it. '*Tamaatar jaisa laal, bhediye ke baal—*'

'I'm not like that any more,' Vijay said, forcing a laugh and glaring at Nikku.

'Oh, don't worry. He used to make up rhymes about everyone,' I told Vijay. 'I mean, just a few days ago, I met him for the first time after years and he greeted me with "Taru Taneja moti hai".'

'Why after years? I thought you both must be . . . well, ever since school . . .'

'Oh no,' I waved my hand in dismissal, 'no way, I mean . . . Nikku, no. Anyway he left right after school.'

Nikku shot me a weird look and Vijay smiled. 'Well, come on, you're in my city. Let me get you some chai.'

We sat near a chai *thela* and Vijay Mathur proceeded to narrate his family history. I nodded along to his chatter, bored soon enough. Nikku narrowed his eyes at him.

'And have you seen the mandir on the corner when you take left from the chowk? The small one, not the main mandir, of course, well, my family got it built,' he said proudly. 'They didn't want me here when I was growing up. The boys are very rowdy here, you know. So they sent me to Siyaka to stay with my mamaji, but you know that. That's why I could never take part in the summer kho-kho championship, because I had to come back home. I always used to admire you in school, you were so fearless. People made fun of me a lot, especially those kind of guys, the ones who were always playing kho-kho.'

Was that a snide remark for Nikku?

'Have I ever told you about my gun business? We have a roaring trade . . .'

And so he went on for about twenty minutes before asking, 'Anyway, what are you doing here?'

'Oh, just some work,' I looked around, wondering when we would be able to get away. I still had to master balancing three pots on my head.

'Tara, I have to say, you have grown up to be so beautiful. I mean, sorry, I didn't mean it like that.'

I just stared at him, unsure of what to say. I looked at Nikku and he seemed as nonplussed as I was. To our chagrin, Vijay went on, 'We, my family, Tara, we have money. And they are not completely against this love kind of marriage.

I know you have that mithai shop back in Siyaka, and for my family, just to see that is enough, they wouldn't want anything else. You know what I mean. I don't know why I am saying all this to you. It suddenly feels like life has given me a second chance, making me meet you. I never expected . . . I always liked you in school . . .'

'Okay, sorry, but we have to go,' I said, getting up. 'Nikku, you have some change for the chai?'

My question seemed to have shaken him as he slapped a few coins into the chai-wallah's hand, ignoring Vijay Mathur.

'Tara, I'm sorry,' Vijay Mathur began as we walked away, waving at him hastily. Nikku started laughing only when we were many lanes away.

'I never noticed how different these were,' he said, looking at me. I looked down at myself and wondered what he was talking about.

'The Siyaka kurta and trousers,' he said. 'I mean, I have always seen them, of course, but now that you're with me I can see how everybody is noticing these and how different they look, isn't it? It helped Vijay Mathur recognize his long-lost love for sure.'

'Eww, Nikku!'

Secretly, I was glad that Nikku wasn't making more fun of this. Maybe he was thinking of a rhyme. I looked at my clothes again. Well, they were quite different. Siyaka pants were made of cotton, straight and generally loose and white. But they ended a little above the ankles. And yes, the kurtas had two circular collars on the top. I wanted to tell him that people were probably staring at us because we looked lost and vulnerable. We reached the courtyard again and I looked around, walking up to the woman who had been balancing the pots on her head the night before and asked if she would teach me.

Without those pots, she seemed like a regular woman with a big nose, expressive eyes and a smile that asked a question. It could have been anyone. It could easily have been me. She folded her arms and looked at Nikku who walked behind me, pointing a finger at him. I don't know what she meant by that, so I shrugged and told her it was me who had to learn. After what seemed like a long pause, she said, 'Three is a lot of pots.'

'I have to do it,' I said.

'What's in it for me?'

I looked at Nikku who seemed to be expecting this answer. He drew a deep breath and asked her, 'Do you like Siyaka kurta and pants? Siyaka salwar-kameez? Meenakshi said they were becoming the rage here but were not available anywhere.'

The woman grinned.

I had to start with something small and strengthen my neck muscles first, she said. She then taught me several neck exercises, which I practised.

'You stand too stiff!' she almost yelled. 'Did they say you have to stand stiff? Is your future husband coming to look at you that you stand so awkward? Loosen your body!' At first it bothered me that Nikku was watching us, but soon I forgot about him. We did more. After some time, she put the turban on my head, saying I must walk around with it in the evening.

'Only this,' she said, holding up an accusing finger as if I had already broken a rule. 'By the evening, it must be a part of your body. You cannot turn your head without thinking about it. You cannot move without the turban inside your head. It is as much of you as the mangled hair on your head.'

'My hair's not mangled,' I said, touching it consciously. I had just washed it. The turban on my head felt like it would slide down any second, and sure enough, it did. I gave her a reproachful look and apologized. 'Sorry, won't happen again.'

Every time I walked now, I was conscious of my movements, walking in a straight line, turning my entire neck instead of just my head. I thought Nikku would laugh, but he seemed rather impressed and joined me for some time. We practised walking across that stage many times, and finally I could do it without the turban falling.

'Well, you better keep at it till the evening.'

Next, we tried this in the crowds, when people started arriving at the temple for the evening prayers. Initially, I got some stares, but most people probably thought I was one of the Rasiyas. 'Toes first,' I muttered to myself, remembering what I had been taught. 'The heel will make you confident, make you arrogant. You start to think you have the whole world, and you start to take the earth for granted. The toe, it always teaches you your place in the world. To live quietly with nature. Make your steps light and graceful!'

Later that evening, my teacher told me that I had been stupid to practise with an empty kulhad. 'You have to fill it up,' she said.

Nikku, meanwhile, had disappeared from my evening session. I had a sneaking suspicion that he was watching Meenakshi practise.

'You have to fill it up to balance it. Put this sand in it. Go on, more than just a quarter of the way . . . yes, that's right.'

She was right. Though the pot was now heavier on my head, it was sturdier. A couple of hours later, I could easily walk the length of the courtyard with the pot on my head. I grinned at her, excited and happy.

'My Siyaka pants and kurta,' she said, eyeing my clothes, 'I wait.'

'Yes, I will give them to you,' I said, my business instincts kicking in, 'but I have to balance three pots first. After that.'

'I know. That's the toughest part. Now you think you can do it, and that's the problem. Go to bed. Tomorrow at 7 a.m., we start again.'

I looked around for Nikku again but figured he must have already slept off in the men's hall. I went to my own mattress and crashed.

Rummaging through my bag, I counted my clothes, wondering how many she would want. Nikku had easily offered her my clothes without thinking how many I actually had. I had six pairs and decided that I could afford to lose a maximum of two. She should be happy with that. I then decided to wear the same pair as last night's, so she would think I had few anyway.

When I went out, Nikku was already waiting in the courtyard, looking groggy and rubbing his eyes. 'Morning,' I said to him, raising my eyebrows, 'you seem tired.'

'Oh, yeah . . .' he said, stifling a yawn. 'Didn't sleep enough . . . that well. How's it going? I was thinking we could save some fuel and you could carry our luggage back up to Siyaka on your head, now that you've so much practice . . .'

'Oh, ha ha.'

He laughed too, getting up to follow me. 'So what about breakfast?'

'I'll practise for a bit first.' My teacher too had appeared by then and I realized that I still didn't know her name. She raised a hand, 'Go run for an hour! You'll need it during the day!'

I looked at Nikku, and he smiled in agreement.

I broke many pots. I wondered how they were going to replace them, but I definitely wasn't planning to ask. In the beginning, it was frustrating. I had half a mind to call Lalaji and ask him why I had to do something so useless. What also ate me up was why I hadn't seen Rohit and Mohit banging their heads against these pots. But once I began enjoying it, I forgot about my concerns. There was this giant thing on my head, balanced precariously, and I was in charge of it. How I walked, took a breath, moved my eyes—all of it determined whether the pots would fall or not. I had to completely shut out the world, align my thoughts and cast them on the path ahead, all the time being fully aware of the pots.

I still couldn't manage the walk I was supposed to though—the main mandir stage was almost thirty metres long. I couldn't even walk ten metres yet, no matter how many times I tried. I was beginning to think that it was impossible. It probably needed months of practise, which was why only special people like the Rasiyas could do it. 'You just need to not think they are on your head,' Nikku said.

'Why don't you try?' I shot back at him as we headed towards the chowk for dinner.

'Sorry, but the rules clearly stated: "A woman who is able to cross the main mandir stage with three pots on her head",' he said as we reached the chowk. Looking around, he asked, 'What do you want to eat?'

'Mmm,' I looked around the street; the usual bustle was on and I could see the bhaiya who had sold us chaat the other day. 'Let's have some dal and paneer. What else—' I turned to Nikku, but he had stopped dead in his track, his face frozen. I looked down: had a scooter run over his feet?

'What? What happened?' I asked, shaking him.

'Taru—a woman! The rule says a woman who is able to cross the main mandir stage!'

'Yeah, so? I know that!'

'It says a woman—but nothing about a *man*.'

'What . . . what do you mean?'

'The rule was very specific in saying a woman, but what if a man crosses with the pots? They will have to give us the next clue!'

At first it seemed stupid. Wouldn't that be the dumbest solution if a man could easily cross it? But the more I thought about it, the likelier it seemed. There was no reason Lalaji would make me do something as stupid as this, and maybe this was just for gags. The main trick was to use your wit to solve the task. To do it without doing it. Could this be it then?

'I can just walk across the stage and the task would be over,' he said.

'Should we go and see if we can?'

I looked at him, past the people trying to push us aside, past the chai stalls and the peacock feather costumes, past the rickshaws paving their own paths. We hurried back and Nikku spotted Meenakshi. We both went up to her.

'We found a loophole,' I said breathlessly. 'It says a woman. A woman must carry the three pots on her head. He's not a woman.'

'And thank God for that!' she giggled.

I held back my retort. Instead, I asked, 'So can he do it? Can he do the walk and we get the next hint?'

She shrugged. 'You should have figured this out sooner. Indeed you can.'

I looked at Nikku, thrilled to bits, and he too smiled broadly. We could be out of there by the evening.

Nikku went up to the stage, ready for his walk. But the woman who taught me found me first, demanding her Siyaka pants and kurta. I told her I'd still give her what I promised, but she asked me why I wouldn't do the walk with the pots.

'I don't need to,' I said.

'But now you *can*. I know it. I've seen you. Why don't you do it anyway?'

She was right. I should do it anyway. Why shouldn't I?

'But I still can't do three pots,' I told her. 'They keep falling.'

'Take his name,' she said with a wink, 'and they won't.'

I knew she meant Krishna. So despite my misgivings, and the ridiculousness of it all, I did.

And I managed it. I balanced the pots. In the evening, when the stage was set up and I looked ahead at its daunting length, I shut my eyes and told myself I would be able to do it. I could hear Nikku yelling for me. I could feel Meenakshi's testing eyes on me. Hundreds of times, as I walked across, I said only one word to myself, the pots balanced precariously on my head, looking at nothing except the path in front of me. Our first conversation with Meenakshi was playing in my head. Nikku waited at the other end, crouching, waiting nervously, clapping his hands often, yelling, 'Come on, Taru'. When I completed the walk, he took the pots from my head and bent to give me a happy hug.

'She said I would be able to do it if I took his name,' I told him, 'Krishna's name.'

'You did it because you practised, Taru,' he said, smiling, 'Come on now, let's find—'

Meenakshi appeared just then and handed me a letter. She winked at Nikku before leaving.

'Come on, let's get our stuff and get to the car,' he said.

I handed a couple of my pants to the woman who taught me and also gave her a tight hug. We walked through the chowk and had barely reached the Fiat when we heard him again.

'Tara Taneja,' his voice boomed. Nikku and I turned around with dread. Vijay Mathur stood behind us, but this time with five of his friends. It was dark and I was suddenly scared. I should have treated him with more consideration instead of walking away, humiliating him. What if he got mad? What did he want now?

'Hey,' I said nervously.

'I believe I deserve the chance to say everything, including what all I can offer you. You should definitely give me a chance,' he continued, while his other friends stood there with their arms crossed.

'No, it's fine actually, you see. Nikku here is my boyfriend,' I said to him, and Nikku nodded. Rather unconvincingly, I couldn't help but notice.

'Well, all the better,' Vijay Mathur sneered, 'let's have a competition and see who is more deserving.'

This had to be a joke. All my life I had waited for Nikku to say he loved me and now Vijay Mathur, who I hadn't seen in years, expected Nikku to fight for me?

Vijay Mathur stepped forward, rolling up his shirt. 'Come on then. What did you call me? Tamaatar jaisa laal, bhediye ke baal, he just kisses—does a kiss—what was it?'

'He just wants a kiss, but is a *tai-tai phis*,' Nikku said unhelpfully.

Vijay Mathur went red again.

'Taru, get in the car,' Nikku said.

Did Nikku actually want to fight Vijay Mathur? He was twice his size and had friends to boot. I tried not to let the ludicrousness of the suggestion show on my face.

'Uh, I don't think—'

'Taru, go,' Nikku said, his face focused on Vijay Mathur. I looked from one man to another before stepping aside and sitting in the car. I was nervous. If it got scary, would they even listen to me?

Nikku positioned himself, looking ready to fight. Vijay got ready too, pulling his fists up. They faced each other tensely for a few moments. And then Nikku made the first move. But instead of charging at Vijay, he ran straight towards the car. 'Go, go, go!' he yelled. I locked the doors as Nikku started the car and sped off, leaving Vijay Mathur and friends running after us.

Chapter 7

We stopped the Fiat once we were quite a distance away from Mathura. It was only then that Nikku urged me to open the letter that Meenakshi had handed to me. My hands shook as I tore open the envelope.

Dearest Taru,
So you've done it—crossed the first task in what might right now be one of the most exciting journeys in your life. This is just the beginning though.

There's a good chance that you must be thinking whether your poor Lalaji has finally lost his mind, asking you to put pots on your head and walk. There is no greater reason for asking you to do this, except—just because.

Sometimes, when I look at you, I am scared because there is so much of me in you: you plan one thing after the next, you are ready to get going and get work done every morning. You build things from the ground up, full of energy, achieving your goals and ticking them off one by one.

But this was a reminder to do things for their own sake, not for a greater purpose, just for their sheer joy. Remember when you refused to go to your Kathak classes because you felt they would add nothing to your life goals?

I was so proud of you then, of my granddaughter who was so single-minded.

But now, Taru, I am older and want you to remember to do some things just for fun. I was in Mathura once, when I was younger than you, loitering around the mandir, looking at people for no reason at all. I didn't even know why I was in the city, except that I had hopped on to a train that was going to Mathura. I had nothing to do, nowhere to go except home, so I just hung around watching the Rasiya. And that's how I met your grandmother. So remember, Tara, that to do something for no reason at all can be the best thing you do.

Yours,
Lalaji

'Of course,' I whispered, holding the letter close, 'how could I forget! Lalaji met her here . . . in Mathura.'

My grandmother had died before I was born. I never met her. As the years went by, Lalaji spoke little about her, and I mostly never thought about that part of his life. His life that he had shared with his wife. For me, he had always been just Lalaji.

'Taru, this is terrible,' Nikku said suddenly.

'What?'

'Lalaji found your dadi here in Mathura, his life partner. Maybe he wants the same for you, and that's why he sent you to Mathura. You met Vijay Mathur but we just ran away from—oww, you're pinching me too hard!'

'Don't take his name again,' I said as he leaned back, laughing. I turned the letter around and there was more from Lalaji on the other side.

Your dadi and I always wanted to see the Taj on a full moon night. We couldn't, but you can. Send me a picture of you at the Taj on a full moon night and I'll send you your next hint. Wah Taj!

'Taj. He wants us to go to Agra! Well, there's no way we can do so right now.'

'It's not that far.'

'Taru, it's almost ten! I had to get out of the city because of your lover boy, but we can't get on the highway. Can you imagine the thugs and the thieves and what not—'

'He's not my lover boy.'

Nikku looked at me in amusement. 'It's a good thing that I'm tired and can't think of any jokes. Let's drive to a motel or something.'

I, meanwhile, tried to get the image of Vijay Mathur out of my head.

Nikku pulled over at the first motel we saw. The board said 'Motel VJ' in neon red and green, and despite my protests Nikku insisted that it would be the best for us.

'Got the bag?' I asked Nikku, referring to our small, important one. We could leave the bigger one in the car.

'Dhak Dhak Karne Laga' played on the TV at the reception, but apart from that it didn't seem as shady as it looked from the outside. The receptionist, whose eyes were fixed on the screen before we came, suddenly stood up. Taking in our appearance, he cleared his throat once and gave a little bow.

'Check-in?' he asked politely.

We nodded. Nikku unshouldered our backpack.

'Come to see Taj? Honeymoon?' he asked. I looked away, embarrassed. Was this guy daft? If it really was my honeymoon, would I have been looking as haggard as this?

'No, not honeymoon,' Nikku replied laughing, handing him our IDs. He looked at us confused. And then he read the names, the smile vanishing from his face.

'No unmarried couples!' he whispered furiously, slapping the IDs back on the table. Nikku seemed completely taken by surprise.

'Excuse me, Mister Manager!' I said. 'We are not a couple, he's my brother! Cousin *hai mera*!'

'*Aaj* cousin *hai, kal saajan hai*!' he said, sliding the IDs back towards us. 'We do not entertain unmarried people in the same room.'

'We don't even want a double bed!' I said, the heat rushing up to my face. 'We want two singles! He's my cousin brother and I am here because I have an exam in Agra tomorrow—a government exam—and my parents really expect me to clear it! Where will I go in the middle of the night, tell me? My cousin is studying in the college here, but of course he's not allowed to have girls in his boys' hostel. That's why we are here! I have travelled the entire day. Please let us stay here or it will ruin my exam. Please? We'll be out of here first thing in the morning.'

He took another look at my pleading face and paused for a full minute before he took our IDs back. 'Payment now,' he said in a harsh tone, 'and just for one night!'

We hurriedly paid him and he pointed us to our room. We crossed the motel bar, a little, dingy room.

'I better not hear any noises from here,' he said before handing us the keys. I pretended to look offended.

'Oh, don't worry,' Nikku laughed. 'She has a boyfriend, and better still, he's a world-famous DJ!'

I kicked him in the shin before shutting the door behind us. Two dreary single beds lay next to each other, in front of which was a very small television. Eclectic curtains were drawn across the windows. Nikku dropped the bag on his bed.

I tried to turn the TV on, but it wouldn't work. 'Well, let's just go to bed, I guess—'

'Did you see the bar downstairs?'

'Yes, it seemed interesting.'

'Let's go there,' he said, already walking to the door, 'we have to celebrate the completion of your first task!'

I looked at him curiously for a few seconds, shrugged and then followed him. This couldn't mean anything. Hadn't he been quick to remind the manager that I had a DJ boyfriend?

I didn't recognize the song that was playing when we walked into the bar, which smelt of cigarettes, peanuts and liquor. The entire place was bathed in a red tinge. There were just men at the tables, huddled in pairs or alone. I felt all eyes on me when we walked in.

'Better let me be your husband here,' Nikku said quietly. I laughed when I remembered the manager's quip: Aaj cousin hai, kal saajan hai . . .

'Yes, Sir,' the bartender said as soon as we took a seat, and suddenly realizing his manners, turned to me and added, 'Yes, Ma'am.'

Grinning, we asked him what was available and accepted his suggestion of their special 'imported' whisky. 'Not many in this area can stock imported whisky, Sir,' he said, pouring it into our glasses and then adding in a lower voice, 'they deal in desi *tharra*, totally locally brewed, and what not. Here, we strictly forbid it. Not fit to be consumed by people like you.'

He turned to me and smiled once more before leaving.

'Never thought I'd seem so fancy,' Nikku said, raising his glass.

'Oh, please! He meant me.'

We clinked our glasses. I drank slowly, not particularly relishing the whisky that burnt its way down my throat. Nikku pulled a face. 'It seems adulterated. So much for his lecture on tharra. It's not so bad, you know. Remember what we drank with Meenakshi? It was almost that . . .'

I raised my eyebrows. 'Looks like you made a friend.'

Nikku quickly took a sip and said, 'Don't be jealous. I can have more than one friend.'

'She didn't want to be *just* your friend.'

'Still jealous,' he said, and I looked away annoyed. Why did I even get into these stupid conversations with him? I had to act cooler than that. I noticed the man sitting next to our table staring shamelessly at us. I looked away in irritation.

'Let's play a game,' Nikku said.

I looked at him in confusion. 'What do you mean? What game?'

'I mean a game for fun.'

'But we're here. How can we play a game? Do you mean "Raja Mantri Chor Sipahi" or something? We need four people for that.'

Nikku rolled his eyes. 'No, I don't mean that, Taru! Something fun, like a drinking game. We used to play that all the time in Bangalore.'

'What do you have to do?'

'Okay, let's see,' he said, resting his chin on his glass. 'I will make a statement—it can be my opinion, or what I think is right. If you agree with it, I drink. If you don't agree, you drink.'

'Okay,' I said, replaying what he had said in my head, 'let's start.'

'Tara Taneja has a strange nose.'

I stuck my tongue out at him and took a sip of the whisky.

'I have to take a sip!' he said indignantly.

'Shut up.'

'Okay, how about this. Secretly you really like my rhymes, especially when it's about people like Vijay Mathur.'

I couldn't help but laugh. 'Okay, fine, you win, I do!'

He grinned broadly before taking a sip. 'You are thrilled that "Bolo Tara Ra Ra" has your name in it.'

I waited for a few seconds and then took my hands away from the glass. 'I love it!'

He took another gulp.

'Let me go now,' I said, clutching my glass and looking around. 'If you agree with it, I drink. If you don't agree, you drink.' In the dim red hue of the place, I caught some eyes looking our way.

'You are scared of Lalaji,' I said. He stared at me for a few seconds, eyebrows in a furrow.

'I used to be, but I'm not now,' he said, signalling me to drink.

'Are you telling the truth?'

'It's the basis of this game!'

'Fine. You still have your *kancha* collection, and clean it from time to time.'

'Damn right I do!' he said, taking another large sip. 'What kind of man would I be if I couldn't maintain my kancha collection?'

I gave him a weird look before going on, and suddenly realized the opportunity I had. I narrowed my eyes at him and said, '1988, our last golgappa-eating competition, after we won the kho-kho championship . . . you cheated, didn't you?'

'You can't ask questions. It's not truth or dare.'

'Okay,' I said. 'Okay, you said you ate twenty-seven golgappas but you actually ate just twenty-three. Remember, Nikku, truth is the basis of this game.'

He waited for a few seconds as his eyes made contact with mine. I knew he was struggling, and I watched him carefully. I knew he didn't have it in him to break the rules of his own game. And I was right. He sat back, his head down, silently admitting to it. I slapped my hands on the table and finished all of my whisky, although it wasn't my turn, and happily asked the bartender for another.

'Nikku-Tikku, the famed champion of the 1988 Golgappa-Eating Competition, carrying around a false victory for years,' I announced to the bar.

'All right, fine. But don't act as if you are very righteous. You've cheated many times too!'

'This is about you, Nikku.'

'My honour was at stake,' he whispered, his voice suddenly vulnerable, and I had to lean forward just to hear him. 'I had done so badly in the exams, I had to do my father proud somehow.'

'I know. That's why I didn't bring it up after you got the prize, although I had my suspicions.'

His father always had such expectations of him, and I knew it affected Nikku a great deal. His father had lived in Siyaka all his life, becoming one of its best-loved men, running Sabharwal Siyaka Stationers, winning the Golgappa-

Eating Competition until his stomach couldn't take it. He had expected Nikku to follow in his footsteps and offered to open a photo studio or a fancy new stationery shop for him. But Nikku had turned the offer down, studying hard and moving to Bangalore instead, leaving his father (and me, to be very honest) heartbroken.

Nikku never talked about any of this though, and maybe him doing so now was the magic of the whisky. He was about to say something when the man who had been sitting at the table next to ours walked over, smiling and his eyes slightly out of focus. 'Don't even try,' Nikku warned him before he could even open his mouth. He hung his head and returned to his seat.

'What were you saying?' I asked Nikku.

'That let's drink this and get back, huh?'

We finished our drinks and I continued to tease him a bit more. I have to admit that my head spun a little as we walked back, and I bumped my shoulder into his arm.

'What?' he asked.

'How'd you do it?'

'Well,' he said, opening the door to our room and ushering me inside, 'the trick really is to direct the attention somewhere else. So when the bhaiya was handing me the golgappas, I put my other hand on my stomach like I had had too many. I really built it up slowly, acting as if I was in pain. And then, after a few more, I rubbed my chest as if the golgappas were getting stuck, like I was going to choke. Then even the bhaiya got scared for a bit.'

'What a con,' I said, as he stood in front of me, his eyes boring into mine. Even as he explained how he had cheated, his eyes seemed sincere and honest. 'But where did the golgappas go?'

He leaned forward. 'I crushed them in my hand, letting the water fall, and then stuffed the remains in my pocket. Trust me, it's really hard, this deception, it's all about practice really . . .'

His face was now inches away from mine. Why had he left Siyaka? *Why?* Everything had been so perfect, and even after all this time, it felt like nothing had changed.

'And now I think we should go to bed because it's really late and that whisky seems to have hit you hard.'

I looked down. 'Right.'

The next morning, Nikku drove through the city, squinting and trying to look at the names of the streets through the glinting sun, even as I yelled at people to get out of the way. We hadn't spoken much during the drive. I had seen Nikku walk out of the bathroom in a towel, water dripping from his body. The last time I had seen him that naked was two summers before he left, or that time when he had been swimming in Dima Lake when he was still a boy and didn't have that chest.

When he laughed at my obvious awkwardness, I simply gave him a cold look and walked away.

He honked at the crowd that refused to budge.

'Arre, *hatto!*' I yelled, 'refusing to move like Tendulkar—get out of the way or we'll ram you with the Fiat!' A bicycle almost hit us from the side and I tapped the guy on the head.

'Taru, there's no need to get violent.'

'He almost hit our car!'

The sweat and grime added to our irritation as we got closer to the Taj Mahal. Finally, we squeezed the Fiat into a little parking spot and stepped out. 'Take the bag,' I said groggily to Nikku, who grunted as we ignored the people ogling the Fiat.

'What if someone steals it?' I murmured.

'Will serve us right,' Nikku said, swinging the bag on to his shoulder as we walked, crossing little stalls of Moradabadi biryani, Agra petha and souvenirs. We were ambushed by a bunch of rickshaw-wallahs who offered to take us to the ticket counter. 'One rupee only, straight to the west gate!'

'Buggy ride, Madam? Buggy for you and Sir? Romantic ride, Madam.'

Nikku suggested we walk. Under the shade of the trees on the footpath, it was actually nice and breezy. I wondered why we couldn't see the Taj Mahal yet if it was so big. It had to be an exaggeration.

'Have you seen it before?' Nikku asked me. I shook my head.

We walked through the crowd to reach the counter, joining the queue. The tour guides around asked us repeatedly if we wanted to take a tour, and I sent them off. There were many foreign tourists wearing hats, sunglasses and holding umbrellas. I snorted at them—it was just a bit of sun. I turned to Nikku, only to find him looking let-down.

'We can't see the Taj at night,' he said.

'What? Why? I'm sure we can. Lalaji said so.'

Nikku shook his head as I shoved him away to talk to the man at the ticket counter myself. I tried every trick: I flattered him, yelled at him, threatened him, and finally resorted to bribing him, much to the chagrin of the people standing behind us. But the ticket man wouldn't budge.

'Try bribing him with your Siyaka pants,' Nikku said as I looked around helplessly.

We finally gave up and moved away from the queue, only to run straight into a tall guy who was dressed sharply in a shirt and trousers, and was smiling at us.

'Come with me,' he said cryptically and turned around, giving us a backward, devilish glance. 'I specialize in couples.' Nikku looked at me strangely and was about to say something, but I put my hand up.

We walked away from the Taj Mahal and turned on to a street that had a number of tourist booths. The man led us inside one little shop, on the walls of which were big posters of the Taj Mahal, Agra Fort and other tourist destinations.

'I'm Khan, the guide,' he said, putting his hands into his trouser pockets, smiling widely. 'Please take a seat.'

Nikku and I barely managed to squeeze ourselves into the two tiny chairs placed in front of his desk.

Khan turned, his back to us, and then suddenly opened his arms up. 'The city of love, the city that cut off twenty-thousand pairs of hands, the city where the dead are enshrined in a tomb the world had never seen . . .'

He turned back to face us, his arms still extended, staring at us. When neither of us reacted, he went on. 'The city that spawned a thousand stories, when it became the seat and throne of the great *shahenshah*, the king of kings . . .'

'Which one again? Who made Agra the capital?' Nikku asked.

Khan folded his arms back and stood up.

'That's the question, isn't it? The great secret!'

'Not really, since we studied it—'

'The Great Agra City Tour: Taj Mahal, special entry to the tomb, Agra Fort, Fatehpur Sikri, the tomb of Akbar the Great, travel in Maruti car, water bottle free, lunch at a famous three-star, only rupees—'

'Can you show us the Taj Mahal at night or not?' I interrupted him.

'Of course, I can show you the Taj Mahal, Madam. It is a splendid structure, one of the Seven Wonders of the World, but looks the best when the rays of the sun are bouncing off the white marble!'

'Mr Khan, please! We are not interested in all this. If you cannot show us the Taj Mahal at night, we will leave right now.'

'Fine. I don't have the tickets to see the Taj Mahal at night!'

Nikku and I gave each other a tired look and got up to leave.

'But I know someone who does.'

We sat down again.

'These are very exclusive tickets,' Khan said. 'One is only allowed to view the Taj Mahal on a full moon night, and two nights preceding and following that night. Very few of these tickets come out for the general public, and most of these are snatched up by greedy, conniving travel agents who offer them to foreigners only. One of these agents, luckily for you, sits right down the street. He will certainly have tickets for tonight's night viewing.'

Nikku leaned forward. 'Well, how can we get it?'

'See, although the ticket is not expensive, it's exclusive. He is not allowed to sell the ticket at a higher price, so he only offers them to people he deems to be rich tourists, so they might take other services from him too.'

'I see what you mean,' I said. 'You want us to pretend we are rich NRIs, and only then will we get it.'

Khan nodded.

'Who should we be?' I asked Nikku. 'I can be Reema Singhania from America, with my millionaire husband Anil Singhania, steel tycoon, best friend of Ambani.'

'I don't know,' Nikku said, sounding unsure. 'I think anybody called Anil Singhania should have a beard. One of those French beards, you know.'

I agreed with him. Anil Singhania could not be taken lightly. I mean Nikku was wearing shorts for God's sake.

'What do you get out of this though?' I asked Khan.

He smiled sheepishly. 'Well, if you can get me a photograph of the Taj on a full moon night, I will use it on my brochure. Then I will be part of the big league of travel agents, you know. I might be able to get night-time tickets in the future.'

Nikku nodded at him.

'I have an idea,' Khan said. 'Let's find some different clothes for you two. There is a local market here that sells rejected imports. Even the rejected import is very important here, see?'

'What is a rejected import?'

'Come with me,' Khan said. 'By any chance do you have a car? We have to make a great impression . . .'

A couple of hours later, Khan was driving the Fiat while both of us sat at the back, uncomfortable at this loss of power. I wore trousers and a blazer, with heels that barely let me walk. The good part about the pantsuit was that it was for really thin guys, so it fit me perfectly and I could make the impression I had in mind: the formidable NRI. I had decided to be a working wife. Nikku too wore a formal suit, but he looked extremely uncomfortable.

'Try to look angry and professional,' I told him.

'Your suit is too big for you,' he said to me.

Khan drove us back to his street, stopping the car just near Pankaj Travel Agency, and told us to go in and do our thing. I asked him to open the doors for us, to create a better impression, and he did so. Once I stepped out, Nikku handed me sunglasses, which I wore with panache, suddenly feeling the character as heads turned to look at us.

'I'm going to wait in the car,' Khan said, 'he might recognize me. But make sure you also negotiate for a ticket for me! To get the Taj photograph!'

'Yes, we know,' I hissed.

Nikku and I held hands, and just for a moment, it could have been the cover of a magazine: my hair flying in whatever little wind a hot Agra morning offered, both of us wearing sunglasses and almost matching pantsuits. I had even put on a dash of red lipstick. The heels made me look almost as tall as Nikku.

A blast of cool air hit us as we walked into the office. It was from the cooler positioned at the window. A man sitting behind the table immediately got up from his chair. I removed my sunglasses, looking around with slight disdain and watched the man's face turn eager. The thing is, I should have been an actress. It was just that acting opportunities in Siyaka weren't the best, or I would have been Shah Rukh Khan's preferred lead. 'Welcome, Madam, Sir, welcome! Please sit, sit! Chotu, *paani la! Jaldi!*'

'Uh, no. Thank you,' I said, putting my hand up daintily although I was thirsty, 'we can't really drink *local* water . . . our stomachs are not used to it, you know.'

'Oh,' said the man, who I assumed was Pankaj of Pankaj Travel Agency, crestfallen. I found Nikku staring at me with his eyebrows furrowed. I pinched the side of his knee in response. My accent might not be the most genuine, but whose really is? And how would this travel agent ever know?

'What can I do for you, Sir, Madam?'

I looked at Nikku as he cleared his throat and placed his hands on the table. I was sure he was wondering how to match his accent with mine, finally imitating some English movies that were often played on cable TV. 'Actually, we have lived most of our lives in America. We don't come here much, once in ten years maybe. It has been Tara's, my wife's dream, to see Taj Mahal under the moonlight. It's my anniversary gift to her, this trip. Today is our anniversary and we want to spend it under the moonlight. At Taj.'

Pankaj clapped his hands together in delight. 'Happy anniversary! Amazing, amazing. Of course, I understand, yes. Yes. May I ask where you're staying, just out of curiosity?'

'Umm, at the Taj! Hotel, you know?' I butted in. 'Very comfortable.'

'Wonderful, wonderful! Most of our guests are from Taj only. And which city are you from in America?'

'New York. City,' I blurted. It was the only city I knew and I hoped that he won't ask for more. I wasn't sure if I would be able to make up an English name for a locality.

'Very nice, very nice . . . and what do you work as, Sir, Madam? If you don't mind me asking?'

'I am, well, a scientist. I mean, I call myself an engineer there, at a big company, you probably don't know the name. It's an Internet company.'

He looked blank. 'What's Internet?'

'I can't possibly explain . . . there's a huge technology lag between America and India.'

'Oh,' Pankaj looked completely enchanted, 'and you, Madam?'

'I'm the president of a charity for Indians in America,' I replied.

'That I understand!' he laughed. Then, with a wink, he added, 'Charity begins at home, huh?'

'Of course! Always!'

'Well, great then. I must tell you that our full moon passes are very exclusive, generally only for foreigners. But, of course, for esteemed people like yourselves I can make an arrangement. You need pickup from hotel?'

'No!' I said quickly. 'We have a driver. Actually, we need one ticket for him too. We don't go anywhere without him. He's kind of our . . . uh, bodyguard, if you know what I mean. Sensitive business, can't say too much.'

'We are best at being discreet,' Pankaj muttered. 'Be outside the Taj Mahal complex at 11 p.m. We'll take you from there. Also, I would suggest that if you like our service, take the rest of your tour with us. We are the best in the city after all.'

'Yes, sure,' I said, trying to sound confident.

'Your names please?'

'Mr and Mrs Singhania.'

'Perfect! Wah Taj!'

The next thing we knew, we found ourselves walking towards the Taj complex on a cloudy, full moon night, at a time when the city was mostly shut and only a stray dog barked somewhere. A scooter whizzed past us.

I asked Nikku what Internet company he was talking about. He shrugged. 'Just made it up. And what was that president of charity thing? He might expect us to bribe him, thinking that we have so much black money that we've opened a charity!'

'He anyway would have expected it. Best to get it out of the way. Let's try and see if we can avoid it.'

Khan, meanwhile, was over the moon. Literally. He kept trying to hold the moon between his thumb and forefinger, saying he would take the best picture ever for his company pamphlets. We got there to find a throng of people waiting outside the gates. I realized that Khan was right. It was either foreigners or rich-looking Indians there. I straightened my pantsuit and held Nikku's hand in an effort to look like a modern couple. The change in his expression was easy to notice. Just as I was about to comment on it, I spotted Rohit and Mohit in the group, both of them looking at us in astonishment.

Chapter 8

The murmurs from the people around had faded into the background. The darkness was punctuated by random beams of light from a distant streetlamp and Pankaj's flashlight. It was hard to miss Rohit and Mohit, who too had dressed up in suits and stood right next to each other. It struck me that Nikku and I were still holding hands. I immediately jerked mine away and noticed a mystified look on his face, but only until he too saw Rohit and Mohit. The four of us stood surveying each other for a few seconds before Khan whispered into my ear.

'Friends of yours?'

Before I could answer, Pankaj appeared and ushered us forward. 'Come to the front Mr and Mrs Singhania. Don't lose yourself at the back!' I didn't dare to look at Rohit and Mohit. Had they caught what Pankaj said?

Seconds later I knew the answer, as Rohit gleefully walked up to me. 'Mr and Mrs Singhania, are you? Is that why you are wearing these fancy clothes? You never called us for your wedding!'

I refused to answer, not wanting to create a scene, but I couldn't help asking him, 'How the hell did you get in?'

'Easy,' Mohit said, his face smug, 'I got him sent Lallan Sweets' finest. We have been here for a few days. Did you just arrive?'

I was so mad. As genius as it was simple. Why didn't I think of bribing him with sweets? Who would say no to that! Of course, the sweets would have to get here first, which smelt of Pappu Uncle pulling all kinds of strings to make sure his precious sons got what they needed. Even if I were to try and use this trick at some point in my journey, who would send me the sweets? Would Mumma possibly be able to help me out the same way?

Nikku shifted nervously behind me. I was about to lead him away when I saw Rohit and Mohit walk up to Pankaj and gesture wildly at us. He wouldn't! *Those dogs!* And then I saw, almost in slow motion, Pankaj heading towards us as the rest of the group walked on. Even in the darkness, I could see his face was red. I clutched Nikku's hand in fear, realizing that his was as sweaty as mine.

'You're Tara Taneja!' he said, a vein in his forehead throbbing as if it would burst, 'and Nikhil Sabharwal, known thieves of Siyaka! You fooled me! Get out of my sight before I have you arrested!'

I couldn't believe it. They told him we were thieves from Siyaka? I hadn't expected them to sink as low as this.

'We are not thieves!' Nikku replied, outraged. 'What would we steal, the Taj Mahal?'

'There is a lot of valuable stuff in there!'

'But how would we steal it? You said so yourself, we are only allowed entry up to a certain point. How would we—'

'Oh, I'm sure you have a few tricks up your sleeves, ones that ensure you sneak away in the dark. I can't believe I let you two fool me! Mr and Mrs Singhania!'

I opened my mouth to defend ourselves but then let it be. Our defence about not being thieves would basically be an admission that we weren't Mr and Mrs Singhania. Pankaj then warned us to not come near the Taj and shouted at the guard to make sure we were sent away. Khan followed meekly as Nikku and I watched the group enter the gates and disappear. The guard shouted at us to go away, and we shot him a dirty look.

'Welcome to the Taneja household,' I said glumly. 'Bringing each other down since the day we were born.'

I could tell Nikku was fuming, but he didn't reply. We sat down on a low wall next to a Moradabadi biryani stall that was shut. Dust gathered in the air, a sure sign of a storm, and I asked Nikku if we should head back to the Fiat. He was so angry that he didn't even hear me. I looked at Khan as he walked towards us, his *paka-pakaya* plan gone bust. And then it started to drizzle. I shook Nikku once more, telling him we should go take cover.

'I want to go in now,' he said. Khan, meanwhile, had reached us.

'Come on, it's raining, Nikku,' I said, tugging at his arm, 'we'll think of something else tomorrow.'

I had never seen him look so angry. He still didn't move. 'We can't give up this easy,' he said. 'We have to get in somehow.'

I looked at Khan in exasperation, who, to my surprise, shared Nikku's sentiment.

'Madam, he is right.'

'It's raining even harder now! Have you both lost your minds?'

'Exactly, it's raining,' Nikku said gleefully, as I watched the raindrops cover his shirt. My own pantsuit would soon be wet. 'Let's sneak in.'

'If it was so easy to sneak into the Taj, people wouldn't try so hard to buy tickets,' I said, looking at Khan for support.

'Let's go,' Nikku said, grabbing my wrist and heading back.

By the time we reached the gates again, we were drenched. We stood behind a tree as it poured all around us, the rain beating down relentlessly against the concrete. I was vicious enough to hope that it would spoil things for Rohit and Mohit too.

'Listen, the guard is not at the gate now, he's inside his little booth,' Nikku said. 'It's our best chance.'

'But this is plain view, he'll obviously see us! We can't just walk up there!'

'I'll distract him,' Khan said bravely, 'and considering it's the Taj, he won't be the only guard posted. I'll bring the Fiat, start honking like a crazy person, drive a bit rough and force them to approach me.'

Nikku clapped his hands. 'Perfect.'

'But . . . but . . .' I said, 'can we just trespass on a national monument like this? What if we are arrested for this?'

'Arre, even if the police takes you, we will say you are lovers and can't think straight. It's your honeymoon, whatever! This is your best chance.'

Nikku nodded and handed Khan the car keys, taking from him the camera that he had got for us. It was still raining steadily and I prayed that it would continue till

Khan brought the car. Nikku and I stood together in silence. I shivered a little, suddenly feeling cold. Nikku seemed to be cold as well, and I was just about to ask him when we heard the Fiat skidding a little way away from the entry gate to the Taj Mahal.

In dramatic fashion, the headlights were turned on and off a few times, and then the honking began. Khan blew the horn like a maniac, lurching the car forward and backward, the headlights going on and off. It was like a spirit had possessed the Fiat. The guard came out of the booth, squinting in the darkness. Khan was absolutely spot on about there being more guards, as a couple more dashed towards the first guard. For a couple of minutes they wondered what to do, before deciding to approach the car. Huddled under an umbrella, they made their way to the Fiat through puddles. As they got close to it, Nikku held my hand and told me to run.

'What?'

'Come on, let's go!' We ran hand in hand from behind the tree and towards the gate. All through I prayed to God that the guards wouldn't turn around and see us. As we sprinted through puddles, it felt like I would never be dry again. We approached the gate and, as expected, it was locked. Nikku looked around wildly, heading behind the guard's booth. At least that offered some cover.

'We have to jump over those railings,' he said, pointing towards it. The boundaries of the Taj Mahal had railings on top of the wall that surrounded it. I didn't want to be a killjoy and tell him how high it was. We dashed towards the railings and he bent, asking me to climb on to his shoulders. 'Now stand!' he said.

It was a precarious balance as I stood on his shoulders and grabbed the railing for support. I was now high enough to be able to place a foot on the railing and pull myself up. Then I turned around to give Nikku a hand up, but he looked doubtful. He jumped, his hands gripping the top of the wall as I pulled him up. With some help, he grabbed the railing and finally pulled himself up.

'You do a lot of pull-ups?' I asked him and he merely laughed in response. I jumped and landed on the other side with just a few scratches. We had had enough practice in Siyaka; many a guava had been stolen that way and we were none the worse for it. Seconds later, Nikku landed beside me with a thud.

'Come on, let's hurry,' he said. We ran across the ticket counter, which was shut, and past another gate. The rain had slowed down and running in the pantsuit was becoming difficult. 'We have to run faster, he'll be coming back soon. From here until the last gate, it's a clean view!'

I wanted to tell him that I was tired of running but decided to save my energy. I couldn't help but wonder how many laws we had broken. This was one of the Seven Wonders of the World, not some rugged fort like the one in Siyaka, the walls of which lay derelict. We went through the gardens, under the archways and past another structure that didn't look white and definitely didn't look like the Taj Mahal.

'This is one of those red brick gates. Maybe a mosque, I don't remember,' Nikku murmured.

We reached the final archway and caught a glimpse of the monument in the moonlight, and realized why Lalaji had wanted to see it. It was easily the most beautiful thing I had ever seen, and at that point I had only seen it through a little doorway. We walked very quietly now, knowing that Pankaj's group, including Rohit and Mohit, could be close.

From the other side of the archway we saw the moonlight bouncing off the white marble. Now that the clouds had shifted and the rain had reduced to a drizzle, the Taj gleamed and seemed to reflect its own light. Even the fountain in front of the main dome seemed to sparkle. The trees blended into the darkness while the minarets stood out in contrast. The other structures on either side of the Taj Mahal cast black silhouettes. I wished Khan was here to tell us all about it.

Both of us were so enamoured by the sight that we fell silent, unaware of the other person until we turned to look at each other at exactly the same time. Nikku's shirt clung to him, exposing the top of his neck and highlighting his chin, which I had never realized was so angled. His trademark floppy ears stuck out as always and his eyes too appeared to be lit up. He smiled and extended a hand to my face, catching the dripping water from my hair, and then turned to face the Taj Mahal again. I reached for his hand and we stood there for a few more minutes, staring in admiration.

'I don't think we can go any further,' he said.

'We don't really need to. Let's take a picture here.'

First, I clicked the Taj Mahal in the best frame possible for Khan's catalogue. Then Nikku clicked a picture of me, standing in front of the main dome, to be shown to Lalaji.

'I think the Taj Mahal also warrants a picture with both of us in it,' I said and we tried to somehow angle the camera into a position away from us. We had no idea if we were even in the picture and had been grinning at each other stupidly when we heard someone call out, 'Hello, *kaun hai wahaan*! Who's there?'

A flash of light fell on us and we instinctively put our hands in front of our faces. As soon as sense kicked in, I grabbed Nikku's hand again, this time in panic. We immediately ran back the way we had come, for that was the only way we knew. So focused had we been on trying to get inside that we had completely forgotten to plan how we would get out. The guards would surely be back in their positions now that the rain had stopped. And we had that wall to climb.

We heard some more shouts behind, but there was no time to look back. Our clothes seemed heavier now, the wall seemed higher and the menacing shouts seemed to get closer and closer. We managed to jump over the wall again but the landing wasn't as smooth this time. I scraped my hands and legs but didn't have the time to feel the sting.

'The guards will be there. Don't even look at them, just keep running straight,' Nikku said. I nodded, limping along. I shut my eyes and ears to everything except the path before us.

We raced past the guards who were definitely taken by surprise. By the time they reacted, we had already reached the street and were looking for the familiar Fiat.

We barely registered what was happening any more and continued to run as we heard people behind us. It was when my legs gave up that the Fiat skidded to a halt in front of us and Khan threw the doors open. We got in, Nikku telling him to hurry. I didn't dare to turn as we traversed through the winding lanes. Both Nikku and I were still panting when Khan banged on the steering in delight.

'You got the pictures, right?'

'Yes,' I said. 'But where now? Where should we go?'

Once we were far enough, he stopped by the side of the road. 'Where do you have to go?' he asked.

'We?' I shrugged and looked at Nikku. 'We have to get these pictures developed, post them to Lalaji, and well . . . wait for his letter.'

'Why?' Khan asked blankly.

'It's a long story,' Nikku answered. 'But where do you think we can go, park this Fiat safely out of view and get these photos developed?'

Khan made a face. 'I want to be nowhere near this Fiat. The police are already looking for it, thanks to my antics to help you get inside! It will be known to harbour the criminals who broke into the Taj Mahal complex. This car needs to go away. It's so easy to spot too, especially in a small place like this!'

I hadn't thought about that, about the consequences. Now we were stuck with being runaways.

'We can't just chuck the car,' Nikku said impatiently. 'And we need a few days, I mean, the photos might take a couple of days, and then we actually need the pictures to reach Lalaji and get a reply.'

Khan was lost in thoughts. 'I have a suggestion . . . I would have asked you to stay in my house, but I live in a single-room accommodation. You take the Fiat, drive up to my house in Bareilly, where my family is. They will be happy to let you stay with them. Meanwhile, I can get the photos developed for you and for my brochure. You can give my Bareilly address to your Lalji for a reply.'

'Lalaji,' I said.

'Whatever ji.'

Nikku and I stared at each other, considering Khan's suggestion. The dampness inside the Fiat, thanks to us still being wet, was making me uncomfortable. Also, all of us were exhausted and hungry, and I would give a lot to share a plate of samosas and be in bed.

'What do you think?' he murmured. 'I think let's just do this. Bareilly is not too far; Khan can send us the pictures there.'

I agreed. Khan said he would let his family know in the morning, but it would be better if we got out of Agra before dawn. I wrote down my home address for him and he promised to get the photographs delivered. We shook hands before saying goodbye. I got out of the car to sit on the passenger seat as Nikku took the wheel again.

With the threat of going to jail not imminent for now, my wounds started to hurt. I pulled my pants up to my knees and grimaced.

'Oh no! Did you hurt yourself?' Nikku asked.

I nodded. Nikku stopped the car on the side and took out a bottle of water. 'Let's at least wash the wounds,' he said. I braced myself, sticking my legs out. It burnt as he ran water over them. I couldn't help but laugh as a strong sense of déjà vu took over. 'It's like a classic day of intense kho-kho,' I said. 'One of us ends up being hurt.' Nikku laughed too, flicking a few drops of water on my face with a chuckle.

'I think you should change your clothes,' he said. 'These pants will keep sticking to the wounds. And we should tie a handkerchief over it.'

I looked around dubiously. 'How will I change here?'

'What? Just do it at the back of the car. I won't look!'

I slowly slipped out of the stupid pantsuit and slid into my salwar-kameez in the cramped space that the backseat offered. 'Could you hurry though?' he called out. 'I don't feel safe out here, the two of us on the highway.'

'Almost done,' I said. Nikku changed after me. I stood in front of the car while Nikku started the car again, whining about having to be out on the road at night. Minutes later, we stopped at a petrol pump, Nikku refusing to step out of the Fiat to check the meter. 'I will not be cheated!' I said in a huff, jumping out of the car despite his protests, and stood watching the meter with my hands on my hips. Nikku too came out angrily, berating me for being irresponsible in the middle of nowhere, looking around with narrowed eyes. There were just a couple of other cars there, which he looked at nervously.

'You don't have to worry about me. I am used to taking care of myself.'

He shook his head. 'I know. I'm worried about myself. Can we go in now? Come.'

'I think you need some music to cheer you up,' I said, turning the radio on. 'Let's see what we have here, shall we?' I tuned in, only to find that the only song on was 'Jaadu Teri Nazar', which didn't do much to ease the tension in the car.

'Is your leg fine now?' he asked me, his eyes on the lookout for signboards that would point us towards Bareilly.

'Yes, I think so,' I said, looking down to examine it. 'I could do with some food though.'

'Yes? Me too . . . we can stop at some dhaba. Not for too long mind you, we'll make it quick . . .'

Was there something different about Nikku since our Taj Mahal moment? A kind of—I don't know how else to describe it—tenderness that was missing? Or was he just shedding his stupid stiffness and warming up to me? Even when we were little, he had taken really long to be friends.

It was his tenth birthday. We had already been best friends for more than two years and I was really excited for his birthday. I had made a huge card with a nice, long message inside. Along with that I had the gift my mother had neatly wrapped, as well as something that could be considered as big a declaration of love as was possible then—my five most unique kanchas.

I had worn a frock for his birthday party, only to find that besides me there were twenty other boys from his class, all of them playing kabaddi. Something came over me and I sat shyly in a corner, his mother constantly asking me if I wanted something else, bringing me samosas and Campa. Nikku didn't speak to me the entire time, let alone feed me the cake when he cut it. It was the most hurtful thing he had ever done.

The next day he made up for it, but I never forgot, which served me well because Nikku did tend to wander off when there were others around him.

Now was as close as we had been in years.

Soon after, Nikku stopped outside a dhaba, surveying it for a couple of minutes. I stepped out of the car yawning and stretching once he approved it, dreaming about the dal makhani and tandoori rotis that would soon be inside me.

'Nikku-Tikku,' I said, grabbing his arm as we walked inside. He smiled at me. I told him to get a table and order for me while I went to use the bathroom. I had decided I won't doze off, thinking about poor Nikku and all the driving he had to do. There was no way I could expect him to not feel sleepy. Maybe we could play some nice songs on the radio, or tell each other one of those horror stories.

I came back to find Nikku looking solemn. A particularly burly group had come to sit behind our table. I decided to keep my eyes down. I may be the feisty Ultimate Mathematics Tuition teacher, bullying all the kids, but I wasn't stupid. Our dal and roti was served almost immediately. As we ate, we were privy to the conversation of the group, which was punctuated by their raucous laughter.

'*Oye*, dal is not so good today,' one of them said to the waiter, a little boy who looked to be fifteen and innocently replied, 'It's the same as every day.'

'Oye, *tu zaada mat bol*. Stop talking now and get me some green chillies.' The boy scampered off. The man who had chastised him looked at us and gave a sly grin.

'Hello,' he said. Nikku looked away pointedly. The rest of his gang, meanwhile, was laughing at something.

Though we tried our best to ignore them, their raucous chuckling refused to die down.

'So, umm, what are we doing when we get there? Should we straight go to Khan's house?' I asked Nikku.

Nikku didn't seem to have heard me. 'What? Yes . . . no, actually, perhaps we can wait, go in at a decent hour . . .'

'Yes, that makes sense,' I said loudly, trying to drown out the noise from the group, but was unsuccessful.

'The last batch was difficult, but we managed to get it ready,' another one from the group said, and they thumped the table loudly.

'It is difficult sometimes,' the oldest among them said, 'but we have to get the job done anyhow. Bareilly is not Bareilly without these, is it? But remember, not a word out. The police have been especially careful these days. We need to teach them a lesson again so that they don't interfere in our work.'

'Okay, I'm done,' Nikku said suddenly, pushing his plate away. 'You? I think we can get the rest packed if you're not. Or better still, we'll stop again later. Yes? Let's go.'

All of them stared at us as we got up. I gave my unfinished dal and roti one last glance.

'You should not travel on an empty stomach,' one of them suggested.

'I'm good, thanks,' Nikku replied without looking at him, putting down thirty rupees on the table and turning to me. 'I don't want the change. Come on, let's go. Our friends are waiting.'

I followed him without looking back and heard the group burst into peals of laughter again. Nikku shut my door behind me and crossed over to the driver's side.

Just as he started the car, there was a loud rap on my window, making me jump. Nikku reached over and locked my door, and put the car in the first gear. One of the men stood outside, holding something in his hands. After a few seconds of deliberation, I rolled the window down just an inch.

'You left something,' he said, holding up my dupatta.

'Oh,' I said, looking at Nikku and then reluctantly rolling the window down to take the dupatta.

'Take care on the road,' he said and gave a broad smile. His teeth were yellow below a big, bristly moustache. I noticed that he was very fair and had sharp eyes. The look in his eyes was unforgettable. He knew he had scared us. As I rolled the window up again, I memorized his face, which was just as well because it wasn't long before I saw it again.

Chapter 9

I woke up to find my head lolling against the window and Nikku whistling a tune. I straightened up immediately.

Shit. *Shit*. I had promised myself that I wouldn't sleep. What is wrong with me? 'How long was I gone?'

'Not that long, don't worry,' he said waving a hand.

'I'm sorry, I don't know when it happened. I wanted to give you company. Where are we?' I asked looking around. It was already dawn, which explained Nikku's cheerful mood: everything around seemed less menacing.

'Very close to the city now,' he said, 'although we still might have a few hours to kill. It's not even six yet.'

'Aren't you sleepy?'

He stifled a yawn as we both laughed. 'I'd love to say no, but . . . well, I didn't feel sleepy in the darkness anyway. There was barely any light and I had to be careful while driving. But I feel good about being here; we have some free days! What do you want to do?'

I shrugged, looking outside the window. The windows were half rolled down, which let in the cool breeze. We passed long stretches of fields, and the morning light soon pierced the sky. An occasional motorbike or car crossed us, but mostly we navigated between trucks. It was then that a question occurred to me. 'What are you going to do now?'

'I was thinking of getting some sleep. I know we can't go to Khan's yet, but probably a park for a quick nap . . .'

'No, no. I meant, why did you come back to Siyaka? What are you going to do in life now?'

He raised his chin. 'Oh. Can't I come back to Siyaka? What, you think it's your city now?'

'It is my city, but you know what I mean.'

He waited a while before answering. 'I got a little bit tired of my job, I told you. I know it's very strange that I just left, everyone was absolutely baffled. Nobody leaves a good job. A good job means a good marriage! Well, anyway, I had to think about some things.'

'Like what?'

'I don't know,' he said, tapping the steering wheel in agitation, 'but I always think there must be something more than this. Something more to life than just work, marriage, kids. I don't want to do things the way people have been telling me to do them for years, and then have them pat my back when I meet their expectations.'

'Maybe you should do something on your own. A business, a cause that will give meaning to your life. Maybe continue the good name of Sabharwal Stationers. Or establish Kuber Photo Studio.'

Nikku snorted. 'You always know what my heart desires.'

I wondered whether or not to ask him what was on my mind, but the words were out of my mouth before I knew it. 'And what about . . . do you, I mean, did you, meet someone there? As in, a girl?'

He looked at me, making me look away. I didn't want him reading my expression. 'I did,' he said, 'but it didn't work out.'

I attempted to modulate my voice as my heart sank. 'Why not?'

'Just, things don't work out sometimes, you know. Not everybody can be as cool and hip as Taru and DJ Buddy.'

I hit him on the shoulder. It was strange that Nikku had brought up Sahil; I realized I had kind of forgotten about him. I couldn't imagine him driving with me instead of Nikku.

We were cruising around the city now and were surprised to see that a part of it looked a little like Siyaka's Victorian town: tree-lined *golchakkar*s, old, white bungalows and British architecture until we reached what seemed to be the old bazaar. Here the lanes were narrow, and rows of shops and stalls sat cloistered next to each other. The city hadn't woken up yet and we kept driving until we spotted a park.

There was a patch of particularly lush grass under the shade of a huge tree. Nikku lay down on his back with a sigh, his arms behind his head. At first I awkwardly sat next to him, but then lay down, at a respectable distance though. He turned to face me and smiled, and then went back to cushioning his head with his hands, slowly dozing off.

Nikku was about to knock on the door when I gripped his arm. 'Wait a moment. What is Khan's first name?'

The thought hadn't occurred to Nikku either. He simply shrugged and said it didn't matter. 'Of course, it matters,' I hissed. 'We can't call him Khan in front of his family, all of whom will be Khans!'

'We could call him Mr Khan.'

'There could be another Mr Khan inside!'

'Whatever, we'll see,' he rapped the door before I could protest. It was a few seconds before a woman opened the door. Both of us smiled our widest smiles.

'Friends of Kifaayat! Come, come, come on in!' she said.

We entered a small house and saw an old woman, sitting on a sofa, staring at a tiny television. The aroma of food had wafted into the room. A little boy ran towards us and hid behind his mother. Nikku kept our backpack on a dining table, which had small knick-knacks lying around. The sofas were plain with a shelf behind them showcasing a couple of trophies, a little teddy bear and a family photograph.

'Bibi, look who is here. Friends of Kifaayat! They will stay with us a few days. Are you listening?'

The grandmother grunted over the television. I looked nervously at Nikku. 'Kifaayatji was very kind to offer us a place for a few days.'

'That's how my Kifaayat is, always welcoming! Come, come, I'm already preparing lunch. We'll figure out where you will sleep . . .'

'We can sleep anywhere,' I said quickly and then wondered if she thought we were married.

'Yes, yes, I think you can sleep with Bibi in her room. She has a cot, but we can spread a mattress for you. And he,' she said looking at Nikku, 'can sleep with our son! Mind you, he starts chattering when it is time to sleep.'

Nikku smiled. 'That would be the nicest thing in the world. I would love to talk to him.'

The woman beamed and Bibi coughed.

'We actually could do with a little nap right now. We were driving all night.'

'Oh, yes! Come on, come on, let me show you.'

We woke up groggy, but well-rested, after a few hours and sat down for lunch. It was absolutely delicious: warm kebabs, chapattis and dal. When the family settled in for their afternoon nap, Nikku and I decided to explore the city. I would have asked the little boy for suggestions, but he had vanished.

'Don't young people these days go to movie halls?' Bibi asked us from her cot, making me jump because I had thought she was asleep. 'Go to Kamal cinema! I only watch movies there.' I thanked Bibi and got a little wink in return.

It would have been great if I could wear jeans, but I decided on my best pants and kurta. Nikku too looked fresh in a crisp white shirt and trousers. In Siyaka, we always dressed up to go to the movies. I felt happy trying to recreate the feel of home. I had been missing Siyaka.

As we stepped out of the house, I told him coolly, 'You don't look bad.'

He chuckled. 'And you! Ravishing beauty! I'd say the nose is a little off, but apart—'

'Nikku,' I warned him. He laughed again and held out his arm. I took it, smiling. We walked like that for a couple of minutes, until a cycle rickshaw stopped next to us, ringing his bell.

'Madam,' Nikku said, bowing a little and holding out his hand for me to use as support to step on to his rickshaw. '*Kahaan chale*, Sir, Madam. Where would you like to go?'

'Kamal cinema,' I told him, and he rang the bell again, cycling ahead with enthusiasm. It was breezy and the roads were beautiful. Nikku and I behaved in a quaint manner, pretending as if we had never seen each other dancing in our underwear under the water pipe, or had an intense golgappa showdown. He even called me Tara; I had almost forgotten who that was.

There were many people outside the cinema hall: families, couples and friends. We could feel eyes on us as we made our way to the ticket counter. 'Well, they clearly know we are outsiders,' Nikku murmured.

'We'd know too in Siyaka,' I said and he nodded. We asked for balcony seats but there weren't any. 'Balcony seats for next show, 6 p.m., after two hours,' the man at the counter told us.

'Well, okay,' I said.

'But old show. *Karan Arjun*.'

'Ooh, even better,' I said excitedly. 'Haven't seen Shah Rukh for so long!'

Nikku shook his head and reminded me of our bet as we headed down to an old park nearby.

'It's a mistake to remind people of bets that you are likely to lose,' I told him and he laughed. We sat on a bench and watched people walk by, clutching popcorn, *budhiya ke baal*, or a Maha Cola for the whole family. There were a couple of ice-cream trolleys by the edge of the park, right next to a row of channa chaat and papad stalls.

'For what it's worth,' I told him, 'I'm really happy that you came back. And that you are here with me now.'

He looked at me, so close that I could count the tiny brown spots around his nose. 'For what it's worth,' he said, 'I am sorry I left, or rather, that I *truly* left. I should have stayed in touch.'

I debated whether or not to say what I wanted to. My heart was racing. If there was ever a good time, it was this—the moment we stood facing the Taj Mahal together had done it for me. In my head, I fought the possible consequences of what I wanted to say, but ultimately decided to brace myself and go ahead. This hesitating, unsure girl was not me; I was the girl who beat Nikku in math and badminton, and was the partner-star player of our kho-kho team. I was the coolest girl in my school because so many people were scared of me. I couldn't be afraid of telling Nikku *this*.

'I was sad to see you go,' I said, my voice low and quiet, 'because I had a crush on you. Back then.'

It was as good an admission as any, and I couldn't look at him after that. I looked at the kids on the swings. When he still didn't say anything, I looked at him but he was facing the other direction.

'I did too,' he said in a rush, turning around. 'Always. I was too scared to say it.'

'Classic Nikku,' I said, trying to lighten the mood.

What else was there to say? My heart thudded as I waited for Nikku to speak.

'Do you remember the time when that guy from Rohit and Mohit's class asked you out?' Nikku asked and I rolled my eyes. 'It was painful.'

He chuckled and threw a little stone into the distance. 'Tara Taneja, will you friend me for life?' he imitated the boy who had asked me out.

'Well, Mukesh's sister had pretty solid hots for you,' I reminded him. 'She called you home for a romantic evening, didn't she?'

Nikku shook his head, embarrassed. 'I was so scared. Everyone was telling me to go ahead, this guy even bought me a condom and told me to be strong.'

'What! You never told me this!'

'I freaked out. All the guys expected me to go there and just . . .'

'And then? You didn't go, did you?'

'Of course not. And they didn't let me forget that for a long, long time.'

I couldn't help but laugh. Nikku joined me. He then got up and said we should go order at the restaurant that would serve us in the movie hall.

I got up and stretched, reminding him to pick up our bag.

'You can also pick it up, you know. Sometimes,' he said, an eyebrow raised in an amused smile. I laughed and apologized, but made no promises of carrying the bag.

The restaurant promised to serve us a proper meal. We were absolutely overjoyed—they never served anything except popcorn in Siyaka.

'Your Lalaji has outdone himself this time, just pure class,' Nikku said appreciatively as we looked for our seats. 'A hunt for the magic ingredient across the country! Ingenious, and so much fun. Imagine if the answer is lying in your own verandah. Ha ha . . . there are our seats.'

As the movie came on, we were served soup, little cut-out sandwiches, shahi paneer and tandoori roti, and then finally a gulab jamun—all to the sound of Shah Rukh Khan and

Salman Khan fighting for revenge. I tonelessly hummed 'Yeh Bandhan Toh Pyaar Ka Bandhan Hai' all the way home when we decided to walk back instead of taking the rickshaw. It was even more breezy now, and Nikku enumerated the ways in which he thought the movie didn't make sense, with me trying to counter him all through.

'And on top of that, what kind of silly song was 'Jaati Hoon Main, Jaldi Hai Kya'? Who dances like that? In a stable? Can't they smell the horse shit?'

'Yes, but they are so passionate about each other that they aren't paying attention to these mundane details.'

'Come on, Taru. Wearing that and running around a farm? Would we ever do this? I don't think so.'

It struck me a couple of minutes later that he had compared us to Kajol and Shah Rukh Khan, and it made me happy. We also stopped at a telephone booth, each of us calling home. I gave my mother the low-down on what we had been up to. I reassured her about our place of stay, telling her we were safe and that Nikku was being very responsible. She paused for a moment and then said that she trusted him and me, together. Getting a hint about where she might go next, I quickly asked her if Lalaji had received the package. She said no. Well, fair enough. Khan wouldn't have mailed it yet. I quickly cut the phone after that.

'Actually, *Karan Arjun* kind of reminded me of Rohit and Mohit,' I said to Nikku as we walked back. He looked at me questioningly.

'Really, why?'

'Just their loyalty towards each other. Rohit and Mohit have always stood by each other, never with me. I mean, there was a point when we were close, but in the end, they would always have each other's back and I would be the third wheel. You know what I mean? Whatever it is, their parents made sure they are absolutely loyal to each other. Instead of Draupadi, they were made to bond over their common dislike for me.'

He gave me a rueful smile.

Once we were back, we chatted with everyone before setting up our sleeping places. After changing into the salwar-kameez I used at night, I laid out my mattress on the floor next to Bibi's cot, and to my surprise, found her with a small hookah.

My eyes widened. 'You have got to meet my Lalaji.'

'What?' she asked unconcerned, taking a long drag from the hookah. 'Just don't mention this to my daughter-in-law. Seems to think it's not appropriate. So what did you do today? Watched a movie?'

'Yes, we watched *Karan Arjun*. It was fantastic and they gave us food as well! Doesn't happen in Siyaka.'

Bibi grunted, unimpressed, smoking her hookah again. 'You also saw Cir-sent House?'

'What? No, what's that?'

'Cir-sent House! Bareilly's very own haunted building. It is one of the most haunted places in India.'

'One of the most?' I was confused. 'Is there less haunted and more haunted? I thought haunted is haunted.'

Bibi made a face. 'Have you ever seen a haunted building? *Nahi na*? So don't show attitude, Nautanki! All you people north of Delhi are just too much!'

'Sorry, sorry. So what is this place? Where is it?'

'On the northern edge of the city, beyond the Cantt area. But go only during the day, mind you. In the night if you go, well, not everyone comes back.'

I was sure my eyes were glittering. I loved such tales. Because they are, at the end of the day, only tales. For fun—a way to entertain people.

'Tell me more about it, please!'

Bibi rubbed her hands, delighted to talk about it but hiding her joy.

'Are you sure you can handle it?'

'I will try my best.'

'Many years ago,' she began, 'it was a troublesome winter. The fog was thick, the sky was alone, the moon was afraid, and the rain was falling, falling, falling . . .'

I looked at her with my eyebrows raised, impressed.

'It was a scary night, as you can imagine. Now see, this is a small place. It's no place to hide a secret. Yet all such stories have a secret at their hearts. A girl had a secret. And the secret was her lover.'

I expected nothing less. Which ghost story was not about a jilted lover?

'They met, away from prying eyes, finding secret rooms in the old Nawab's abandoned haveli, in the bushes at the back of the gardens, in silent and dark alleys near the *ghantaghar*, the menacing clock tower. Anywhere they could be with each other, where no one could find them. It was passionate, it was brave, it was love . . . but it was just not possible. You see, he was a Hindu, she was Muslim . . . the rest of the story, society decides. It happened then as it happens now.

'They were found together one evening and beaten up, torn apart. But somehow they still managed to meet each other. She, doe-eyed, looked at him as he held her hands with a sad, browbeaten face, whispering words of love, cursing society, this cruel world that wouldn't let lovers remain lovers.

He promised her he would do anything for her. And so she made her final demand, that he kill her, so they may be together in heaven.'

'Of course,' I whispered.

'But that was not all: she asked him that he kill her in a way that her family, the city, would not even find a part of her to grieve and mourn over. She asked him to hack her to pieces.'

I clapped my hand over my mouth.

'Yes, my dear. Bound as he was by his own words, he did it. Cut her up into a hundred little pieces and then took his own life. Till date, people speak of that horrific day when they found him dead over little pieces of her.'

It was a little too gruesome for my taste. 'So is it the ghost of the boy or the girl that haunts this Cir-sent House?'

She laughed like a maniac. 'Both. They say a hundred little pieces of her wander over the house, and the city too sometimes. Why do spirits always take human form? We don't know what happens. A hundred pieces of her came alive that day, hell-bent on ravaging the city. But he, poor boy, he keeps her in check, calming her rage and telling her to stay in Cir-sent House. And so that happens. *Mostly.*

'And now I must sleep,' she announced suddenly. 'What are you thinking of, keeping an old woman up like this at night? Don't you know how much our joints ache? Go to bed! And hope you don't have nightmares!'

I jumped at her abruptness, promptly turning to my side to sleep. Dream I did, but not of this particular couple in suffering.

I dreamt of Nikku and me running from one place to the next, going through the cinema hall, the temple and the Taj Mahal, finally catching our breath at one place. I was leaning against Nikku, the back of my head resting against the back of his head. Knowing what to do next, I turned to face him, and he did the same. We both knew we had to do it. We laughed nervously, almost shaking our heads at the dream for making us do it. I moved forward, brushing my lips against his, but also drawing back instantly, realizing what I had done. Seconds later, he kissed me back, and we continued till we were out of breath. I woke up dazed.

I was quiet as I got ready, and later too when I went to sit on the parapet, which is where Nikku found me. 'Why are you sitting here? It's so hot!'

'Yes,' I said shiftily, not looking at him. We wasted the morning hanging about the house. I mostly avoided Nikku and his attempts to speak to me. Sometime around noon, when he suggested that we step out of the house, I agreed.

'What is it? Why are you acting funny with me? Is it because I haven't sung your song in so long?'

'No. I'm not acting funny.'

He stopped in his tracks. 'Wait. Did you dream about me?'

I gasped. It was as good as, if not better than, a big and resounding yes. 'How did you know!'

'This happens,' he said, 'if you spend enough time with someone. So what was it?'

I refused to answer, crossing my arms over my chest as he hovered about me like an annoying fly.

'Did we find the magic ingredient? Did you admit that I'm a better badminton player? No? What could it be—wait, did we kiss?'

'No!' I yelled. My indignant refusal was again a dead giveaway. Nikku, however, seemed very pleased. I refused to discuss it any further and instead told him the story Bibi had narrated.

'Do you mean Crescent House?' he asked, and I realized that Bibi must have mispronounced it. 'Yes, Faroukh told me about it as well, the boy. Let's go visit!'

Because it was far from where we were, we took an autorickshaw. 'I almost forgot,' Nikku said as we passed through the bazaars, 'I'm going to buy you some earrings.'

'Why?' I asked him, puzzled. I didn't wear earrings often.

'Arre, so we can sing that song,' he said, '"Jhumka Gira Re, Bareilly Ke Bazaar Mein".'

I grinned at him. 'I thought you didn't like Bollywood songs.'

'I like the old ones, and the new ones that make sense. Not your Baba Sehgal-types. Although Bally Sagoo has started to grow on me.'

'Hey, "Thanda Thanda Paani" is not so bad!'

Nikku rolled his eyes. 'You know that it's a rip-off of "Ice Ice Baby", right?'

'What?' I gripped Nikku's arm and squeezed it, making him flinch. 'That's why it sounded so familiar!'

'Yes, also you're hurting me—'

My heart seemed to sink. I couldn't believe it: I had admired this song, and fought for it. I had defended it before Sahil and all his wannabe DJ friends who always laughed at my choice of music, making fun of me for being 'stupid' and 'local'. Is that why, because I couldn't understand music? I couldn't even recognize a rip-off! Why didn't they ever tell me? I looked at the streets blankly as we skirted through narrow lanes and then the Cantt. Nikku knew better than to disturb me as I wallowed in an abyss of pity and doubt.

Finally, we found ourselves in front of a large haveli. It had a dilapidated gate that swung noisily. There were a few more people besides us, staring and giggling at the house. Nikku paid the autorickshaw driver and I chastised him for not haggling.

I could not help but wonder what the haveli must have been like in its prime. People bustling about, dressed in their finest silks and *jutti*s, rows and rows of biryani plated and prepared, women giggling, those gigantic doors welcoming visitors . . .

'Pretty run down, huh?' Nikku said. 'I wonder why it's called Crescent House. Come.'

The haveli was two storeys high and spread out over a large area, with a huge garden at the back. The paint on the walls had almost peeled off and it was dusty everywhere, but we could still spot some mosaics. As we walked around, I could see why people would think it was haunted. Each room seemed endless and was connected to another room. Someone said it was because people were always sleeping with everyone else, yet a pretence of decency had to be kept up. So through interconnected rooms, the cheater could always escape. There were a few pieces of furniture strewn about the house, and many, many alcohol bottles and cigarette butts in corners.

We walked further inside, startling a pigeon or two, only to find ourselves in a room facing the park that said, '*Hatheli Padengi*—Murti Devi—special palm reader'. I looked behind the pillar to find a woman sitting on a cushion with a low table. She had wild curls, expressive eyes, and wore several rings around her nose and ears. When she caught me looking at her, she smiled. 'Come on in, Star Child. Let me tell you a little about yourself.'

Chapter 10

'What did you call me?' I asked her.

Her lips were a strange shade of purple. She was skinny, her veins showing prominently against her skin. She moved her hands a lot, her long and skinny fingers hard to ignore. She wore a green sari, sat cross-legged and invited us to sit across the table. 'Star Child, are you not? Come!'

Nikku and I exchanged a look before walking over to her. I looked at her curiously. 'How do you know my name?'

'Your name is Star Child?'

Taken aback, I replied, 'No, it's Tara, but I thought you . . .'

'Star Child? I call everyone that,' she said, and then laughed wildly. 'I'm kidding, of course, I knew your name!'

I saw Nikku staring at her suspiciously before asking, 'What's my name?'

'I don't know your name. It's harder for me to get men.'

Nikku snorted. I looked around the place where she sat. There were random scribbles on the wall: 'Raj loves Rama', 'Aashiq' and broken hearts sketched roughly. Here too lay some broken bottles. A couple of other visitors passed us by.

'You read hands?'

'It's the only thing I know how to read,' she said briskly and then shifted her position, settling down more comfortably. 'Give me then.'

'Wh-what's your fee?' I asked. I didn't want to be ripped off later.

'You will know what fee to give me once I am finished,' she answered smugly. I hesitantly extended my hands.

'First, only right,' she muttered, putting on her glasses and holding my right hand in hers. It was easily upwards of ten minutes that she stared at my hand, and all throughout Nikku clicked his tongue impatiently, even crossing his arms across his chest in protest. But her concentration didn't waver. She stared at my hand, barely blinking. My hand was soon clammy and I wondered how she was still holding it. She then took my other hand and joined it with the first, now staring at both. I could feel Nikku fidgeting and getting restless.

'You don't seem to be lost, but I wonder . . . ah, here it is,' Murti Devi mused as Nikku stared at her in scepticism. And then she abruptly let go of my hands and wiped her own on her thigh.

'You are in search of an answer.'

I looked at her curiously while Nikku made a 'pfft' noise and asked, 'Isn't everybody?'

She gave him a disparaging look before continuing. 'The answer is set up, and will evade you for a while, but the answer lies at home.'

'What?'

'What you seek outside was never outside. It's all inside you. A search, a quest, only makes sense if the final destination is home.'

'If the final destination is home,' I repeated.

'But you must go through the journey nonetheless, because that is what will ensure you know the answer when you see it.'

I stared at her and held back my hand. 'And what is it? The answer?'

'It's not what you think it is. You will find the answer, but not the one you are looking for.'

I looked at Nikku, who had an expression of utmost disregard on his face, and chose to ignore him. 'Tell me more,' I said.

'You think the answers will take you to the future, will create your future, but that's not true: the answer will take you further into the past. There is unfinished business. The answer lies where you started, and until you go back there, nothing will move forward.'

Murti Devi took my hand again and held it tightly. 'As for the immediate future, trouble lies ahead. And it's very close too, hovering over your heads like a black hawk. Yes, yours too, Mister, you can make all the faces you want. These lines, where they criss-cross, are not a good sign. Three times.'

'Three times what?'

'Three times you will fall and three times you will have to get up. It's essential you get up, because if you don't . . . lines change. Fate changes. I can see it's in your fate, if you hold on to it. Anyway, another important line I see: men. You will be disappointed.'

'Really?' I asked, looking at Nikku who snorted once more.

'Oh yes, but honestly, aren't we all? They will betray you, at some point. But well, that really is the story of us all.'

I giggled. 'Three times I will fall, you said. Isn't there a cure? A preventive measure?'

She gazed at my hands for some more time and then said, 'The first time you fall, don't lose faith. The second time you fall, don't lose hope. The third time you fall, don't lose your way. That will lessen the effects of your fall.'

'How specific,' Nikku said and Murti Devi's nostrils flared when she looked at him. 'You can say what you want now, Mister, but I caught a sneak peek at your palm. Oh, you'll be mincing your words soon enough, I am sure of that.'

Nikku still seemed unperturbed as she went on. 'You think everything there is to know is already known? There are worlds and knowledge that are still not obliterated, passed down from generation to generation, to those who are schooled in the ways of their community. You think magic does not exist, ghosts do not haunt and spirits do not guide? There are crafts well-hidden and concealed from the rest of the world, that you may not know until you're in the midst of these worlds, and maybe not know even then. Beyond this haveli lies a forest as old as life. You will never know what happens there because there are some things you will never know.'

For the next minute, none of us spoke. I then asked Nikku for my purse and handed her a ten-rupee note as Nikku glared at me. Before he could say anything, I took his hand and led him towards the exit. He wasted no time in telling me that I was absolutely crazy to believe her and hand her money.

'There was something about her. And she's right. I mean, how can we presume to know everything that exists?'

'She was a right old fraud,' Nikku grumbled as we walked. 'Saying super vague stuff, "you're looking for an answer".

Anyone would say yes to that! And isn't losing hope and faith the same thing?'

'No, losing faith is when you already had faith in something. She basically said hold on to it. And hope is more like you can't see how things will get better, but you stick it out anyhow.'

'How earth-shattering,' he said sarcastically, 'and what a waste of time. Now you will see similarities in your life with what she said, because you want to, and that's why everything was so vague, so it could apply to anybody. It's a self-fulfilling prophecy, that's how these things work. It was the same thing when you had to balance the pots chanting Krishna's name. The only reason you balanced those pots on your head was because you practised!'

We bickered all the way until we were back in the town in an auto. We were about to enter a little eatery when I noticed something: a newspaper vendor right outside and a man sitting there, holding a newspaper open. The headline read: 'Siyaka Thieves Break into the Taj Mahal, Steal Valuable Marbles'.

I drew Nikku's attention to it and we hurriedly bought a copy. The article went on about how two notorious thieves from Siyaka had broken into the Taj Mahal in the dead of night and stolen valuable marbles. It also mentioned how the thieves had escaped in a blue Fiat. All the life seemed to have been sucked out of me. Nikku too looked pretty shaken up. So we were thieves now? No doubt Pankaj had built on what Rohit and Mohit had told him. And how in the world could we have stolen marbles? We couldn't be sitting down and breaking them up with a hammer!

'I have to do something about the Fiat,' Nikku muttered, 'hide it somewhere, because anyone who reads this newspaper and sees it . . .'

I nodded.

Back at Khan's house, we were mostly quiet, watching television with the family. An episode of 'Padosan' was on and I pretended to laugh, but I couldn't stop thinking about Murti Devi's predictions and the newspaper article. Suddenly, all of it hit me. I felt hopeless and aimless, stuck in this little town without knowing what to do next, living with strangers, safe only because of their kindness and large-heartedness. Not knowing how to thank them, I offered to Bibi that I would make laddoos for the whole family. I told them that my family had a mithai shop and I knew how to make good laddoos. This brought a smile to everyone's face and Faroukh ran around excitedly, yelling 'laddoo'. The next day, Nikku and I bought all the ingredients after fighting off the family's requests to use what was at home.

We had a fun day making the laddoos, with Nikku trying to sniff out the difference from the original Lallan ke laddoo, hoping to guess the magic ingredient. In the evening, we spoke to Khan on the phone and talked to him about the Fiat. He said the police still seemed to be looking for it and that the matter would settle down in another two to three days. Later that evening, Nikku headed out for a walk while I decided to go to bed early, tired as I was from all the laddoo-making.

I was in very deep sleep when I was suddenly woken up. Bibi was snoring peacefully next to me. Nikku's face shone above mine, illuminated by a flashlight, and I just about managed not to scream. Nikku had his palm clamped over my lips to stop me from reacting and then he put one finger on his mouth, indicating that I should keep quiet.

Worried, I followed him to the living room where everything was dark and quiet. All I could hear was the tiny, sky-blue fridge whirring. Rubbing my eyes, I waited for him to speak, but he didn't. Instead he walked out of the house and up to the terrace. I followed him. The city was quiet and only a couple of crickets buzzed. I looked at Nikku for an explanation and noticed that he looked shell-shocked. I gently asked him what had happened.

'I saw it,' he croaked.

'Saw what?'

'The ghosts.'

I stared at him. 'What are you talking about?'

'The Ghosts of Crescent House, Taru. The boy and the girl! I saw the ghosts.'

'There are no ghosts! What in the world—were you dreaming?'

He shook his head vigorously. 'I had gone out for a walk, and then just for kicks, I hitched a ride to Crescent House again. It sounded ridiculous, a stupid small-town tale. But when I was there, I saw it . . .'

'Saw what? The ghosts?'

He nodded. I couldn't believe what I was hearing. 'I went inside the gate with the flashlight. As soon as I got in, I saw them clearly. The ghosts. There were two: one white and the other grey and black.'

'God, Nikku! Do you hear yourself? Is this a prank? Are you joking with me, Mister?'

Deep down I knew Nikku wasn't this good an actor. On his face was a combination of horror, confusion and daze. 'I saw the ghosts, Taru.'

'How do you know they weren't people?'

'They didn't look very solid!'

'What if it was light reflecting?'

'There was no light around, except for the one in my hand! And my light wasn't even shining in the direction of what I saw. One was black and grey, like, half-human. I couldn't tell. I was so scared that I ran all the way back to the bazaar, thinking they might be following me.'

I was worried for him. Was this really Nikku? Did he not get enough sleep? Or did someone sneak some bhang into what he ate or drank?

'You're a lot less accepting of this than your palm reader,' he said, noticing my sceptical expression.

'Palm reading is a science, Nikku! There are books on it, people who have been learning it for centuries. It's not some ghost story, which honestly seems a bit far-fetched.'

He looked hurt. 'It's not a story. I saw what I saw.'

The next morning, for Nikku's sake, we went to the haveli again. I was certain that if there were ghosts, they wouldn't make an appearance in broad daylight. And what was more, we could ask Murti Devi. If she said the ghosts were real, I would be a lot more convinced. I didn't think Nikku was making it up, but it was possible that it was just the tiredness and stress of the past few days playing tricks on his mind.

He didn't talk much on the way there. When we reached, of course, there was nothing there. Just the usual run-down haveli with curious visitors. We went looking for Murti Devi, but she was not there. 'She must be one of those travelling psychics,' I guessed.

'Can you decide which one she is: a psychic or a palm reader?' Nikku asked.

'Well, big words from someone who thinks he saw a black and white ghost here last night!'

Irritated at each other, we sat down on the haveli's verandah that opened up to a garden, beyond which was nothing. Just fields as far as we could see and thickets of trees on the side. We sat idly for a while, lost in our own thoughts. Whatever Nikku might say, I believed there was some truth to what Murti Devi had said. *A search, a quest only makes sense if the final destination is home . . .*

What if Lalaji had set all of this up, laughing to himself, waiting for us to figure out that the answer lay in Siyaka? What if the answer was in the shop? In Lallan Sweets? Yet I couldn't help thinking there was nothing there. Lalaji had guarded the secret with his life. He had told us to go on this trip, at the end of which we would find the magic ingredient. But if the end was Siyaka, and I skipped everything and went straight back, wouldn't that be cheating? It would, however, be a sure-shot way of winning against Rohit and Mohit.

Pappu Uncle used to say to us, when we were younger, much to the amusement of Lalaji, 'Why slog like a donkey if you can cheat like a monkey?' I was sure Lalaji won't send us on this random cat-and-mouse chase if it wasn't pertinent.

'Should we go there?' Nikku asked, pointing towards the field.

I stared ahead. 'Whatever for though? It looks like there is nothing around.'

'Didn't your psychic say there was a forest there as old as life? Why don't we go and have a look?'

I agreed, mostly because he was in an odd mood and already annoyed at me. We bought some water and snacks before heading off in the direction. Going through the fields was rather fun, with the mustard reaching up to our waists. We walked further. 'Wouldn't it be iconic if someone were to take a picture of us here?' I asked Nikku and he nodded in amusement. A while later, we found a grassy spot and decided to rest for a while. This was just before we reached a highway. 'Is it the same road from which we entered Bareilly?' I asked Nikku. 'We shouldn't venture too far.' Nikku shrugged in response and we walked to a tea stall where a couple of bikers hung around.

'Where does this highway lead?' Nikku asked casually.

'All the way to Lucknow,' the chai-wallah said, pouring out tea from the pan into little cups in a huge waterfall swoop. '*Jaana hai?*'

'No, no,' Nikku shook his head. 'Just like that. And what's beyond this?'

'Jungle.'

'Have you been to the haveli?'

'Yes, sometimes we go there to smoke or drink,' he said with a laugh and Nikku laughed along.

'So, you think it's not haunted?' Nikku asked, pretending to be unconcerned.

The chai-wallah made a noise of dismissal. '*Kuch nahi hai ji!* It's all a conspiracy to keep people away from this area.'

'What? Why? What's in this area?'

'What usually happens on the outskirts of small cities, Sir.'

I couldn't think of anything. Nothing scandalous ever happened on the outskirts of Siyaka. There was just the ashram for devotees and hippies, and Dima Lake on the other side.

Nikku waited a minute before asking, 'And, uh, what is it?'

The chai-wallah looked up, surprised, but then shook his head and whispered, 'The old factory, Sir.'

Nikku looked at me to check if I too was as clueless as he.

The chai-wallah added, 'The factory! The moonshine factory. They are making the local moonshine.'

'Oh.' Nikku seemed underwhelmed.

I looked at him, confused. 'Does he mean tharra?' I whispered and he nodded.

'So, uh, there is no ghost, nothing? The Hindu boy, Muslim girl, separated, hacked to death? No ghosts at all?'

'*Kahan,* Sahab!' the chai-wallah said, slapping his hand on his forehead. 'They pay off the dak master who sends a couple of men to come here and make scary noises, scare off the city people. Increases the tourism also. No haunting here, just the moonshine factory.'

I tugged at Nikku's arm before he could argue further. I could see it on his face that he was unwilling to accept this version.

'I want to see the factory,' Nikku grumbled.

I told him not to be stupid. 'It could be kilometres away! We can't walk all the way back. It will be dark soon!'

He nodded reluctantly as we paid for our tea and began walking back, but he continued to stop at every roadside vendor to ask whether the haveli was actually haunted or not. He soon had enough affirmations to confirm the chai-wallah's claim. As we got closer to Khan's home, I asked, 'You're checking on the Fiat, right?'

'Yes, it's parked in the compound,' he said absentmindedly.

The next couple of days were uneventful. Each of us was lost in our own thoughts, me trying to decide whether I should head back to Siyaka, while Nikku was busy thinking about the ghosts he had seen. One evening, I sat down with Bibi and told her the whole story. She was delighted to hear it and said that I was meant to go ahead. Her words made me feel more confident when Lalaji's letter finally arrived. I ripped it open, Nikku peeking over my shoulder.

Taru,

I had dreamt a great many things for you, but to feature in the newspaper, as part of a half-page article—your mother will kill me if she reads this—but I am quite proud of you. Yes, your brothers told me. I'm sure you have learnt it by now, but I want you to remember, because for me it's the most important rule of business: everything in life is negotiable.

Everything. You think you have heard a 'no' from someone, but then you go and find another way to get the job done. I am guessing breaking into the Taj Mahal and stealing the marbles wasn't such an easy job, but you didn't take no for an answer.

The next stop for you is Delhi. Can anything in India be complete without Delhi? In my day, they used to say that if you managed to survive in Delhi, you could do anything.

That's exactly what you have to do, Taru, survive in Delhi. It's very well working at your old grandfather's mithai shop in sweet, old Siyaka, but can you work at a mithai shop in Delhi? I will tell you where and what to do. Once you reach Delhi, call me.

Yours,
Lalaji

'Work at a mithai shop in Delhi? Oh boy.'

I couldn't help but agree with Nikku on that, but surely it sounded a lot more doable than balancing pots on my head or breaking into the Taj Mahal.

It was our last night in Bareilly and the family had prepared a special dinner of delicious mutton korma and naan. After dinner, we spoke to Khan and thanked him for everything. 'Come to Siyaka once we are back, and bring your Bibi. My Lalaji loves the hookah too.'

We said our goodbyes to Khan's family too, since we planned to leave early the next morning. Nikku then remembered that he hadn't bought me the *jhumkas*, so we loaded our big bag into the car, to avoid doing it in the morning, and went for a short drive. At that hour, I didn't expect to find anything, but a few stalls were still open around the choodi-waali gali and bada bazaar. We parked the car and walked through the lanes. We stopped at a stall that had a little lamp over it, and I chose a pair. I was about to put them on when Nikku insisted I drop them once, so the song *really* came true.

Back in the car, Nikku had an excited look on his face.
'What?' I asked, suddenly nervous.

'Let's go to the haveli one last time. Just to say goodbye.'

'Nikku, come on. There are no ghosts there. You heard those people the other day!'

'I just need to see it one more time.'

'Oh God, you're crazy.' Yet we drove towards the haveli and parked outside it while Nikku kept staring at its windows from the safety of the car. We waited for some time but nothing happened. I finally rolled a window down, feeling hot. An owl hooted in the distance. The crickets kept buzzing and, after a few minutes, I asked Nikku if he was okay to leave.

He nodded, resigned. 'I don't know, I was just so—'

There was a huge bang on the bonnet and Nikku's hand flew to my door in an attempt to roll the window up, but it was too late. To my horror, an arm inserted itself through the window, opened the door from the inside and dragged me out. More people surrounded our car as Nikku yelled something that I didn't understand. I turned to face the man who had smiled and handed me my dupatta back at the dhaba.

'I told you to be careful on the road,' he said menacingly.

Chapter 11

It was like my insides had frozen. I was unable to move or process anything happening around me. I just stood straight, my hands forcibly held behind me by one of the men. Panic descended on me as I wondered what would happen to us.

The sound of a smack brought me back to earth as I saw someone slap Nikku. I screamed his name and the guy behind me forced a rough hand over my mouth.

'Ow!' Nikku said, clutching his head as if it would fall off. They pushed him towards me until he was standing next to me. The guy with his hand on my face tightened his grip and whispered hoarsely, 'Don't scream.' I nodded.

I looked around to assess the situation. There were five men in all, one sitting on the bonnet of our Fiat, two at the back, and two in front of us. As far as I could see, there weren't any guns. The men said something to each other and laughed, but I barely understood. They were the same men who had sat next to us in the dhaba on the way to Bareilly. Yes, I was sure, I recognized two of them. I tried hard to remember what they had been talking about when we were there. I remembered something about a batch being ready, but beyond that my memory failed me.

We stood quietly as they went through the Fiat and our luggage. They emptied out the suitcase and my clothes fell out. They pocketed Nikku's wallet that lay on the dashboard and then sized up the car for a few minutes as Nikku and I looked on helplessly. Now there was just one of them standing behind us. I tried to look at Nikku without moving my head but wasn't able to catch his eye.

The men then pushed us into the centre of the little circle they had formed around us and made us get down on our knees.

'You two,' one of them said, 'we met you on the way here. Why are you in the city?'

One of the guys hit Nikku from behind as he spluttered, 'Just to visit—to see the city!'

He kneed him again and Nikku let out a groan.

'Stop it!' I protested. The men turned to me.

The man who had been hitting us said, 'Be grateful that we haven't touched you yet.'

'We knew there was something dishy about you,' said the man who had pulled me out of the car. Really? Something dishy about *us*? He seemed to be the leader. *Maybe they think we are the marble-stealing thieves!* But how could that be, it wasn't like our picture was in the newspaper.

'Oh no, you got it wron—'

This time, the man standing behind us hit me on the back of my head. I could feel a buzz as my head spun. I heard Nikku say something and tried to get back to my senses.

The leader spoke. 'Who do you work for? What do they want? And why have they sent you here?'

It was clear. They thought that we were sent in to spoil some business of theirs. It was imperative that we clear the confusion about who we were, swear to secrecy, assure them that we had no interest in their business and hope they would let us go. With renewed confidence, I looked at Nikku, waiting for him to set the record straight, but he wouldn't speak.

'Listen,' the man continued, 'we did not mix the pesticide in our batch! That happened after we sent the batch to our distributor; it was not our fault. So don't even think about taking over this area. Maybe we should send your heads to your boss as a warning!'

'We're not who you think we are!' Nikku said, holding up his hands in a gesture of peace. They hit him again.

'Please!' I protested. 'Stop hit—'

Another slap stung my face, and this time I took longer to recover. The men, meanwhile, kept talking to each other. I could see Nikku was thinking. I tried to catch his eye, but he was lost in his own thoughts. 'Don't say anything,' he finally said in a low voice, 'let me handle this.'

He addressed the men again. 'What do you want from us?'

'First, tell us who you work for and what kind of mission you were sent here for,' the leader said.

'But we are just tourists here!' Nikku protested. At that point, I didn't quite agree with his definition of 'handling it'.

'Then how do you have this stolen car, huh?' the leader yelled, banging the Fiat again. 'You hear me! We know about this car! We stole it from a man in Delhi, and then it was stolen from us. We thought it was a rival gang and clearly it is! I saw you both that night, at the dhaba, I saw the car as well but I just didn't register that this could be our Fiat. Later, when I read that two thieves had broken into the Taj Mahal and escaped in a blue Fiat, I knew that it was our car and our thieves. We were so close, and we let you go! But tonight when we saw the Fiat again . . . seems that our stars have been shining bright.'

'Fine,' Nikku said, 'fine. I'll tell you everything. But you need to let her go. Let me sit down and then we start.'

The man burst into laughter. 'Let the girl go? Do we look like idiots? So she can call your bosses and get us killed? No way.'

'No letting her go, no deal.'

I wish Nikku hadn't said this because now the man seemed to be getting angry. His nostrils flared and his face was contorted. He walked forward and grabbed Nikku by the chin. 'You want her to go? Oh, she will go. With us. So if you want, I can send two of us with her, deep into the forest, if that will make you talk. Deal?'

'No! Okay, fine. We will tell you everything, give you all the information, but she needs to be right here. And we need to sit properly; give us some water. Then we'll give you information you never thought you'd find out.'

The leader glared at Nikku, while his other cronies muttered among themselves. He finally nodded and I felt my muscles relax. Nikku got up and gave me a hand, and we sat on the Fiat, while the others huddled in front of us.

When I looked at Nikku, I could almost see his mind whirring. I too prepared myself to back him up. But what about after we had told them a bunch of made-up stories? I highly doubted these people would let us go.

Another owl hooted. I looked up to see a cloud shifting. The haveli looked even more menacing, but the real menace, of course, was in front of us. If Nikku had actually seen those ghosts, why couldn't they show up now when we actually needed some haunting?

'The year was 1944, when India was on the brink of independence. That's when he was born, in a small town in what is now Pakistani Punjab. In the face of the brutalities of Partition, he made the treacherous journey towards this side. As is true for many of us, and with the rage of all that had happened, he decided to establish an empire.'

I drew a blank but tried my best to not let it show. The men seemed to mirror my thoughts.

'What the hell are you talking about?' the leader asked. I was eager to know too.

'That's when Genghis Khan was born, and that's how he set up his empire. Khan's is the biggest alcohol mafia from Siyaka to Chandigarh. We began working for him a few years ago. Thrown out of school and out of money, we started working for him and climbed the ranks pretty quickly.'

'Wait. Genghis Khan? Running the alcohol business?'

'Yes, but that's not his real name. You think he's stupid enough to do that! He played his cards right and things were going well for him until one day he discovered something new—an ingredient that could be added to the moonshine, increasing its potency and bringing down overall cost. Several batches were made and the new moonshine, with the secret ingredient, became a huge hit. People from Siyaka to Chandigarh were charmed. So Genghis Khan, of course, thought of expanding. It was quite a small belt he had been operating in until now. And everyone knows Uttar Pradesh and Bihar are huge markets. Khan heard that people were mixing pesticide into the moonshine, that some of those people had died, so he, uh, he sent us to scan the market.'

I was floored. It was a very good story, considering it was made up on the spot and that he had got only a few minutes to think about all this. Apparently, the leader of the gang that held us captive also thought so because he nodded enthusiastically and said, 'So my guess was correct! This is what you are here for. Which brings me back to my earlier suggestion—we should cut off your heads and send them to Genghis Khan. Then he'll get the message that nobody messes with us.'

'I am not finished,' Nikku said in an exasperated tone. I really don't know how he managed it since our lives were under threat. 'You think Genghis Khan cares about us or our heads? We are just pawns in his big game, my friend. He will send others after us, and you hurting us will just aggravate him. Why he sent us here was to have a look at the market, yes, but also because very near to this place grows the new secret ingredient. He hasn't told us what it is, mind you, but he told us where it is. And, well, we can take you there. For the right price, of course. I'm sure it'll help you retain your territory.'

The leader stared at him for a long time before nodding thoughtfully. I kept quiet and knew that Nikku was revising in his head all the nonsense he had just spewed. A couple of the men protested, saying they were not sure which parts of our story to believe. They also seemed doubtful about the secret ingredient. I had half a mind to jump in and tell them how much of a difference secret ingredients could make, but I chose to restrain myself.

'Listen, we have nothing to lose,' the leader said. 'Let them lead us to the sight of the secret ingredient. Then we can do as we want.'

'Hey!' Nikku protested. 'That's not fair. How do we get the assurance that you won't kill us as soon as we show you the magic ingredient? We need a safety net.'

The leader stepped forward and growled, 'The fact that we haven't harmed you yet is your safety net. You're our prisoners. Now, I don't have a taste for killing, let me be frank. Girls, yes, but not killing people. Although if what you are saying is a lie, I won't mind beating you to a pulp.'

Both of us nodded, terrified. 'So, where to now?' he asked.

'Well, past all these fields, and just before your factory, is the main road that leads to Lucknow. On the way, a few kilometres from here, is a road that leads into the interior, which is where the secret ingredient grows.'

'Okay,' the leader said nodding, looking at his team, 'we can go. And you come with us. Both of you.'

'We should probably wait, boss. It's too dark right now,' one of them said. The rest of the gang agreed, opening up some of their own tharra and offering it to us too, which we refused politely, making them laugh. They soon started chattering, keeping a close watch on us. I didn't dare to talk to Nikku. In fact, I was wondering how the hell we were going to get out of that mess when we heard police sirens and some car doors slamming. Everyone froze.

'Calm down,' the leader said, 'just be very, very quiet. They are on their regular patrol to the haveli. Just don't make any noise.'

The policemen were quite a distance away. I craned my neck to have a look. There seemed to be just a couple of them. 'I pay these policemen every week,' the leader said. 'They can't harm us.' Yet he didn't sound convinced, and I knew it.

Mustering my shrillest, loudest voice, much more than the one I used to advertise Ultimate Mathematics Tuition Centre, I yelled, 'HELPPPPPP!'

Everyone heard it. The footsteps paused and there was a second of confusion writ upon the leader's face, followed by fury and Nikku's panicked movements as the men around us scampered. The leader lunged at me as I opened my mouth to yell again, but Nikku seemed to have anticipated this and threw a stone at him, jumping off from where we were sitting and pulling me along. Now we both started shouting for help, even as the gang got into the Fiat and drove off, leaving us standing there. They stole our Fiat. *Our* Fiat. Technically, it was theirs, I reminded myself seconds later.

The policemen had reached us by then. We held up our hands as they rounded on Nikku. I quickly intervened to clarify that I hadn't called for help because of Nikku.

'Well, why then?' one of the policemen asked me, annoyed and clearly doubting our intentions.

'There was a, uh, big dog. He was almost at our throats, and then we heard footsteps and I yelled . . . so he went away.'

The policemen looked like they didn't believe my story one bit. 'What the hell are you doing here in the middle of the night anyway?'

Neither of us had an answer for that. I blurted out that Nikku was my husband and that he was sure there was a ghost in the haveli, and that we had come to check and then decided to get a little romantic. The policemen gave Nikku an appreciative laugh and offered us a ride back to town.

Neither of us said a word all the way back. As soon as we were alone, I flung my arms around Nikku and let a little sob escape. We stayed that way for a while and then started to walk back to the house. Just then Nikku stopped dead in his tracks, clapped his hands to his head and sank to his knees with a sigh of anguish.

'What—what happened?' I asked, kneeling down next to him.

'Our stuff, Taru, our stuff! It was all in the car! We lost everything! All my money, my IDs, our clothes, everything was there!'

So relieved had I been after getting away from those men that I hadn't registered the loss of our car, let alone think of all that we had lost with it. My entire luggage. 'I have my purse at home,' I tried to console him. 'We didn't take the backpack, remember? At least that's still at home.'

He nodded. 'Yes. I had taken my wallet to buy the earrings.'

I touched the earrings that I was still wearing, the ones we had bought before being attacked. We decided to sneak into the house, get the backpack and leave, as we had already said goodbye to the family and didn't want to explain why we didn't have our car any more.

Just a little before daybreak, we caught a bus headed towards Delhi and sat on the seats at the back. It was a run-down local bus. Before we knew it, a third man squeezed in on the seat next to Nikku, squashing me against the window. As soon as the bus started, he took out what looked like a dirty piece of cloth and pulled it over his head. If he thought that he was fooling anyone, he wasn't: the man was obviously smoking a beedi under there. None of us said anything though. I crossed my arms over my chest.

'Why the grumpy face?' Nikku asked.

I raised my eyebrows. Seriously? 'I mistrust Delhi. I don't want to go there.'

'It's not that bad. I've been there a few times.'

'I know, but still . . . I went there a couple of times too when we were really young, but I remember being wary even then.' That, however, was a half-truth. Nikku and I used to talk about visiting Delhi together once we were older, see all the sights we had read about, walk through its crazy markets. But then Nikku went to Bangalore, for which he would travel through Delhi. It made me mad to think that he visited Delhi without me. I didn't want to set foot in the place again. Nikku too seemed to be thinking along the same lines. 'Well, at least we get to visit Delhi together now, isn't it?' he said.

'Why did you have to take us to the haveli again?'

'Listen,' he said turning towards me, one hand on the seat in front of us and the other behind me, 'I know you must think I am crazy. But I saw what I saw, Taru, and I swear to you I wasn't dreaming.'

'Look where it got us though.'

His head drooped. 'I'm really sorry. Truly. You yelling out, the way things happened, even though we lost the car and my bag, we still got really lucky. I can't imagine what would have happened if we hadn't escaped. I'm sorry for putting you in danger like this.'

'And yourself.'

'And myself. I just didn't expect . . .'

'I know, Nikku,' I said, placing my hand over his. 'It's not your fault. I'm sorry you lost all your stuff. And you did a good job, making up that story in that situation.'

He stared at me intensely for a few seconds and was about to say something when the beedi guy interrupted. '*Maachis milegi?*' He then offered to share his beedi with Nikku if he would buy him matches.

I groaned and put my head on Nikku's shoulder, trying to get some sleep.

When I woke up, the bus had stopped and Nikku was asleep, his head lolling on the shoulder of the beedi guy. I put my head back on his shoulder and closed my eyes, the events of the last week replaying in my head: the gang catching us, Nikku telling me about the ghosts, our buying the Bareilly *ke jhumke*. It seemed so long ago that we had watched *Karan Arjun*. And last night it had felt like we were in it. I looked at Nikku to tell him my joke, but he was still asleep. I also remembered how he admitted to having a crush on me and immediately felt a little better about being stuck in the bus.

'Papaji told me strictly that I am not to drink under any circumstances,' the girl sitting in the seat behind me was telling the one next to her. 'He said he will not tolerate his daughter drinking alcohol. Even on our honeymoon in Goa, we received a free bottle of wine, but we didn't dare to drink from it, you know. But I did carry it back with me in the train. I hid it in the luggage, he he! It's been lying in the house for a year.'

I didn't want to listen to this any more. I woke Nikku up. Both of us stuck our heads out of the window, only to discover that the bus wasn't moving because the road ahead was completely blocked. Everyone around speculated that it would be atleast a couple of hours before we started moving again. Irritated, we got out of the bus and walked to the nearest concrete structure we could find. I asked them if they had a toilet and was pointed towards the open field.

'I miss our Fiat,' I whined to Nikku later as we sat down for chai.

'You have been spoilt, miss. A little struggle might do you some good.'

'Shut up. What are we going to tell the mechanic? Won't he kill us?'

'I don't know,' Nikku said mournfully, massaging his temples. 'I don't even want to think about it. And you can't really report a stolen car, can you?'

'We used to play "Made in India" in the car . . .'

'It's the only song we ever played . . .'

'Arre, Bhaiya,' I said to the chai-wallah, 'Radio *hai toh chalao*?'

He gave me a thumbs up and turned a little radio on. 'Dekha Hai Pehli Baar, Saajan Ki Aankhon Mein Pyaar' started playing. The stupid song made me feel glum. Why couldn't there be a Shah Rukh Khan song playing?

'What do you think?' Nikku asked quietly. 'How far ahead are Rohit and Mohit?'

'I feel I always misjudge them. In some way or the other, they do end up outsmarting me at times. When we got to college, for months everyone at home thought they were going to study, but they were actually going to play cards.

I shouldn't take them too lightly. I mean, everywhere we reached, weren't they there already?'

Nikku crunched on his rusk thoughtfully. 'I bet your Lalaji is doing this just for kicks. Sending us on this chor–police adventure.'

'It wasn't really supposed to be like this, you know. We added this element on our own.'

Nikku laughed. 'You think your father knew the magic ingredient?'

'I think he did. He definitely knew more than he let on . . .'

I generally avoided talking about my father, even thinking about him for that matter. I was so young when he died, and so much about his last few months was shrouded in mystery, which my mother never talked about. He had apparently started wearing the mala from the ashram then. I had seen it in a couple of pictures. My mother had only told me that he had become a regular at the ashram sometime before the accident and that he spent a lot of time there. He knew the magic ingredient, I was sure about that. I felt sad that he didn't write it down anywhere to be passed on to his daughter. But then again, he didn't know he had such little time left. My parents had even thought of having another child.

'Maybe we should give the ashram a little visit when we go back,' I suggested. 'Just to see what it's all about. I mean, we have done all other kinds of weird tourism already. It can't get stranger than this.'

'Cheers to that,' Nikku said, raising his empty chai glass. We then got back to the bus in a much better mood.

Many bumpy hours later, we reached Delhi, the city of cities. Despite my misgivings about the place, when Nikku and I got down from the bus, we felt strangely free. 'Maybe because we don't own anything now,' Nikku joked. 'You can't worry about losing anything if you don't have anything.'

We felt a strange calm as we stepped into that giant monster of a city, swept along with the crowd within seconds. Little did we know that this was just the calm before the storm.

Chapter 12

We roamed around the city for an hour. We ate at a little diner, comforted by the food that was steaming and delicious: thick, hot dal and oodles of shahi paneer.

When we stepped out of our accommodation again, it began raining. There was nowhere we could run to for shelter. Nikku cursed under his breath. I couldn't help but giggle, my mood suddenly lightened. That made him smile too, and he handed me his jacket.

'What! No. I don't need your jacket!'

'Come on, take it. Your hair's getting wet.'

'No, I can't take it . . .'

'Just wear it and let me feel like a man,' he said, his voice resigned, making me laugh even more.

'So if I wear it, it will be for you and not for me?' I asked.

He laughed along, giving me a wink. 'As you will.'

'Why do you keep a jacket on you anyway?'

'A habit from my Bangalore days. It would rain anytime there, you know . . .'

At some point, after taking directions from random strangers and getting on an overcrowded bus, we arrived in Paharganj, where people had suggested that we look for cheap rooms. We got off at Shri Shri Shani Mandir, standing in puddles of rainwater as people swept past us. We passed a cobbler sitting outside Swagat Dhaba, next to a board that suggested several travel itineraries: Delhi to Taj Mahal, Delhi to Haridwar, Delhi to Jaipur. If I thought that the Victorian town in Siyaka was full of touristy stuff, it was nothing on this.

We passed shop after shop selling kitschy doorknobs, beads, woodblocks, shells, decorative boxes, bangles, key chains and purses. Autorickshaws stopped and yelled 'Auto?', horns cackled as if on fire. We passed more shops selling Kolhapuris and fresh Bisleri water, brass ornaments, puppets, and we also crossed some broken buildings. I aggressively nudged a man out of my way when he brushed past me too close. Nikku looked at me with his eyebrows raised. 'That was too close,' I said and shrugged.

Another man, slightly bent, shuffled up to Nikku, his eyes moving left and right. 'Chillum? Ganja? Hookah? Hashish?' he asked. Nikku looked up at the sky as if in deliberation, while I told the man to get lost. He gave me a sleazy look and I couldn't help but notice how red his eyes were before he yelled at me, 'You like a fake!' and ran away. Nikku chuckled and I glared at him. 'Let's just find a place to sleep, okay?'

We eventually came across a cheap hotel called K.K. Palace, the words written on a lopsided board on greying, parched walls. It was quite dark inside. A red lamp gleamed behind the reception desk. The man on duty seemed to be busy with something under his desk, so Nikku cleared his throat loudly. He looked up, surveying us diligently before standing up and opening the ledger.

'How many hours do you want the room for?' he asked, flipping the pages.

I looked at him strangely. 'What do you mean how many hours?'

He ignored me completely and addressed Nikku instead. 'How many hours? In the daytime, we also give rooms by the hour.'

Nikku coughed, spluttering on his next words. I was sure I was missing something.

'She's not—I mean, we're not—is this place for . . . I mean, can normal people stay here?'

The man stared at us, confused, and it seemed like both of us realized what was happening at the same time. I stomped my foot in indignation and the man at least had the decency to look embarrassed. 'Sorry, Sir. Most people who come at this time—anyway, of course, you can stay. AC room, Rs 40, Non-AC Rs 25 per night. How many nights you want?'

Nikku looked at me, but I was still too angry to respond. 'How could you think I am a prostitute?' I turned to the man.

He held up his hands, embarrassed but still defensive. 'You have no luggage! Why would you have no luggage?'

'Still, come on! I am from a respectable family.'

'So what? I wasn't judging you! We make most of our business from this kind of work.'

'So your hotel is full of these—these kind of women?'

'Not full of them, but we do get a few . . . but don't worry, it is completely safe. My guarantee.'

I looked around in distaste while Nikku took a couple of seconds to figure out what to do and then shrugged and took the keys. He looked at me pointedly and said, 'You have to pay, Taru.'

'Oh,' I took out my purse, feeling quite smug. 'See, I'm not the prostitute,' I said to the man and then looked at Nikku, grinning, 'he is.'

The room had pale pink and green walls, one sad, brown cupboard, a chair and curtains that were even sadder. I tried to ignore the elephant in the room, the double bed that took centre stage. The waves of embarrassment and awkwardness were palpable between the two of us. 'Uh, let's see the toilet. Okay, it's fine,' Nikku said. I didn't miss the quiver in his voice. He then sat on the chair while I stuck to the side of the bed opposite him and slowly stretched out.

'On the bright side,' Nikku said, his stupid grin returning as he removed his shoes, 'we don't have to unpack.'

I couldn't help laughing either. And then we caught ourselves staring at each other, conscious of the point when you realize how wholly and deeply somebody had decided to laugh at something you said. We both realized this at the exact same second and looked away. My gaze rested on the small quilt on the bed.

I looked up a few seconds later to find Nikku staring at me, about to say something when we heard a loud bang, followed by hoots and claps. Nikku looked curious and I followed him to the door to take a peek.

Near the steps at the end of the corridor were three people huddled around something on the floor, banging their hands against the wooden cupboard in the corner. Curious, Nikku walked over to see what was going on. I followed.

They stared at us as we approached them, two men and a woman, looking like they belonged there. I wondered if they were prostitutes. But why would they huddle in the corridor if they were?

'*Maafi*,' one of the men said, 'did we interrupt, uh, something?'

Nikku looked into the huddle before processing what he had just said, forgetting to reply and smiling instead. I was confused at Nikku's reaction and so took a peek myself—kanche. They were playing kanche! Of course, I mean, what else in the world could make Nikku forget everything else?

'You want to play?' the woman asked. I gave her a sharp look. She was beautiful with long lashes and dusky skin.

Nikku looked at me, not in question but as an answer. I am sure he would have rolled up his sleeves if he had any. 'Well, they don't call me *Kancho ka Sikandar* for nothing, do they?'

'They never called you that, Nikku,' I muttered. 'You called yourself that.'

'Taru, don't be jealous just because you could never master this game.' That much was true: I just didn't have the hand for it. He sat on his haunches, ready to play, looking at the other three people.

'I'm Nikku,' he said, extending a hand, 'one of the best kancha players Siyaka has ever seen.'

The woman responded first with a huge grin. 'I'm Preeti. That's Appu and Monty. Welcome to our gang.'

The kanchas glimmered in the light that came in through the entrance to the corridor. The others looked at me. 'I'm Tara,' I offered reluctantly.

It was not until Nikku failed a couple of exams in school that his kancha obsession ended. It was one of the rare activities that both he and his father enjoyed equally. They had turned their verandah into a stadium, with arrangements for different games: three different-sized circles drawn with a chalk for *chakri*, holes at different points for the basic version of the game, dhai, and a especially designated area for the team version of chakri. Nikku proudly proclaimed that all his original kanchas were collected from soda *bunta*s, but I am sure he had bullied people and bought some of those, especially the exquisite orange and hazel ones; there was no way he could have found those in bunta bottles.

Even though he was rusty and out of practice, Nikku soon won all of Preeti, Monty and Appu's kanche, but was devastated to learn that they would simply head over to a shop and buy new ones. He dramatically put his hand to his mouth, asking them how they lived with themselves. 'What do you mean?' Preeti asked, confused.

'You can't buy these things,' Nikku said derisively. 'You have to win them, earn them.'

'Ignore him,' I advised, 'he's too sentimental about the game.' I was also tired by then. They had been playing for a while now, while I flitted in and out of the room. I wanted to remind Nikku that it was already sundown and we had no clothes, no food, no car... just a shady hotel room and dodgy people for company. But he looked so focused and happy, his hair falling lightly over his eyes, that I didn't have the heart to say anything. I knew by the way he had handed me his jacket that he blamed himself for us getting into trouble.

While they were playing, however, I went to phone Lalaji. He gave me the names of two shops: Bombay Halwai and

Ram Lal Jalebiwallah. The instructions were to find a job, any kind of job, at either of these shops. 'It's very important, Taru,' he had told me, 'and you have to do this task well. You cannot break the rules with this one. Find a job and tell me once you do. I will tell you the next steps.' Slightly annoyed by this air of mystery, which I had found exciting at the beginning of the trip, I hung up. Did he even know what we had gone through? The stupid thugs? The stolen car? Not to mention all that we would have to face when we were back.

But on the other hand, I was equally proud that he didn't care: for him, I was equal to Rohit and Mohit, not someone who needed to be extended an arm of protection. I was appreciating my good luck when I heard Monty say, 'Let's go.' I saw Nikku get up.

'Where are we going?' I asked.

'To eat. At a wedding,' Monty replied.

'Whose wedding?'

'We don't know. Someone's. We are crashing one.'

Nikku seemed completely okay with the plan, following them as they headed out. I was glad when he waited for me at the bottom of the stairs, looking at me with his stupid grin.

I sighed and said, 'Fine. Let's go.'

He laughed and took me by the hand as we headed out into the mad street again.

It was only once we were outside the wedding pandal with Preeti and the others that I realized it was a Delhi wedding, not a silly, small Siyaka wedding. The tents covered a huge park, with generators blaring in one corner. A carpet was laid out before the entrance that had a ribbon running across it, and we could see women standing at the gate with thalis in their hands. There were lights everywhere, so many in fact that it was almost blinding. Balloon sellers hankered outside the pandal, waiting for stubborn kids to coerce their parents into buying them one. Even though we could not see it, we could hear the baraat approaching, thanks to the band's trumpets and drums.

'It's not far,' Preeti said, turning towards us in a businesslike fashion, rubbing her hands. 'I think this is a good one. It's neither too small for people to understand that they don't know us, nor too big for them to know we don't belong here.'

Everybody nodded, as Monty put an arm around her, which she shook off irritably. 'Not now, Monty! We have a wedding to crash.'

She then surveyed me and shook her head. 'You could have done better.'

'We lost all our clothes!' I said defensively, throwing a look at Nikku who rubbed my back in consolation. 'Come here,' she ordered. I stepped forward obediently. She dabbed some things on my face, finishing off with a line of kohl. Then she settled my hair with her bare hands. 'These Siyaka pants are in fashion, I admit, but yours are too dirty,' she murmured. 'Here, take my earrings.' I took the huge silver hoops and slipped them on.

In a few minutes the baraat arrived and we made our move, as that was apparently the best time to break in. I looked around in wonder: if this happened in Siyaka, it would be the wedding of the year, or maybe even bigger. The suits and saris were dark and glittery, shimmering under the numerous fairy lights. Most of the women wore heeled sandals and gold jewellery that looked real, while the men wore suits. Though Nikku's jacket and Preeti's earrings did make me look less shabby, if someone took a close look, I thought they would be able to tell we were misfits.

But as we started blending into the crowd, I realized that there were all kinds of people there—well-dressed, dressed down, and some simply . . . not dressed at all. As I watched, some men dancing in the middle removed their shirts. Preeti advised that we walk around separately but keep meeting once in a while. 'Act as a couple,' she said, 'then people will think you are the groom's friends. And you should dance, only a little bit though, not too much. We will pull you on the dance floor. First protest, but then give in. Okay?'

We nodded meekly and were soon lost in the sea of people dancing with one hand in the air and sipping Pepsi in small glasses from the other. Once we were inside, I saw Preeti, Monty and Appu head towards the chaat counter. So we went in the other direction, towards the snacks. Nikku told me to wait there and went off to the bar, bringing back a couple of whisky colas. I downed mine quickly, which made him laugh. I then sniffed pretentiously at the glass. 'It's a lot nicer than the moonshine we produce.'

Pretty soon, everyone around us turned into a blur. Aunties wearing shifty red and pink suits, more regal women draped in saris, poised but sweating because of the humidity, and the DJ floor that was now teeming with enthusiastic relatives and kids wanting to impress their parents. A little, fat girl in glasses tried to clear everyone away from the floor, so she may have all the attention. I cheered her on, hooting enthusiastically. Nikku found this hilarious and had to sit down because he was laughing so hard. 'This is when we say, "*Begani shaadi mein Abdullah diwana*",' he told me.

Then this song came on that really pumped the girl up. She spread her arms and I could see it in her eyes, through her glasses, that she was really into it. 'Mera Laung Gawacha,' she sang, her head bouncing as she danced. Nikku grabbed my hand and led me away to the others. I zoned out while they spoke, staring at people as they went by, waiting for Nikku to devote his attention solely to me. Even in my drunken state, I knew something had changed between us. No more did he hide behind the mask of being my annoying best friend who made up stupid little songs about my nose. We looked out for each other even when we didn't have to, catching each other's eyes and smiling widely. I'd catch him staring at me and not look away, nodding and grinning instead. I noticed how he would not pay attention to anything else when we spoke.

It wasn't long before the DJ put on 'Bolo Ta Ra Ra Ra'. I jumped in delight, dragging us both on to the dance floor. The girl who was dancing earlier joined Nikku and me. We danced for some time before Preeti found us and told us we had to leave. We blew kisses at the girl and walked out arm in arm, the others leading the way.

'Why do you like this Daler Mehndi so much,' Nikku asked seriously, 'when your boyfriend loves all these English songs?'

I felt a stab of annoyance at Nikku mentioning Sahil and ignored the question. 'Bolo Ta Ra Ra Ra' still played in my head and I bumped my shoulders against his, giggling. He smiled at me. Even in the darkness I could see that his eyes had a tinge of brown, and there it was again—orange-flavoured Poppins.

'I forgot to tell you,' he said, bending down to my ear and almost whispering, 'you look very pretty with these earrings.'

'Really?' I touched them. 'I thought it made me look like a . . . like Preeti.'

He laughed as we followed the others and I replayed his compliment in my head. Entering the street on which the hotel was seemed to have a sobering effect on Nikku, as he no longer looked as light-headed. We said goodbye to Preeti and Monty, who were already making out on the stairs, and entered our room. There was a buzz in my ear, but I didn't feel that drunk or confident any more. Nikku took a pillow and the quilt and settled on the floor. I wanted to tell him not to but found my voice to be lost. I collapsed on the bed, thinking about the night, about all our days before, feeling a sadness in the pit of my stomach, the need to say something but being too paralysed to do anything about it.

Nikku came with me the next day when I set out in search of the two mithai shops Lalaji had mentioned. Both of them were in Chandni Chowk, the famous old city of Delhi I had heard so much about. Nikku had been there and warned me that it would be exhausting, but the fact was that there were some things Nikku and I just saw differently. What was tiring and stressful for him to watch was one business opportunity after the other for me.

It was so big that we must have walked for half an hour straight without the street ending. In Siyaka, if you walked for half an hour, you'd have walked from the Victorian town to the lake, which is not that hard as the terrain is flat and the breeze from the lake blows across the city.

In the space of just a few metres, we crossed a bhandara, several different halwais and a range of different markets, all the while manoeuvring between rickshaws. We crossed Chote Bhai Patangwale, a range of kite and *manja* shops selling kites in every possible colour and design you could imagine, followed by a range of hardware shops that displayed locks, handles, holds, knobs, hinges and bathroom fittings. Further down the street was the utensils bazaar with huge varieties of weighing scales, frying pans, ice trays, and a range of pots and pans in different sizes. My mouth fell open as I walked on, pointing out to Nikku all the things we could invest in for Lallan Sweets.

We asked around for Bombay Halwai and got swift, no-time-to-waste replies. 'Walk straight, Fatehpuri Chowk. Ask anyone!'

A few steps ahead sat a man in front of a signboard, singing a song, '*Na khaane mein mazaa, na peene mein mazaa, jeena lage ek badi sazaa! Khujli ho ya daad, hum karenge ilaaj!*' Nikku burst out laughing as I read the board:

Shri Hari Kishan Lal Hakim

Khujli, Daad, Sex Problem, Performance Problem, Husband–Wife Problem: One Solution!

'You want to try?' I asked Nikku. He snorted in response.

'Right now, you're my biggest problem, Taru. You think he can help me?' I whacked him on the back. Soon, we found the long queue that snaked out of Bombay Halwai before we saw the board. People stuck to each other, not leaving space even for a fly to pass. That was the kind of queue I would die to see at Lallan Sweets. I took a proper look at the board:

> Bombay Halwai, Estd 1954
> Tastes Like Home!

We had never had a tagline. I made a mental note to give ourselves one, now that I saw how classy this one looked.

'But why do you have to work here?' Nikku asked me as I stared at the shop. 'Did this man steal your Lalaji's ghevar recipe or something, and now he wants it back?'

I answered with my eyes still on the shop. 'You know, you think you are making a joke, but it might actually be something like that.' He shrugged in agreement as I gasped suddenly, clapping my hand to my mouth.

'What? What's wrong?'

I stared at Nikku, indignation making my voice quiver. 'They charge for extra aloo sabzi? One rupee! What kind of despicable, money-making business would do that?'

It took him a few seconds to understand what I had said, and then he rolled his eyes, putting his arm around me. 'Go inside and get them. Get that recipe that Lalaji wants.' I nodded at him, empowered, and walked in.

Inside was a mad hustle, with men running about slamming dabba after dabba of mithai, packing them carefully and swiftly. I noticed with delight that they packed a couple of their special sweets in little tin boxes, with their name and 'Tastes Like Home!' inscribed on top. I could see there was no kitchen there for the sweets, just for samosas, kachoris and their maddeningly expensive aloo sabzi. I held my dupatta in anticipation, looking around for the boss. Spotting him, I went up to him.

'Namaste, Sahab,' I said with the right mix of hesitation and veneration in my voice. If I didn't sound helpless enough, he would never hire me. He looked up, surprised at being addressed, the moustache on his face covering half his upper lip.

'Sahab, need work here, please. I can do anything. I have worked at a mithai shop before. Whatever you want,' I said.

He shook his head brusquely. 'No work here! Go!'

'Sahab, please,' I said, undeterred. 'I can cook, clean, pack the boxes, even the billing, Sahab. I am very good at math.'

He seemed even more surprised at being talked back to and so changed his strategy, speaking in a patient, but firm, voice now. 'No women. Do you see anyone else here? Only men!'

I was angry but still let a smile come over my face. 'Sahab, I know much more than all of these men, all of them combined, in fact. I have been making mithai all my life!'

'So you make at home and sell. This isn't the place for a woman. Boys get distracted, work is slow, we lose business... some *cheda-chedi* and our whole day is lost in arguments. No, I avoid all of that.'

'But I will keep to myself. I know a lot, trust me! Ever since I was little, there was a mithai shop in front of my house and I saw how it worked, right from—'

'Come here,' a voice boomed. I looked to the right. A much older-looking man with a white moustache, sitting at the back, called me over. I assumed he was the father of the man. He had rotund cheeks that almost took over his eyes and small rectangular glasses with a gold rim. I walked over to him, entranced. Was this the man whose story was intertwined with Lalaji's?

The older man wore gold rings on his stubby fingers and a gold chain around his neck. 'Where are you from?' he asked me.

'UP, Sahab,' I said. 'Mathura.'

'You don't sound like it.'

'When I came to Delhi, I shed my accent, Sahab. I wanted to be like the Delhi people.'

He smiled and asked, 'When did you come here?'

'Two years ago, Sahab,' I said.

'Married?'

I nodded meekly and knew instantly that it was the correct thing to say. Relief showed on his face, as he obviously assumed that a married woman would be less trouble.

'Now you want to live in Delhi?'

I nodded again as he chuckled. '*Yeh Dilli hai na . . . meethi jail hai.* You come here once, you never want to leave. But at some point, you don't want to stay either.'

'Sahab, please give me some work here. I need the money, and I will be very good, I promise. You can give me some work and test me if you want.'

'Oh, we will,' he said. 'Come tomorrow at 10. Then we'll see.'

I clapped in delight, thanked him profusely and backed up to walk out.

'Wear your sindoor! I will not have these boys being slow at their work, thinking they have a chance!'

Chapter 13

Nikku waited outside the phone booth for me, holding the bags containing clothes we had finally bought from Janpath. The pitter-patter of the light rain sounded comforting as it bounced off the booth. Nikku smiled at me from outside. I tried to avoid the hurry-up look the booth manager kept throwing at me, as a couple more people lined up. It was not my fault that Lalaji was being so painfully slow. First, he took forever to come to the phone and now he was stalling before telling me the story.

'Can you tell me what to do now?' I hissed. 'And where are Rohit and Mohit?'

'Eh, they are at the other shop, Ram Jalebi. That shop is also theirs, Bombay Halwai's,' Lalaji said.

'Really?'

'Two brothers.'

'So, I guess I will see them.'

'Oh, Taru! Now the story.'

I was glad he couldn't see me roll my eyes. 'Yes, please, if you would be so kind.'

'This Natwarlal and I were the best of friends, but we only got to know each other once we moved to Siyaka. We were young with big dreams. He came from a similar background.

That time Siyaka had nothing, you know, just forests and land. You wouldn't even recognize it!'

'Okay, Lalaji, but what is the point?'

'Well, Taru, we entered adulthood together, got married almost together, which was when Lallan Sweets was just coming up. The thing was, he had some money, so he set it up with us. We were kind of partners, isn't that how you say it these days?'

'Uh, yes. I guess?'

'But what you might not know is that we got the idea of the magic ingredient from him.'

'What do you mean? He came up with that ingredient?'

'No, no. I mean, he got lucky, you know. He was perhaps the only man in the village who got to marry the girl he was in love with. Don't get me wrong, your grandmother and I loved each other, but this rascal had set his eyes on a girl in the village, and he would always be dreaming about her. I don't know what kind of luck he had, but one day her family proposed a match! Have you ever heard of that? The very same girl!'

'Wow,' I said, wondering where this was going. It was really shameful how Lalaji's life had been way more exciting back in the fifties than mine was now. I mean, it took me years to admit to Nikku that I had a crush on him.

'Well, he used to make amazing mithai, all on his own. We started joking that he used some magic, a secret ingredient to make his mithai taste so good. By then I obviously had my own ingredient, but I hadn't revealed it to anyone. He in turn would joke back, so in love, you know, that his wife was the secret ingredient. And that's when I realized that I needed to use my magic ingredient to make my mithai popular!

I needed to use it as a marketing tactic. He will not be able to tell you what the ingredient is because he left soon after. We split up, you know. He had different ideas. His ultimate aim was to expand into Delhi, while I preferred to stay in Siyaka. That should never be a reason, but well, it was, and we couldn't work anything out.'

He gave a long pause as I waited for him to finish the story.

'I want you to tell me, Taru, I want you to find out—are they happy?'

'Who?' I asked blankly.

'Natwarlal and his wife! After all these years, are they happy or not?'

I clutched the receiver tightly as the operator banged a couple of times on the booth. 'How in the world am I supposed to judge if they are happy or not?'

'That's the challenge, Taru, isn't it? It can never be a stamp on your forehead, can it? How do you know if someone's happy? How do you know if you've lived a happy life?'

I was too nonplussed to question any more but made up my mind that Lalaji had completely lost it. I hurriedly said goodbye and exited the booth. I repeated the conversation before Nikku. He first laughed and then grew quiet. 'Is he happy?' he murmured. 'Wow, that's weirder than anything you've got yet. How will you ever find out?'

We walked a bit around Connaught Place. I was really loving it. It was like our Victorian town, only much bigger. There were all kinds of fancy brands there. What fascinated me the most was a huge place called Wimpy's that looked like it was straight out of TV. Outside, there were rows and rows of candy shops with Phantom cigarettes, Uncle Chips, Fanta and Cola, Poppins, and so many other treats I had never heard of. I saw bakeries, the names of which I couldn't even pronounce, and girls smoking cigarettes on the street! The cinema halls made my eyes almost pop out. Nikku and I held hands, so as to not get separated by the crowd.

Every few minutes we would look at each other, exchanging stupid grins and taking in the craziness that the capital had to offer. It felt like it was Nikku and me against the rest of the world, and we could brave it together. While I was staring at Nirula's from the outside, I caught Nikku looking at me and started laughing. I asked him what it was, suddenly feeling self-conscious. Maybe he thought I was too much of a small-town girl. Nikku, meanwhile, shook his head, still laughing. 'It's nothing. You had such a big smile on your face, it amused me.'

I shrugged. 'Come, let's treat ourselves. You just got a new job,' he said, pulling me inside as I looked around in wonder. There were huge, colourful menus behind the counter with pictures of burgers, pizzas and French fries on them. On another board were pictures of ice creams and some other kind of food I couldn't identify. 'Wow, they also have food from France and all,' I said to Nikku, impressed. He stared at me for a few seconds and then chuckled. 'What do you want to eat?'

'Maybe the pizza,' I said to Nikku. 'I've never had it before. It looks fascinating.' He nodded and went to stand in the queue. I followed him. 'They don't bring it to the table?' People all around us were eating, burgers wrapped in paper and pizzas looking round and delicious, ice cream and chocolate topped with some kind of nuts in big glasses. They slurped on Coke and Fanta in plastic glasses, and I was scandalized to see the prices. Didn't people know they could get it cheaper outside?

The red-and-white theme of the restaurant felt so modern. When our turn came, I waited for Nikku to order. It was a little intimidating. Finally when our food came, Nikku sat next to me, rather than in front of me. We had little bites of the pizza and Coke.

'I don't like the onion,' I said.

'Yes, it tastes a bit off on this pizza,' Nikku said, as I picked at it, and then bent his head towards me, adding with a wink, 'Plus it's not good if you have to kiss someone after.'

I raised my eyebrows, taking a sip of the Coke. 'Don't act like you have a lot of practice in the department.'

He laughed and we finished the rest of the food like that, talking more than we ate. I didn't want to think too much of all the flirty little things he said since he was always saying stupid stuff like that, but it stayed on my mind, right until we went to bed. I asked him to sleep on the bed, but he waved his hand. 'You're a strong, independent woman. You're going to start earning for the both of us tomorrow, so I want you to have it.'

'You're so stupid,' I said stifling a yawn.

Tying a dupatta around my shoulders and waist, with the tiniest hint of sindoor on my forehead, I reached Bombay Halwai well before time. I took off my slippers at the back and stood in the corner. If I looked up, I would catch some of the boys working there staring at me, but they would look away immediately. I was more than used to it. When new people walked into Lallan Sweets, they never expected a girl of five feet and a few inches to look them squarely in the face and ask them what they wanted.

The older man I had met asked me to call him 'Bauji' and took me straight to his desk. His white moustache looked like it had a life of its own. 'You said you're good at accounting, right?' I nodded, and for the next hour, tallied some of his bills, handwritten ones that of course he couldn't show officially. By the end of it he offered me a cushion next to his chair, asking for a little table to be set up in front of me.

Then he made me check his accounts, week by week. He hadn't said it, but I could sense that it was over some suspicion or leak. I checked and cross-checked every number on the handwritten bills, as he sat over my head, excited to have found an assistant who actually knew math. While his son protested about showing me the bills, Bauji shut him down. 'She's a silly little girl! I'd rather show her my bills than any accountant you bring home!'

I wanted to point out that the greatest mistake a man could make was to assume someone was just a silly little girl, and think she could do nothing, but I let it go. The silly little girl had a job to do.

We fell into an easy routine. Because I was working directly with Bauji, none of the men at the shop tried any mischief with me. Either that or it was the sindoor. Every hour or so, I would receive my favourite Karachi halwa to munch on. The job was also good for keeping my own knives sharp. I didn't want the kids to have a stupid teacher when I finally went back to Ultimate Mathematics Tuition Centre. I found it very mind-boggling that the shop was busy all through the day. As

I went through the bills, I realized that such sales could never be achieved in Siyaka. The sheer number of people who came to Chandni Chowk was far more than our little Victorian centre had ever seen.

Once, when I looked up from the ledger, I saw a brown mala around the neck of one of the customers, identical to the one I had seen ashram-goers in our town wearing. I would have asked that man then and there if he was from Siyaka, but Bauji was sitting right next to me. Later, when I was back at the hotel, I asked Nikku to take a break from his games with Preeti and gang, and make use of the libraries in Delhi to see if he could find out something about the ashram.

'What do you want to find out though?' he asked, popping a peanut into his mouth. 'I mean, we already know about their swamiji. He comes once every few weeks, they have their own school, they profess love and peace and all, but through complete control over the mind which you can apparently only achieve by joining the ashram.'

'Not like that,' I said, struggling to find the words. 'It's just that I want to know what people think about it. You know my father was also into it, before he . . . and I just feel that I need to understand this. It will help me to know him a bit more. Just, can you find books or articles and read up a bit on it, or find out more from people? Anyway, you were always much more of a reader than me. I never had the patience.'

'All right, I'll go to the library tomorrow and check the newspaper archives.'

'I'll call you and check in after lunch,' I said with a nod.

'If I don't answer, it'll mean I'm picking up girls.'

'So you'll answer on the first ring then?'

For the first time, Nikku had no answer and accepted defeat.

We now had a set routine. I worked from morning until seven in the evening, sitting with Bauji, tallying his receipts, which got boring after a point but was always punctuated with entertaining titbits like Bauji going off on one of the boys for sloppy packaging of the sweets. Another time, one of the servers dropped a whole tray of badam halwa. I looked forward to kachori time around 4 p.m. and my banter with Bauji when I was done for the day. He would accuse me of conspiring against his shop and I would accuse him of trapping a young girl in a mithai shop. I hoped to build enough of a rapport with him to somehow get the answer to Lalaji's question, although I had no idea how I would ever get to that.

Nikku spent his time trying to find information on the ashram, as well as playing kanche with Preeti, Appu and Monty. Although I felt a bit jealous, there wasn't much I could say. And it made him super happy. He also sent for his cheque book from home, taking out some money from the bank so he wouldn't 'feel like such a gold-digger'.

I was absolutely scandalized and quickly clarified that there was no reason he should feel like that. I already felt guilty for putting a dent in his savings, but he insisted it was worth it. I told him I would find a way to pay him back.

On my fifth day there, I met Mohit. He had been sent from the other shop to fetch something. I spotted him as soon as he stepped in, watching him like a hawk, but it took him a full five minutes to realize I was there. He then stared at me for so long that he may as well have blown both our covers. He did try to hang around for some more time to see what I was up to, but couldn't. When the day ended, I went over to the other shop and waited for him.

'What are you doing here then?' I asked him, my arms folded, as we both spoke standing inside a tiny nook on the street, lest we were spotted together.

'Same as you.'

'I mean what job, idiot!'

'I am cleaning the dishes and Rohit is frying the jalebis. You know he has a steadier hand. But don't you tell anyone who we are or we will tell everyone who you are!'

I narrowed my eyes and almost hit him. 'You already did, at the Taj Mahal! You realize what a low blow that was, right? And the trouble we got into? I'll take my revenge, Mohit.'

'Don't even try. You tell on us and we'll tell on you. Right now, it's better to stick to our own game and finish what lies ahead of us.'

'And what lies ahead of you? What is your task?'

I figured it could not be the same. He pursed his lips and I could see he was going to tell me. He had come to the same conclusion, that our tasks must be different. But just then Rohit walked by. Mohit suddenly straightened up.

'None of your business, Taru,' he sneered and both of them walked away, even as I watched them with narrowed eyes.

On my way back to the hotel, all I could think about was how much I hated them. It had always been like that, their family and them, always trying to one-up us. They always took for themselves the bigger area in the house, the best of things. Memories of Aunty diving for the best pieces of the chicken for her sons came to my mind and made me angry. Ever since my father had died, they had given us only leftovers, especially when I was younger and didn't know how to fight for better. They made us feel like a burden, like we constantly took and used what didn't belong to us. While my mother maintained her dignity, it made me angry and competitive.

Nikku was my escape from all this. I was thinking of him as I got off the bus at Shri Shri Shani Mandir and began walking towards K.K. Palace. For years, all I had done was to go to Nikku's house and forget about everything. And now I had in him a partner to beat Rohit and Mohit, a partner who was older than them, a boy who chose to hang out with me and not them.

When Rohit and Mohit had felt threatened by Nikku being my best friend, they had tried everything to break us apart, including inventing stories about how he was my boyfriend and how we planned to run off together and get married. Every time they messed with us, we paid them back, twice over, and that's how, over the years, I started to get my due respect. They stopped poking their noses in my business and didn't dare to tell me what to do, going into the defensive rather than offensive mode.

When I got back and found Nikku counting all the kanchas he had won, I gave him a hug. He laughed and patted me awkwardly on the back, making me laugh as well. I then composed myself and told him I had seen Rohit and Mohit. He nodded at everything I said but couldn't help adding, 'But in the end, they are your family, right.'

'They have always acted otherwise, Nikku!'

'I understand the rivalry and jealousy, but after all is said and done, there is no way to go around these things except for kindness and being the bigger person.'

Although at that moment I told him that he didn't understand, that the family members only brought each other down instead of pulling each other up, over the next days I couldn't help but admit that there was some merit to what he had said. I didn't let on in front of Nikku, but in the big streets of Delhi where I didn't know anyone, when push came to shove, I missed Siyaka and its quiet charm and intimacy, how everyone painted their houses in different colours instead of the boring grey here. I missed how the jasmine bushes at street corners made you stop and take in deep breaths, how they wiped out every other thought from your mind.

So, despite the competition against Rohit and Mohit, I smiled at them every time I saw them after that. This obviously made them put their guard up, as they struggled to understand why. But I really meant it. One day, when I saw Mohit being yelled at for dropping a whole tray of jalebis while bringing them over from the other shop, I said it was my fault, that I had bumped into him and accidentally knocked over the tray. I got sweared and grunted at. Some even went so far as to say that 'women ruin everything'. But it soon blew over and by the next day, Bauji was in a good mood around me again.

I looked at Bauji thoughtfully. Here was a man running two successful mithai shops in the biggest market of the biggest city in the country. If there was anyone I should ask about the mithai business, apart from Lalaji, it should be him.

'Bauji,' I said, and he hmmed distractedly. I paused before going ahead, choosing my words carefully.

'All this mithai we make, we source all the ingredients on our own?'

He didn't seem to have heard me, so I repeated my question. He nodded but then asked me what I meant.

'Well, I mean, all the famous mithai shops, they have something special in their ingredients, don't they? One thing they put on their own that others don't. I was wondering if you find special ingredients, or just use what's available in the market. Is there something special that you add? For example, when my mother makes biryani, she always fries the onions in a bit of sugar, you know, because the onions we get are a bit too sharp. Using sugar always makes it a little better.'

He looked up at me, and for the first time I noticed that his eyes were actually a very light shade of brown, much lighter than Nikku's.

'You are right, Tara,' he said, nodding at me, 'a successful mithai-wallah will always have that one ingredient, but he must never reveal it. It's like a magician should never reveal his secrets. If he does that, people stop thinking it's special, although others might be using something similar as well. The fun is in the mystery and so is the appeal.'

'Yes,' I said, bending forward, 'I like to guess the ingredient of each shop whenever I have mithai. But I am not always able to. Can you tell me what shops use generally?'

'See, the biggest misunderstanding is that people assume it is something extra that will be the secret. But more often than not, it's the same thing, made using better quality ingredients. You can't add random ingredients to your mithai and start saying that's what's special about it, because it has to be in perfect balance with the other ingredients. But maybe the milk, or the way you dry your dough, might do the trick.

I know that an old friend of mine used to add a pinch of salt to the mithai he made. He said it gave the mithai a little extra something.'

I nodded, having a fair idea who the old friend might be. But what he said had a point. Maybe I had it wrong all along. Maybe he was right and there was no special, extra-secret ingredient.

'You say your mother fried the onions in sugar, huh?' Bauji asked sharply.

'Uh, yes, sometimes . . .'

'Funny, I never heard someone from Mathura doing that,' Bauji said, staring at me.

'Uh, someone taught her, it's nothing special,' I blabbered and went back to the bills, but I could feel his eyes on me for a long time after that.

Nikku was going up the stairs when I reached the hotel. He didn't see me and I ended up accidentally stepping on his sandals, making him stumble. 'Sorry,' I said. He smiled and then stepped on my foot as a joke. As we reached our room, he opened the door for me and bowed. I thanked him and began telling him how my day had been. We opened the windows and curtains, and put our stuff in the corner, picking up clothes from the chair, where we had left them to dry earlier in the day. The first few minutes when we were inside the room together were always the tiniest bit awkward. Whatever time I spent with Nikku, I wanted his full attention. It felt as though I couldn't let conversation between us stop, for fear of it becoming awkward, but I also didn't want to waste a single second not talking to him.

Today, he sat on one side of the bed, instead of his usual position on the chair, and opened a beer bottle. He was saying something about the book he had read, something about the ashram, but I found myself unable to pay attention as I stared at him, finally sitting down beside him. I smiled and nodded along as he spoke but barely registered anything. All I did was fiddle with my thumbs.

I felt his eyes on me and looked away, pitching in a little so that it would seem as though I had been listening. He talked in a low, quiet voice. I sneaked a look at him and found him staring. I opened my mouth to say something, but then thought the better of it and looked away.

And then he kissed me.

Chapter 14

It felt like something had finally fallen into place. When he kissed me, I was convinced about what had until then been a nagging thought in my head—I had always loved him. From the very day that he had brought his grandfather's walking stick to help me get home past the stray dogs, when I could see the fear in his shaking arms. The first time we got drenched under the water pipe in his verandah. All the times we took long walks on summer nights, eating kulfis. Or when we took a boat from Dima Lake towards the caves and stumbled upon what looked like a hippie party full of drugs . . .

It was like coming home. Nikku *was* home, and a much better version of it at that, without the cattiness and politics of the Taneja household. Every afternoon that we spent under the two-thousand-year-old tree spinning *lattoo*s, walking around in the Thursday sabzi bazaar, taking in how magical it seemed with the sellers sitting in the middle of all the vegetables, with their yellow lanterns and dark faces peering from behind, a place full of secrets. Our squeals of delight every time the electricity went out at night, which meant that we brought out our charpoys into the verandahs and Nikku and I were allowed to hang out again, despite being together the entire day.

He even smelt like it, like Siyaka's summer breeze, or when the rain fell on mud, of endless summer days and the stunning winter sun. He smelt like the excitement on a Holi morning, and the fifteenth of August, which was spent entirely on the roof, flying kites and yelling 'ibo'.

The next day, all thoughts of the magic ingredient and the contest were wiped from my mind. I constantly forgot things and messed up my calculations with Bauji, and had to force myself to stare at the numbers on the bills to stop thinking about Nikku and what being with him was like. As soon as I would get a break, my mind would immediately go back to thinking about being with him. I went to Bombay Halwai thinking about Nikku and came back thinking about him. Suddenly, Delhi and its eccentricities were lost on me as all I could think about was returning to our Paharganj room as soon as possible, straight to Nikku.

It wasn't just me. I could see that Nikku felt the same. He hardly thought about the kanchas any more. He was always staring at me and imitating my laugh, the way I made a face. Instead of the banter, now I would just laugh and he would kiss me. The moment I would leave his side is when he would wait for me to return.

I clearly wasn't doing a good job of hiding my emotions. When Bauji caught me smiling to myself while staring at the bills, he banged his hand against the table, shaking me. 'Well, I might as well show these bills to the idiot who's sweeping the floor over there!' he said. Chastised, I dropped the bills from my hands.

'Sorry, Bauji,' I said, hastily picking them up. 'So sorry. I am paying full attention. You won't find any mistake, God promise.'

He stared at me for a few seconds, his moustache flaring because of the angry way he exhaled, but then his face seemed to relax. 'No mistake is good. Now who is it?'

'Who is what, Bauji?' I asked, not looking at him.

'I know you are not married because you never mention your husband. So who is the boy? Who is making you smile like that?'

I was about to deny his claim and insist that I was married. I wanted to say that nothing distracted me from my work and that there was no boy. I wanted to keep up with the lie. But another part of me wanted to tell him, just to see his reaction.

'There is a boy, Bauji. Nikku, I mean, Nikhil.'

Bauji grunted in response and took his time before speaking. 'And does your mother know?'

'Yes, I think so, Bauji.'

'Is he any good? Can he add numbers like you?'

I laughed. 'He can't add numbers, but he can do other stuff. On the computer, you know. He's very talented.'

He grunted once again, and this time I knew it was in approval.

'You can be different people and still love each other,' he said, a wistful look in his eyes. 'They are idiots who say two people have to be the same to get married, all this *chattis guna* and all. You just need to agree on the important things in life. Have a similar kind of attitude to dealing with situations, but apart from that you can be completely different. My wife doesn't like alcohol, you know, but I love it. My son would buy me a bottle of expensive whisky often. For thirty-six years, I hid my whiskys from my wife, and for thirty-six years she pretended not to know. Yet she would leave a washed glass for me, sometimes even a bottle of soda. We've lived together all our lives. She knew I loved it and I knew she hated it. For me, that is love.'

I couldn't do anything except to smile. I wanted to ask him more, I really did, but at the back of my head I already knew I had my answer. I finished the rest of the day in a relative state of calm. It was only when I went back and found Nikku playing kanche with Preeti and Monty, and I was able to sit down, that I gave some more thought to it. Bauji was right, that was love. His words rang over and over again in my ear. It made me think about Sahil as well. I was sure that he was not the one for me, based on what Bauji had said. I felt bad about being with Nikku without telling Sahil. So did Nikku, I could tell. At times, he would suddenly ask if I wanted to call Sahil, but I knew there was no way we could talk about this on the phone. I was sure of my decision, of course, especially after hearing what Bauji said.

I was sitting in our room, going over all of this, when Nikku walked in. I looked at him and smiled. He nodded at me too, smiling.

'Nikku, I think I have it. The answer.'

'To? Lalaji's question? Whether they are happy or not?' he asked, putting his arm around me as he settled on the bed.

'Yes!' I said excitedly and turned to face him. 'He told me this story, of how he hid whisky from his wife all his life, but she always knew and never said anything, and even put out a glass for him!'

Nikku shrugged. 'Sounds like a classic marriage. You don't like something but still put up with it.'

I had no reply to that, but I somehow knew that this would pass off as an answer.

'Would you like it if I hide something from you your entire life, but you still know it?' he asked.

'Depends on what it is. If it's your stupid jokes and songs, I would be so glad.'

'Which song? Taru Taneja Moti Hai, Uski Naak Choti Hai—'

Kissing him was the only way to shut him up.

I reached the shop a few minutes early the next day and requested Bauji's son to let me use the phone. He nodded with a sullen face. I had to dial twice until someone finally picked up: Aunty. We had a painful couple of minutes of small talk. I could sense her reluctance when she finally went to bring Lalaji to the phone.

'They are happy,' I said immediately and quickly narrated why I thought so.

'Really?' Lalaji murmured, more to himself than to me. 'Never thought he was that fond of a drink. No, Taru, I don't have anything against him, remember that. I actually—she had a friend—well, never mind. We'll talk about this later. We split up on not the best terms, him and me. It was not supposed to be like this, you know. We were supposed to build a mithai empire. Now he has his own little kingdom in Delhi, I have mine in Siyaka, but we could have been great together . . .'

'Well, why did you want to know if he was happy?' I whispered, as I saw Bauji enter the shop.

'Just curious. You always wonder, don't you, how people who part ways with you end up. I knew how his shop was doing. I wanted to know if he was happy.'

'You should have just asked him yourself. You could still have been friends.'

I heard the regret in his sigh and couldn't help doing what I did next. I told him to hold and hurried to Bauji, an urgent look on my face, asking him to come to the phone. Bauji was extremely confused initially and refused to move until I literally begged him to.

Standing where I was, I saw his expression change from one of confusion and shock to revelation. Bauji looked at me finally, his eyebrows raised. For a second I was really worried that he would yell at me. But then he gave the widest smile, one that made the bristles of his white moustache move. I felt safe enough to walk over and hear his side of the conversation. 'No, I know, Lallan. *Na iraade humaare kum the, na iraade tumhaare kum the* . . . both of us wanted the best. We throw the dice and then sometimes it falls how you want, and sometimes it falls the other way . . .'

It was going much better than I had expected. I stood with my hands clutching my dupatta, too afraid to move away, lest the conversation go downhill.

'And so now you send your granddaughter to spy on me! Classic Lallan trick, eh? I should have recognized it . . . yes, you're right, I'm out of practice . . . well, truth be told, I don't mind keeping her. She's very good, in fact. I've a son, he's quite the eligible bachelor, what do you say we join our shops now, huh, after all these years. I should ask her, but wait, she said she has a boyfriend.'

My eyes widened as I heard Bauji say this, for had I not assured Lalaji that Nikku was not my boyfriend? I quickly shook my head at him, and Bauji, after exchanging a few more jokes, hung up. He made a gesture for me to follow him. He then sat on a chair, his arms folded across his chest.

'I knew you were not from Mathura,' he said. I hung my head in shame. 'So you lied to us about so many things. But why lie about working here? So you could make me talk to Lallan?'

First I thought about saying yes, letting him think that this whole thing was Lalaji's plan to get Bauji to talk to him. But I decided to tell him the truth, about looking for the magic ingredient and Lalaji wanting to know if he was happy. I did, however, leave out the part about his wife.

'This does make me feel a little uneasy,' Bauji said, waving a newspaper as a fan, 'but since I know your crazy grandfather, I know it's not as strange as it sounds.'

'He mentioned that when you were young, you were very lucky. You married the same girl who . . .'

'Oh yes, she was always with Kalawati and we used to eye them together. Your grandfather didn't tell you about Kalawati, his girlfriend? They were always together before she disappeared, and then of course he married your grandmother.'

This was interesting. I did have to ask him about the other thing though. 'But what about the magic ingredient? Do you know anything about it?'

He twirled his moustache, looking upwards. 'I really don't think we talked about any magic ingredient, except I would always say my wife was the magic ingredient. But that was just a joke. I really didn't think your Lalaji would make a clever marketing tactic out of it and use it for business. Let's think now. How many ingredients do those laddoos of yours have? Besan, ghee and sugar, all very basic. Some dry fruits and other stuff on top. Maybe he adds a couple of drops of gulkand, or something like that, but that's about it . . .'

'Doesn't taste like roses,' I said.

'It would be very little. Hmm. So I was just one of your tasks?'

'But I still had a great time here.'

Bauji smiled and went to his desk, handing me some cash. 'You were good.'

I tried to refuse, but he wouldn't hear of it. Finally, I hugged him goodbye and was out on the street again, rickshaws ringing their bells in my face. I walked to the other shop to check on Rohit and Mohit, only to find that they had already left. They must have finished their task too.

I stopped at a phone booth on the way back and phoned Lalaji again, first asking if Rohit and Mohit were done with their task (they were, those rascals!) and what I had to do next (he cryptically gave me an address in Chandigarh and said I'd find out when I got there). I then casually threw a question about Kalawati at him, but he said he couldn't hear me (coughing unnecessarily at this point) and handed the phone to my mother.

Guilt took over me, making me feel terrible about not keeping in touch over the past few days, too distracted by Nikku. She continued our conversation as before, saying that Pappu Uncle was always on the phone with his sons and that Lalaji would disappear for long periods of time. She also told me that some of the kids had begun asking when the first tuition class would be.

'Soon, I think. We've already spent so many days on the road,' I said. 'Did Sahil come by the house?'

'Yes, a couple of times. He has got a new haircut. He also gave me a new cassette, saying he had recorded those songs.'

This news only added to my stress and guilt, and I promised to call her again soon.

I wanted to tell Nikku all this, but when I got back he was not there. My mind whirred as I waited for him. Rohit and Mohit must already be off.

I went outside to the corridor and heard some noises, a giggle. A door opened and Nikku exited from Preeti's room, nodding in greeting.

'What were you doing?' I asked him immediately.

'Just hanging out,' he said. His nonchalance annoyed me.

'Nikku! You know what she is . . .'

He shot me an exasperated look and shook his head. 'Relax, Taru . . . we were all making plans to go for a party tonight. I would like to. I've never been to a nightclub in Delhi. I've heard they are the real things, you know, like where the big new year parties happen, where stars come . . .'

'I did it,' I interrupted him. 'I talked to Bauji and Lalaji, and this task is done. We are ready to leave for the next one.'

I was glad that he looked delighted. He gave me a hug that lifted me off the ground, instantly making me feel better. 'Let's go for this party now. I think one night is okay.'

'I think so too,' he said, nodding happily.

'What will we wear though?' I asked him in despair. 'They will never let me in like this.'

My dirty, overworn Janpath salwar-kameez, exposed to the streets of Chandni Chowk, painted a sorry picture.

'I asked Preeti the same and she said she will arrange clothes for us,' Nikku said.

'Oh wow, that's nice. So have you just been busy playing kanchas or did you also find out about the ashram?'

He laughed and sat next to me. 'I did and found some interesting stuff.'

'What's that?'

'Well, in the late fifties, Swamiji, the main man at the ashram, took over this land in Siyaka, and the government didn't do much to stop him. There was some token fee, some bribes, and the land was his. Ever since, the ashram has expanded swiftly, with zero tolerance for any kind of protesters. Nobody walks on their land without their knowledge. There's an ashram where all these hippies work, a meditation centre, some private complexes, some 'jungle' and a little lake of its own. But what they also have, something interesting here, are the secret gardens. Apparently a lot of mysterious things are grown there.'

'Like what?'

'That wasn't mentioned. That's why it's mysterious.'

'But what about inside the ashram? What happens there?'

'What happens inside? The same thing that happens inside all ashrams. Hippies sing and dance, probably do some drugs, make it seem exotic to the rest of the world.'

'What is their philosophy?'

'How do you not know this already though? It was all over when we were young. Don't you remember? Sometimes those people would come to our school and tell us about the ashram, about what a wonderful place it is? "In the centre of mind, body and soul, we find ourselves"? It was something about the centre, the basic centre . . .'

Now that Nikku had said it, it rang a bell. But it still didn't tell me a lot. I was going to say the same to him when there was a knock on the door.

'Hello ji,' Preeti said with a wide smile, handing us a packet of clothes as Nikku opened the door. 'See you outside in half an hour?'

We went in an auto together: Nikku, Preeti, Monty, Appu and me. When I said we were like *Hum Paanch* and sang 'Yeh Number 1, Yeh Number 2, Yeh Number 3, Yeh Number 4', nobody laughed except Appu, but that could be because I suspected he had a little crush on me. I guess the TV show was too hip for their tastes.

Preeti wore a sparkly, silver gown and I wore a long black one with silver tassels. I had to admit, I had never looked like that in my life, like a movie star. Preeti had spent some time putting make-up on my face. When I had looked into the mirror, it was like magic. I was a different person. Even Nikku's mouth almost fell open when he saw me, but he contained himself at the last minute and started rummaging around for the room keys.

The boys didn't look bad either. They wore smart half-sleeved shirts buttoned to the top, with sunglasses pushed up to their heads. I had no doubt that we would gain entry to the clubs. I was sure they wouldn't be able to guess that we had no money to spend inside. Which is why we actually went to a much-smaller place to drink first, where Preeti ordered Monty to buy beer for everyone.

'We can pay for our own beer,' I offered, looking at Nikku.

Preeti held up a hand. 'This is just the first round, don't worry. Here it's cheap, only ten rupees. Inside the club, thirty, forty, fifty even.'

I nodded at her, obediently taking the beer she handed. 'How do you know all this?' I asked her. It was fascinating to me. I could never expect to know so much about these kinds of things. I realized how little I knew of things that didn't involve mithai or math.

'Practice,' she said. 'A lot of men make big claims, take me to Ghungroo, Djinns, Wheels, but then they go inside and realize they have no money to spend. So I say to them before we enter the club, "But, darling, I want to drink now", so we buy cheap alcohol. Cheers guys!'

We clinked our bottles. Nikku and I smiled at each other.

I would be lying if I said my mouth didn't fall open at the sight of the hotel. I had never seen anything like it. We had taken a taxi for the last one kilometre between the bar and the hotel because Preeti said an autorickshaw would never be allowed inside. I could totally see why. I wouldn't have had the nerve to go inside alone and was extremely glad for Preeti's presence. Even Nikku seemed enthralled.

It felt like we were about to enter a palace. The building itself was huge and had a strange shape. I tried to count the number of floors but lost track each time. All lit up from the outside, it felt forbidden: I couldn't believe I was there.

We crossed huge manicured gardens, the taxi stopping in front of a huge lobby that I couldn't stop staring at. It was something I had seen only in the movies. The security guard, looking regal in his jacket and hat, opened the car door for me. I smiled self-consciously, straightened my dress and looked for Nikku who got out on the other side. The entire place had such a rich feel to it that I immediately wanted to run away. This was not for me. I was worried people would instantly be able to tell that we were fake, that we drank beer at a cheap bar and were staying in a small non-AC room in Paharganj. I felt like everyone knew that we came the whole way in an autorickshaw and just the last kilometre by taxi. I wondered how Preeti did it.

She was smiling generously, walking in a way that I hadn't seen her walk before. She held her shoulders high, looking confident. She must have noticed how queasy I looked, for she whispered to me, 'Fake it till you make it.' Nikku held my hand as we followed Preeti. I admired the rich and ornate marble floor and how our shoes made a noise against it. I was afraid of dirtying it.

Outside the club was a huge crowd with three burly security guys looking fiercely at everyone, giving a slight bow to the people they thought belonged there. I tried to look casual and unimpressed but didn't do a great job of it as my mouth kept popping open at the things I saw—the lengths of girls' dresses, the way they did their hair, their expensive-looking purses, the velvet ropes.

'Thirty rupees each,' Preeti said, putting her hand out.

'What?'

'Thirty rupees entry,' she repeated.

Nikku took out the money and Appu handed it over for the three of them.

'I didn't know there was an entry ticket,' I said.

'It's not a ticket,' Appu said. 'More like a fee. You have to pay to go in.'

'Why? It's not the Taj Mahal.'

'Yes, but if people could go in for free, anyone would go in and the crowd would be bad. And in Ghungroo, crowd is everything.'

After some waiting at the door, we finally entered. It felt like the kind of club Sahil would describe to me. It was mostly dark and there was a huge disco floor with multicoloured lights flashing beneath the floor. Waiters in white shirts and black bows swiftly carried drinks around. The music was deafening, yet I could hear people sing along as they danced. The girls there moved expertly and sexily, while the guys held drinks in their hands and danced. People were smoking everywhere. Soon, we were pushed to a corner. The crowd was like Chandni Chowk, it was just that the people dressed and smelt better. I noticed that nobody sat down. Instead, everyone twirled and spun each other round.

It wasn't long before the combination of the music, lights and alcohol started hitting me, helping me relax. The club only played English songs, which were half-remembered tunes for me. At some point, I had heard them with Sahil, but in that inebriated state I couldn't identify them.

I took Nikku's hands and started dancing, taken in by the atmosphere. It felt good. I was looking the best I ever had, I had paid money to enter this club, and they had let me. Bloody hell, I was on an adventure trip to discover a magic ingredient. I *deserved* to be there.

'Ooh, I know this one!' I squealed to Nikku. 'It's called "Tiger's Eye"—"Eye of the Tiger"!'

He gave me a pat on the back as we battled our way through the crowd to head to the bar. All five of us were there and Appu passed on a drink to me. It burnt my throat as I gulped it. At that moment, I didn't want to think how much money we were spending. After all, it felt like it was worth it.

We went back to the dance floor and I recognized another song, 'Summer of 69', although I didn't know the lyrics. Some people climbed on to the tables and chairs, and I thought about doing the same. I turned to say this to Nikku but realized that he was not there. Another man came up to me and said something, but I couldn't hear him at all, so I just smiled and nodded as he pointed to his table. He seemed friendly and so I decided to follow him.

There were other people at that table, who welcomed me. I drank from the glass they offered, wondering where Nikku was, hoping he would come over too. I danced with them for a bit before ducking away to find the others. Now strangers in the club were beginning to seem familiar. They greeted me as if I was one of them, holding me by my side, giving me big smiles. A man walked up to me and introduced himself, so I told him my name.

'Your name's Tara?'

'Yeah, like Daler Mehndi's "Bolo Ta Ra Ra Ra".'

He didn't understand my joke so I walked around till I found Nikku, laughing, as Preeti leaned into him. When he saw me, he simply waved at me to come over. Preeti took out a cigarette and lit it as I glared at her.

'Where were you?' he asked, putting an arm around me as I refused to take my eyes off Preeti, who blew smoke into my face. I felt a bit sober after seeing them and refused when Nikku offered me his drink. Then they began to play Bally Sagoo, which lifted my mood. I jumped up as the beats of 'Chura Liya Hai Tum Ne Jo Dil Ko' hit the floor. Everyone went mad. Nikku took my hands and led me to dance, cutting through the crowd. We danced for what seemed like forever.

We finally stepped out for some air and I don't remember how long we sat on the steps. Preeti and Nikku sat with their heads close together. I inched a bit closer and heard Nikku say, 'Yes, but that can't be it, right? Life is a lot more and I want to experience all of it, not be stuck in some small place. I want to settle in another country, I think. Ha ha, you wouldn't mind it? Of course, who would? There's nothing here.'

This was certainly news to me. Suddenly, the reality of our situation came crashing down on me. This was Nikku, the original version, always wanting to leave. Run when things were going well because he couldn't bear to settle down. I grabbed his hand and took him aside without saying anything.

'What are you saying?' I asked him.

'What?' he asked me, lighting another cigarette, annoying me in the process. He looked sheepish suddenly. His eyes were a little red too.

'You don't want to live here? In India?' I asked him. I actually meant Siyaka but decided to start with India.

'Not if I get a chance to leave,' he said casually. I stared at him. He had spoken like I didn't matter at all, as though I didn't factor into the decision. Perhaps I had assumed too much too quickly.

'Why are you asking me about this here, let's go back in—'

'Why are you so friendly with Preeti suddenly?'

Nikku held up his hands as if I was going to attack him. 'What, Taru! She's pretty and has interesting stuff to say!'

There was something about his expression that brought on a strong sense of déjà vu. He ran his hands through his hair.

'What about Meenakshi?' I asked him, remembering how he had behaved around her. He had never finished the story of his first crush.

'What?'

'Did you sleep with her?'.

He didn't answer. He wasn't outraged. That was answer enough. I turned away and he caught my hand. 'Taru, we weren't then—it was before—'

'How does it matter,' I said icily, 'because you wouldn't be here if you had a choice anyway, would you?'

I jerked his hand off and walked away from the stupid nightclub. What had seemed so impressive a few hours earlier now looked fake and superficial.

Chapter 15

On the small TV set, Juhi Chawla attempted to strip off her yellow dress, after which Shah Rukh said 'I love you, Kiran', and 'Jaadu Teri Nazar' began playing. I was rewatching Shah Rukh Khan playing his most complicated character ever on a TV at a little chai shop at the bus stop. For some time, I completely forgot everything and lost myself in Shah Rukh's obsessive love and Sunny Deol's coolness.

I had mistaken everything. I had thought of Nikku as Sunil, ready to be with me at every step, failing to realize that for him it was all fun and games, and a break from everyday life. His words still stung. That was classic Nikku, always thinking our minds were small, that he was the true-blue high-flyer who would see and capture the world. Instead of Sunil, he had turned out to be the Rahul of my life.

'Shah Rukh, eh?' said a man sitting next to me on a stool, smiling, with a glass of tea in front of him. 'He lived in my gully only. We used to play cricket together!'

I ignored him and concentrated on the movie as he attempted to initiate conversation a couple more times. That was until I finally banged my hand on the table and yelled at him to leave me alone. I didn't need any man. A bus arrived and the conductor, with half his body out of the door, yelled, 'Chandigarh, Chandigarh, Chandigarh!'

I bought a ticket.

Despite a rickety ride, I had a vivid and intense dream. It was a beautiful summer night and the breeze from the lake hovered ever-so-lightly in the park, carrying the sounds of our laughter across town. The grass was soft and cool beneath our feet. There was barely any light, yet we could see each other well enough to 'kho' and run. First we did tip-top to divide the teams. Strategies were developed, traps visualized and positions finalized. The team in the opposition was to expect no mercy. Nikku and I were in opposite teams, and I was determined to beat him because he hadn't picked me. I wanted that to cost him big. It would be hard, for he was a great player, the default *beech-ka-bichhu* because it was so hard to get him out.

The game began and I ran, barefoot, my mind sharp and ready. 'Kho!' I yelled and the game began. The speed of our khos was almost jealousy-inducing. No wonder we had won the championship for the past two years. Two players were out but Nikku hung on like an irritating fly. I wanted to take him out on my own. I chased him, but he started running away. I yelled that he had stepped out of the boundary, but he kept running. I was out of breath as I chased him. He kept running and we entered a market with people yelling, asking if I want to eat some kheera . . .

It was at this point that my eyes opened and I saw that the sun was out. The bus was speeding through the city, close to the bus stop. I closed my eyes again, angry at myself for dreaming about Nikku. I felt so confused. Why did he have to be like this, so frustrating and pompous, but also so nice and kind at the same time? I gritted my teeth and decided not to think about him. It wouldn't serve any purpose. By the time I would get back, Nikku would already have left to chase all his big dreams. It was all for the best, I decided. Who knew what kind of stupid plans my mind would have started making had I spent more time with Nikku?

Chandigarh reminded me of Siyaka, with its well-ordered roads, patches of green and people who seemed friendly. That elation lasted only a few minutes though, as I quickly realized that Chandigarh was bigger than Siyaka and a lot more confusing. The real problem, however, was that the address Lalaji had given me apparently didn't exist. Not one person I asked knew or had heard about it. Was this my task then? To find an impossible address?

I collapsed on a park bench nearby, annoyed with the world, willing my mind to not think about Nikku. I bought a bhutta and munched on it. It was still early morning and a couple of ducks dallied about. Two guys and two girls sitting on another bench nearby threw crumbs at them. I decided to walk up to them.

'Excuse me,' I said, holding up the address, 'do you know where this place is?'

One of them took the paper from my hands and read it. He looked directly at me and nodded. 'Yes, we'll take you there.'

I was taken aback by how strikingly handsome he was. He had a dimple on one side and a chiselled jaw. He was unperturbed as I looked at him.

'You definitely know where this place is?' I asked again.

'Yes. You can come with us.'

The others, meanwhile, stared at me and laughed. 'Are you trying to fool me, because a lot of people told me they had never heard of the place?'

'I would never lie to you,' he said, smiling while the others laughed. He stared at me intensely, making me step back, taking the paper back from his hands and turning away. He put a hand on my shoulder and I turned around to face him in indignation.

'Excuse me, Mister, watch it,' I snarled.

He immediately put his hands up in surrender. 'You look like a girl in search of something.'

'Genius,' I smiled sarcastically, 'as if I just didn't ask you.'

'What I mean is, so are we. In search of something.'

'So is everyone in the world.'

He clapped his hands. 'Well said. Are you a poet by any chance?'

I gave him a weird look. 'Why the hell would I be a poet? I'm a mathematician. And a businesswoman.' I didn't want to call myself a math tuition teacher and a mithai seller.

I walked back to my bench. Later, I heard them singing, all four of them. They stood in front of the water and sang 'Main Khiladi Tu Anari'. They obviously needed some schooling in who the best hero was. I laughed out loud when the guy who held one of the ducks actually broke into the Akshay Kumar dance.

I walked over to them again and told him that he was not a very good dancer. He held out his hand, asking me to teach him. I looked at his friends who seemed to be surveying me.

'I have an address to find,' I said.

'I told you I can help you find it.'

'Why does anyone else not know about it?'

'Because technically it doesn't exist now. They reorganized the sectors, but I know where this exact point is.'

His eyes were deceptively light, his face that of a superstar, and he was still smiling at me. He seemed innocent enough.

'You know where this place is?'

'I swear I know it. It's the promise of this evening.'

'It's the morning.'

'Shit.'

I giggled. Of course, he knew that. I held out my hand. 'I'm Tara.'

'You're what?'

'Tara, like "Bolo Ta Ra Ra Ra".'

He responded with a deep laugh. 'I'm Aman. And that's Jassi, Gurpreet and Heena.' I smiled at them confusedly, wondering which one was the name of the other man in the group.

'Come, our jeep is out there. Let's take you there.' I followed them, unafraid. It was broad daylight and I had seen worse.

The city went past in identical landscapes. Everywhere I looked, the scene was exactly the same as one that had just passed by. The sky was blue, the trees around breezy and green. It was a smooth ride. I pretended like I couldn't see Aman glancing at me from the rear-view mirror. When I did catch him, he smiled, a little embarrassed, and looked away.

'So where is this place? This A-17?' I asked.

'Near Sector 17,' the other guy said. 'It was like a local meeting point, you know, for people to meet up. Before the sectors were reorganized, everybody says, it was the crossroads, a couple of shops and the red light. Now that doesn't exist any more, but those who have been here for a long time still say, "Let's meet at A-17."'

'And what do they do there?'

'Nothing. They just meet there.'

'Oh. Funny.'

'What do you have to do there?'

I told them I couldn't say.

'Where are you from?' Aman asked.

'Siyaka. I like Chandigarh though.'

'You like it, eh?' Aman asked me, smiling cheekily. 'Would you like to live here? *Yahaan rishta dhoondh de*? Settle down here.'

I laughed but didn't reply, looking out again. Motorbikes zoomed past us. I was surprised to see they wore helmets. I didn't even own one. There were many stalls on the corners: popcorn, channe, budhia ke baal, bhutta . . .

The girls murmured amongst themselves but didn't say anything to me, so I kept quiet. We went around a corner and Aman stopped the jeep, pointing to a narrow lane. 'That's where it was,' he said. 'A-17.'

It looked like an ordinary residential lane. There were houses on either side, electrical wires that ran overhead on poles, a stray dog here and there, and some kids playing stapu at the end of the street. I jumped off the vehicle and found them all staring at me.

'Okay, but I have to go to the exact point,' I said.

'Want me to come with you?' Aman asked.

I was about to refuse but then thought it couldn't do any harm. I shrugged casually, 'If you want.'

Aman jumped down from the jeep. I tried to ignore him as he walked next to me. As we walked a little further, he pointed out where A-17 used to be. There was a single-storey, cream-coloured house there. It looked like the houses in Siyaka. Most of the gates to the houses in the lane were open and clothes had been hung out to dry. Scooters were parked by the sides of the houses. A lone vegetable seller stood with his cart at the other end of the lane.

Aman pointed out the crossing ahead, the one that used to be the meeting point. A small board outside a shop read 'Sharma Uncle ki Dukaan'. There was nothing else around. I went up to the shop and Aman followed me uncertainly.

Inside, I looked around: trails of Uncle Chips, in at least four flavours, were on display. On the counter in a row lay many boxes, full of Rola Cola, Mango Bite, orange candies, Chatmola, Cadbury Gems, Pan Pasand, Lacto King, Fatafat and even Phantom cigarettes. On the side were 'adult' snacks, packets of biscuits, including Marie and Nice. In a box on the floor were glass bottles of Gold Spot, Campa, Pepsi and Coca-Cola, with a sticker that announced 'Cold Bottle Available'.

We waited and looked around. A white table cloth covered the counter and a small clock hung on the wall in front, which was otherwise bare. I was about to walk further into the shop, which led to the entrance of the house, when a woman appeared. There was a dupatta around her head. She wore a pale blue suit and thick, rectangular glasses, and walked with a limp. I assumed she was Sharma Aunty.

I cleared my throat and suddenly didn't know what to say.

'We have ration,' she offered. 'Rice, gehoon, oil, masala . . .'

'Umm, I want a Poppins,' I said, reminded of Nikku, and swallowed, 'and a Pepsi, please.'

Drinking from the glass bottle would allow me to stay there for a while, as I would have to return it. Sharma Aunty limped back inside and brought a cold one for me, opening it with the opener.

'You wanted to come here to drink cola?' Aman asked me.

I ignored him and fished out the money to hand over to her. 'Sharma Aunty,' I said. 'Where are you from?'

'Huh?'

'Originally.'

She took the money from me and said, 'Originally from Pakistan, some years in Siyaka and then finally settled in Chandigarh.'

I beamed. She was my girl. 'I'm also from Siyaka! That's why I'm here!'

She peered at me from behind her glasses. 'From Siyaka?'

'Born and brought up.'

'That's why she has that accent,' Aman said. I glared at him.

'Those two boys who came,' Sharma Aunty said, sitting down on a chair, 'I already gave them the sari she wanted.'

Bloody Rohit and Mohit! So a sari had to be carried. What in the world was I supposed to do now? But for whom? I had to pretend that I knew what she was talking about.

'You know my grandfather?' I asked excitedly. 'Lallan? Taneja?'

She stared at me curiously. 'Of course, I know him. He only requested me for the sari, on behalf of Kalawati.'

Kalawati! I knew if I asked her who she was, she might think I was an imposter.

'So nice to meet you, Aunty,' I said pleasantly, at which she smiled.

'Come, come inside . . . I wouldn't have taken the money from you; I feel so ashamed.'

We walked to the next room and sat on a divan, while Sharma Aunty went to call Sharma Uncle who came with his own walking stick. He too wore the same rectangular glasses as her. Both of them sat down on the chairs in front of us and asked if we would like to have some chai. Both of us refused and thanked them.

'When we heard, we were surprised, but I saw no harm. That's why I sent the sari.'

'To the two boys, huh?' I asked to be sure. 'Rohit and Mohit?'

'Yes, exactly! See, I have not spoken to her ever since she stole my steel almirah. That's why all these problems happened. But whatever, *raat gayi baat gayi* . . . you know about the almirah?'

'Uh, I don't think so,' I said.

'I got that almirah all the way from Multan! You know how dangerous it was, to bring these things? Then, when we were in Siyaka, before she got married, she cleverly strategized and stole the almirah from right under my nose. It was full steel, Beta! It has been around since my *par-nani*'s time, and we wanted to give it to our daughter when she got married. What has that almirah not seen? Saris of four generations, gold, riots when those hooligans descended upon us. People died, Beta, but the almirah saw and survived it all. And Kalawati took it away from me. Then we both got married and moved out of Siyaka—who keeps in touch! We didn't have phones like you do now. For fifteen years, I didn't go to visit her, but then we met at a cousin's wedding. I didn't forgive her, but I was very nice to her and asked her how she had been.'

I nodded sympathetically. 'But you gave her the sari, so all is well.' My mother was also obsessed with our steel almirah. She always spoke about how she got it for her wedding.

Sharma Aunty looked at Sharma Uncle and I was struck by the affection between them. 'Yes, he told me, "Rajjo, what is the point? You won't take the almirah to heaven, will you? We are okay here, aren't we?" Nice little shop, it's quite famous, you know, Sharma Uncle ki Dukaan. You've come in the morning but wait till the schoolchildren come. There are queues outside. It would have been great to have a house by the lake, but we are fine, our kids are married and settled. Sometimes, the neighbourhood children ring the bell and run away, but we have learnt to live with it.'

And then she asked abruptly, 'Are you going to Siyaka after this?'

I nodded.

Sharma Aunty got up and hobbled inside. After a few minutes, she returned with another box. 'Can you also give this? I want her to have it. It's nothing big, just a silver chain, but well, it's a new start, so might as well.'

I opened the box. The silver chain was a bit blackened from the edges but otherwise well kept. I smiled and nodded. I hoped this would count towards the task. I was also hopeful that this would help patch a friendship that had gone sour.

'Thank you very much. I'm sure she will appreciate this gesture greatly.' Really, Lalaji had lost it. Why was he involving me in getting a random necklace for a random lady I didn't even know?

Sharma Aunty didn't let us leave without treating us to glasses of cold Gold Spot and a plate of Marie biscuits, which I munched on quite happily. I put the necklace safely in my bag and walked up the lane with Aman.

'So your business is done?' he asked me.

'I have more left, but it's done here. Thanks for your help.'

We stood across from the two girls playing stapu and I just about stopped myself from yelling out to her that her angle of throwing the stone was wrong. It wasn't going to land on '7' so easily. A woman, meanwhile, wiped the window grills as two kids ran up and down the stairs of the house.

'You're welcome,' Aman said, and I caught myself staring at his dimple again. 'But you forget something. You owe me a dance.'

I laughed. 'I'm not going to dance with you.'

'I'm not going to dance with you,' he said, imitating me. 'You people from Siyaka have such a cute accent!'

'I do not have an accent. It's you Chandigarh people who have an accent. It's so rough!'

'Why don't you spend the day with us? We have some stuff to pick up in the evening actually, near the lake. We can also show you the sunset, and if you want we can feed more ducks.'

I laughed. Rohit and Mohit were already ahead of me. There was no doubt that they had reached the next stage. But I also remembered the lessons from this journey—to do things for the fun of it all. What would be the point of all this, going through all of this twice, if I failed to remember the very things Lalaji was trying to teach us?

I nodded.

It turned out to be the best day. Jassi, Heena and Gurpreet were very warm, and not making fun of me, as I had thought earlier. We drove the jeep along tree-lined streets. I wanted to ask Aman how he had got the jeep. Only Ishaan had one in all of Siyaka. But as a former purveyor of stolen cars, I really was not in a position to question other people's possession of cars.

Aman flirted with me and I basked in the attention of his handsome face and beautiful dimple. We ate the best chicken I had ever had and played the songs that I liked. When 'Made in India' came on, I asked Aman to change the song. In the evening, we drove past Piccadily Square and then headed towards Sukhna Lake.

All along the lake, people were jogging, drinking juice or eating chaat. I pined for Siyaka as I told my new friends about Dima Lake. It also brought me back to Nikku. I hated all the things that he had said. I imagined him watching me with my new friends and wished that he could see me being worldly and friendly and interesting.

When the sun went down, the sky turned a violent pink, and then mellow shades of blue and purple. We watched the boats come back to the shore. The breeze caressed our faces. It dawned on me that I had completely forgotten to call Lalaji.

'What are you thinking?' Aman asked me, brushing a strand of hair off my face. His closeness left me dazed.

'About leaving actually. I have to go.'

'I have to go as well.'

'I'm sure you're not going where I am.'

'Depends on how the rest of the evening goes, doesn't it?' he asked, grinning, and his comment suddenly made me feel shy.

'Aman, we have to leave,' Jassi said, 'for the pick-up.'

'Yes, okay,' Aman said. 'Come, Tara, let's go.'

'I was thinking of heading back,' I said.

'Just some more time? I really enjoy your company,' he said, smiling his dimpled smile again. How could I say no to that?

It was almost dark by then and we turned the headlights on as the Jeep made its way away from the crowded markets. There was some whisky at the back and we all took a swig. This time, I sat in the front, thinking about my next step. Though it was dark, the worst that I would have to do would be spending some time at the bus stop after calling Lalaji. I was sure the next clue wouldn't be straightforward either.

I wondered how many more were left. Hadn't we already proven our calibre? Mathura seemed so long ago now. It reminded me of Meenakshi and Nikku, and I dug my nails into the car seat. I realized that I couldn't think of the past without thinking of Nikku, so I just focused on Aman, smiling at him.

We stopped at a street corner that was very quiet. Aman told me these were the outskirts, where the city almost ended. He hopped out and asked me to follow him. I walked ahead with him while Jassi and the others followed, quieter and more mellow now.

Aman and I reached a bench, where he sat down. I looked around.

'What do you have to pick up from here?' I asked.

'It's a bit sensitive,' he said, signalling me to sit next to him.

'What?'

'Well, it's question papers—from our college. Of an exam, if you know what I mean.'

I frowned and nodded. 'Yes, people in Siyaka also do that. I don't believe in it. I am a math teacher, you know.'

He smiled slowly, his arm on my back. 'I wish I had you as my teacher. I wouldn't cheat either.' I shook my head and laughed.

He was staring at me now, and I knew what was going to happen. I couldn't look away or at him, so I held my gaze until I saw him leaning in towards me. He kissed me, softly at first and then more intensely. I didn't know how much time had passed when he pulled away and smiled at me again. I had to blink a few times to bring everything back in focus. He put an arm around me and drew me close. Before I could process what had just happened, a bike arrived from the other side of the street and parked next to the bench.

Of the two men on the bike, one of them got off and glanced at me, his questioning eyes on Aman.

'She's with me,' Aman said, waving a hand. The man regarded me for a few more seconds before handing Aman a package. In the same handshake, Aman seemed to have handed him the money. The man turned around and counted it, gave a final nod, and got back on the bike. They rode away as quickly as they had arrived.

'Let's go,' Aman said, extending his hand. We walked in the direction of the Jeep. Aman nodded at the others and told them everything was okay. They took out a couple of cigarettes and smoked them. The package was carefully hidden at the back.

Aman still held my hand, but I knew that I really needed to go. I couldn't stop thinking about Nikku and needed some alone time. I was about to tell Aman this but they started playing a song and singing along.

'Shit,' Jassi said suddenly. I saw panic writ large on everyone's faces. I turned to Aman to ask what the problem was and saw a shadow of dread cross his face.

'What—what happened?' I asked. Before he could answer, I heard it too. A police siren, loud and clear, and approaching us. I was going to tell him to relax, that the police were probably not looking for them, but remembered that they had also been drinking in the car.

Aman turned to me and asked, 'You okay, Tara?'

I nodded and he handed me an envelope. 'One second. Just hold on to it, let me just . . . do you have some money on you? Your backpack? Yes.'

'What?'

'How good are you at calling attention to yourself?' he asked me urgently.

I stared at him, confused. 'What? You want me to distract the cops?'

He gave me a searching look and, from the back, Jassi opened the car door on my side.

Aman looked at me and, for a second, I thought he meant it.

'I'm sorry, Tara,' he said. And then, with a violent shove, he pushed me out of the car. I landed hard. My forehead and cheek hit the ground. I felt the warm blood on my face as they shut the car door and drove off into the darkness.

Chapter 16

'I told you already,' I repeated for about the tenth time, but I may as well have been talking to the wall, 'these are not my drugs. I don't know what these are. I don't even know how to use them—smoke, swallow, snort or drink. I have no idea how these work.'

'But you do know that these drugs are either snorted or smoked!' the inspector said, banging his hand on the old, wooden table and holding up his index finger at me.

'Yes, because I am a living, breathing human being!' I replied in irritation, struggling to keep my tone respectful. The atmosphere at the police station wasn't helping—the policewoman standing next to the inspector had grinned maliciously at me, like a nosy old aunt who had caught the kids making out on the terrace. She had her arms crossed over her chest. Her expression said, '*Aaj toh tumhaari khair nahi*'. I didn't know if I would be spared.

The inspector, on the other hand, was hell-bent on proving that these were my drugs.

'Admit it, Madam, you were smuggling drugs, if not consuming them—and that also we can find out with a medical test! Do you know what the punishment for doing drugs is?'

'Arre yaar, I told you! These are not my drugs. That guy, Aman, he said these are question papers. When he heard the police siren, he handed me the package and threw me out of the car. You see these scratches on my face? Why, and actually how, would I hurt myself? He is the culprit, as are his friends Jassi, Gurpreet and Heena. You are just wasting your time interrogating me. This is what he wanted, to distract you. That's why he left me bleeding on the road!'

The inspector shook his head expertly. 'Good story, Madam. But why were you with him in the first place, huh? He kidnapped you and put the drugs in your hands? Why the hell would you allow all this if you didn't even know him properly?'

I had no answer to that. Why in the world was I with him in the first place? How had I been so careless that I got distracted by the sight of a good-looking guy smiling at me? I was Tara Taneja, supposed to be one of the smartest girls in Siyaka. How had one dimple done this to me?

I couldn't believe I had fallen for his act, all that I-want-to-spend-more-time-with-you and you-Siyaka-people-have-such-a-cute-accent. How could *I* have fallen for that? *I* had been the first one to catch the Manchandas sneaking around our shop, trying to steal our recipe. *I* was the one to figure out that Rohit and Mohit would sneak off to play *taash* every day instead of going to college. Bloody hell! *I* was the one who foiled Ayush Singh and his group's plan to prank Nikku. Since when had I started acting like such an airhead? I let him kiss me for God's sake. I wished I could tell the inspector that.

Instead, I just cried. All my life I had tried to hide my tears, so that I didn't come across as weak and fragile, an emotional fool who would never match up to her boy cousins.

But at that point, I wept in front of the police. It started with a tight sob that escaped from my chest. And then the tears flowed generously and my eyes became like little slits, so much so that I could barely see the inspector in front of me, who suddenly looked uncomfortable. Every time I wiped the tears from my cheeks, more would make their way down my face. Finally, I put my head down on the table, on my arm. I heard the policewoman walk out of the room and sensed the inspector's hesitation while he tried to say something to me.

The policewoman returned almost immediately with a glass of water, which she kept next to me, and handed me her handkerchief. I blew my nose loudly and took a long swig of water.

'What to do,' I heard the inspector say in a low voice to the policewoman, '*Hai toh akeli ladki* . . . she's totally alone.'

I hung my head and proceeded to summon as much shame as I could. 'He promised me,' I began, 'he said he would come to Chandigarh with me, we would get married, and this and that. I ran away from home and came here, he made me meet his friends and then . . . you know. I am too ashamed to go home. But I swear to God, Inspector Sir, I swear, I had no idea these were drugs. He used me and then threw me out of the car to save himself, so your car would have to stop. You can take my medical test. Go on, do it!' I stuck my hand out for good measure.

The inspector scratched his head. 'Listen, I understand your situation . . . these things happen. But we found the drugs on you and have to investigate . . .'

'But does my word count for nothing?' I teared up again, but this time the tears weren't real.

'It does, but . . . just have some more water and relax. Write down everything you can remember about this guy and his friends, okay?'

'Can I at least call someone?'

He thought about it for a while and then nodded. 'One call.'

The policewoman pointed me to the telephone as I took out a diary from my bag. But who could I call? I didn't want to call Lalaji and admit that I was a loser, unworthy of being bequeathed Lallan Sweets. More importantly, I didn't want to tell him that Nikku and I had parted ways. There was no way I was calling Nikku. I could call Sahil, but really, what would he be able to do? I flipped through the diary and stopped at Ishaan's number. His father was an MLA, perhaps he could do something? I looked uncertainly at the policewoman. She raised her eyebrows.

'Can I take some time to think? It's just . . . I don't know who I can call right now.'

She nodded sympathetically and I went back to the wooden bench I was sitting on. It was quite late by then and I was tired. I hadn't slept for more than three or four hours on the bus to Chandigarh. It seemed like I had been here for a week, although it had just been one very long and eventful day. I checked my bag to make sure the necklace was still there. Satisfied, I placed it on one edge of the bench, put my head on it and shut my eyes. Nobody objected. I must have napped for a while because when I opened my eyes again it was much quieter. There was nobody there. Where had the policewoman gone? And the inspector? They were nowhere to be seen. Maybe he left? It was late, after all.

I looked around the room and peeked outside too, but I couldn't see anyone. I knew it was perhaps my only chance to get out of there. Making the bare minimum noise, I picked up the backpack and tiptoed outside. If anyone caught me sneaking out, they would definitely think I was guilty. Just then, I heard a door click open somewhere and assumed it to be the policewoman, probably coming back from the toilet.

I hurried out of the police station, pulling my dupatta over my head and walking right past a *hawaldar* who was peeing on one side of the road. I broke into a run, wondering how to get around at that time of the night. The city suddenly felt sinister and made me grit my teeth. I tried to stay calm, half-expecting a police car to drive up behind me and carry me away, handcuffed this time. But nobody came and I soon found an autorickshaw. In the sternest voice I could manage, I asked him to take me to the bus station. He spat out the paan he was chewing on and asked me to hop in.

The police in at least one state, if not two, were looking for me. My partner on the journey had abandoned me. Okay, maybe I had abandoned him after he basically told me we had no common future goals. Mohit and Rohit were much ahead in the race, at least as far as I could see. Things were, in general, terrible.

As if this wasn't bad enough, my next task, Lalaji told me, was to stay with Rupi Masi in Ludhiana while Rohit and Mohit would be staying at Kanu Masi's. They both lived close to each other; if Rohit and Mohit and I considered ourselves rivals, we were nothing on Rupi Masi and Kanu Masi.

It had all started with a beauty pageant. They weren't actually my masis. Rupi Masi and Kanu Masi were Lalaji's neighbours before Partition. When they came to India, they lived together for a couple of years in Ludhiana before being rehabilitated to Siyaka. Both of them had then been married into the same family, to two brothers, and moved to Ludhiana. Though it should have strengthened their love, the relationship had become complicated. They moved to separate homes, though still on the same street, and stopped talking to each other. The fight extended to their husbands too.

It had begun with the Mrs Ludhiana pageant. Legend has it that both Rupi Masi and Kanu Masi had reached the finals. The stakes were high, and the sisters, in the heat of competition, let go of all sisterly feelings. In any case, ever since they had got married, they had been more sisters-in-law than sisters, especially after they moved into separate houses. The contest was the last nail in the coffin.

Rupi Masi insinuated that at the most crucial moment, when it was time to walk down the ramp, Kanu Masi had come to her and, in the guise of trying to help her adjust her sari, had managed to crumple it and even take the safety pins off her back. Nobody seemed to have noticed it. Rupi Masi had tripped spectacularly on the stage, her sari coming loose, much to the embarrassment of the judges, the audience, and of course, herself. Kanu Masi had gone on to win Mrs Ludhiana. When Rupi Masi accused her, she claimed that her sister had no proof. That had been the end of their cordial relationship.

Rupi Masi cut off all contact with her sister and immersed herself in the learning and teaching of Kathak, becoming the most formidable Kathak teacher in the city, hailing from the Lucknow gharana. When little girls were sent to Rupi Masi to learn Kathak, it was believed that they often peed in their clothes. 'There is no Kathak without discipline,' she always said, 'and if you are here to giggle and pass your evenings, I will ensure that I make a proper, well-behaved woman out of you.'

But why was I being sent there? Of course, Lalaji had to have it all planned out. Rohit and Mohit would stay with Kanu Masi and I would be with Rupi Masi. Both the masis had always bragged about knowing the magic ingredient.

'I want you to check if they truly know the magic ingredient or not,' Lalaji had said. 'I want you to see what they use in their cooking, in their water, in their tea, anything they do in the kitchen,' he had added and insisted that we would know the magic ingredient if it was in the house. In the meantime, he told me, you will help Rupi, and Rohit and Mohit will help Kanu.

'Help with what?' I had asked blankly. I didn't know the 'K' of Kathak. I felt as if I could see Lalaji smiling over the phone. 'To win Senior Mrs Ludhiana, of course. Don't you know they are participating against each other again?'

Senior Mrs Ludhiana! Honestly, I was tired of it all but didn't dare to complain to Lalaji. I told him nothing about the Chandigarh incident and was extremely grateful to be on a bus to Ludhiana without the police chasing me. I shuddered to think of what would happen had they caught me. I shut my eyes and my thoughts kept going back to Nikku and the evening at Ghungroo.

'Is Appu coming?' I had asked Nikku then, brushing my hair.
'Yes, he is.'
'All right, we'll have fun.'
'Ouch.'
'What?'
'Sounds like he's the reason you want to go.'
I had laughed at that. 'Why, you want to be the reason?'
'Don't pretend as if I'm not.'
'Don't pretend as if you don't want to be,' saying which I had giggled and kissed him. Little did I know that it wouldn't be enough for him. I had loved him, truly, for as long as I could remember. If that didn't inspire him to think of us together, what was the point?

I groaned and forced myself to not think of him; there were other problems at hand.

Rupi Masi was delighted to see me. She was expecting me, of course, but just wasn't sure about when I would arrive. Rohit and Mohit too, she told me, had come to meet her the day before but were staying with Kanu Masi. Her lips twisted into an ugly grimace when she took Kanu Masi's name, though she did try to conceal it.

'What will you eat, little Tara? You know, when you were little, you always tried to pull my earrings out. You were such a fat, naughty child, always running after your Papa. How is Mummy these days?'

We chit-chatted for a while as I surveyed the house. There were light curtains over the grilled windows. When she went to the kitchen and I stood with her, she tried to shoo me away. 'You go and rest in the drawing room, na!' But I refused to budge. This much was certain: I would be in the kitchen for as long as I could and find that damn ingredient.

'Where is Uncle?' I asked her, popping a rasgulla into my mouth.

'He will see you in the evening. He's at work, na!'

Finally, seated on the sofa next to her and allowed to relax, I felt a wave of relief wash over me. After the last couple of days, I was glad to be with a familiar face. Rupi Masi and Kanu Masi used to come to Siyaka often when we were kids, bringing clothes for us. Rupi Masi always gifted me a night suit. Each time. The two masis stayed with their chachi in Siyaka. The two of them and Lalaji had adopted each other as brother and sisters after living together for so long, first in Pakistan and then in Siyaka.

'So Lallan Bhaisahab actually sent you on this hunt for the magic ingredient?' she asked me, her face piqued with interest.

'Yes, Rupi Masi,' I said, trying not to sound too excited. 'What can I say! I am really tired of it all. I've been travelling for so many days, I've seen so much, the stories I can tell you . . .'

'So tell me, na. What are you waiting for! But wait, were you not going to come with someone?'

'Yes, he had to . . . leave!'

'He, oh Tara, what is this "he"! With a boy? From Siyaka?'

'Masi, tell me about the competition! I'm here to help you.'

'This is not right. Lallan should not have involved the kids in this.'

'Still a fight, is it?'

Rupi Masi turned her face upwards, refusing to answer at first but then looking at me. Her eyes were full of hurt. 'You know how many Kathak batches I run now, Tara?'

I shook my head meekly.

'Five! Five batches of Kathak. In Ludhiana! Every little girl wants to learn Kathak from me, although I am past the age when I can dance. But just one look is enough to teach them, that and my older girls and my strict voice. This has been the most successful Kathak class Ludhiana has ever known. Yet, I never got credit. All people remember is that Rupi fell face first in Mrs Ludhiana and Kanu won the contest. So angry with the outcome was I, people say, that I broke all relations with Kanu, with my own sister, despite the fact that we live on the same street! Do I want to die like this? With this black *dhabba*, taking the blame for killing our relationship? No, Tara, no. I will participate in Senior Mrs Ludhiana. And trust me when I say, this time I will beat Kanu.'

I was fascinated. Rupi Masi was always impeccably dressed, with kajal lining her eyes, her sharp silver nose ring, hair tightly plaited and her dupatta always tied on one side, ready to dance.

'Rupi Masi, is that what I'm here for?'

'Yes, Beta, but I just don't want to involve you! Anyway, my husband says that I am being a fool, that I should let go of these old rivalries, that jealousy doesn't suit an old woman, that all this Mrs Ludhiana is nonsense, but he doesn't know!'

I got up and put a hand on her shoulder.

'I know what it's like, Rupi Masi. I know what it's like to constantly be in competition, to feel like someone is trying to one-up you all the time, to be bested even though you know you are capable of all that they did, and more. I completely understand and I want to help you.'

Her eyes might have teared up as she hugged me.

'This time we will win for sure,' she said to me in a tone so matter-of-fact that I had to ask her why.

'Because I have a fundamental advantage this time,' she said with a smirk. 'The first round is a dance competition.'

Over the next few days, I not only polished my dancing skills, but I was so occupied between following Rupi Masi around all day and helping her prepare for Senior Mrs Ludhiana that I didn't have much time to think about Nikku. Of course, when I lay down to sleep at night, thoughts of him would be the first thing to creep into my mind. I felt hurt and betrayed that he hadn't even called me. I couldn't help but think that if he called my home, they would obviously have told him that I was at Rupi Masi's. He could have called me here. But nothing of the sort happened and I constantly forced myself to not think about him, keeping my eye on the goal.

To begin with, Rupi Masi showed me her best Kathak moves and I advised her which ones we could take up. We finally shortlisted a thumri, but I wasn't satisfied. 'People know you for your Kathak, your thumris. You organize the annual programme for the girls every year. If you perform a spectacular thumri, it won't surprise them, will it? You will be fabulous, but I feel you will win more points if you do something you're not already an expert at, something that shows your vulnerability, which shows that you had to work hard at it. Everybody loves an underdog, they want to feel your pain, see you climb a mountain. You can't already be at the top.'

Rupi Masi nodded diligently, holding my hand. 'What must we do then?'

'Let's bring the house down,' I said, gritting my teeth in determination.

We choreographed a dance on 'Gur Naal Ishq Mitha', and although uncomfortable, Rupi Masi pulled it off with the utmost determination and perfection. Uncle shook his head and laughed at us. 'This is going to be hilarious. How many times do you see a *buddhi* dancing like this?'

'Mister, I am not buddhi. I am a senior citizen!'

In the mornings, we had a detoxification and beauty routine planned—lots of water followed by haldi-chandan paste on the face and neck, followed by oiling of hair with jasmine oil. After this we would practice our dance steps, post which it would be time for Rupi Masi's Kathak classes. All through the day I would follow her like a puppy, staring at what she put into the food, even when she made Uncle's chai. Was it possible that she was hiding it from me? I wondered if I should ask her directly but then decided that I would need her on my side if she was actually going to tell me the magic ingredient. That moment would come once she won Senior Mrs Ludhiana.

I even paid a visit to Kanu Masi. Though we were competitors, she greeted me warmly. Along with Rohit and Mohit, we actually had a fun time reminiscing about the past. When it was time for me to leave, Rohit and Mohit joined me, and we had a rare moment of peace and friendship.

'Where is Nikku then?' they asked.

When I didn't reply, they nudged me. I replied testily, 'Agra's *pagalkhaana*. That's where he's gone.'

'Come on, Taru, tell us,' Rohit said. 'Is he following another lead?'

I ignored the question.

'Anyway, Taru,' Mohit said, 'we were talking about it and we think that, when we win, because we will win for sure, Lallan Sweets will be yours too. I mean, don't think that you will forsake all claim to it just because you lost this competition. We will talk more about this when we win, but . . . just to let you know. You will still be our sister.'

Despite the cocky tone, I was touched. Perhaps it was the Rupi-Kanu Masi effect. Our families might have set us up to spar, but we were probably beyond them, beyond their stupid fights. I smiled and extended my hand, trying to quash the thought that this might be a trick to catch me off guard. They shook it one by one.

Chapter 17

Ludhiana's Vatika Banquet Hall was decked up and abuzz. People strolled in wearing shimmery saris and neat shirts, greeting everyone, trying to sneak a look at the participants list at the reception. Old Hindi music played in the background. The city's who's who had turned up to watch the very exciting Senior Mrs Ludhiana and the famous rivalry that would play out on a public platform. Though Miss and Mrs Ludhiana were better-attended events, this one had its own charm. Old ladies dressed in chanderi saris walked around with dignity, some of them coming up to me as I stood next to Rupi Masi, telling me that they were a former Mrs Ludhiana, or a runner-up, just like Rupi Masi.

I nodded and smiled patiently at them but had something else on my mind: since family was not allowed in the dressing room and there was still some time, I had a plan to head back to the house and search Rupi Masi's kitchen in peace. This was the best chance I could get, when both Rupi Masi and Uncle would be busy here.

Someone tapped me on the shoulder. Both Masi and I turned. A man with glasses, and a slight hunch, stood with a notepad and pen in one hand, the other extended towards her. 'Jaspreet Singh from *Ludhiana Times*. Care to talk for two minutes?'

I raised my eyebrows as Masi settled her hair. I had no idea Senior Mrs Ludhiana was such serious business.

'Rupiji, many congratulations on being here. I am sure you will perform well. I would like to ask you a couple of questions for the newspaper, if that's all right.'

Masi nodded, looking like it was much more than all right.

'Sources tell me that you will be presenting your best Kathak performance, the one from the annual show in 1991 for which the Governor had given you a prize, to beat your own sister in the pageant. Is it true?'

Rupi Masi suddenly looked uncomfortable. 'What . . . I mean, of course, I will give my best. It is a competition, after all. But I am also competing against other beautiful women, not just my sister . . .'

'Well, word on the street is, and I have to say I'm inclined to believe it, that the two of you will be in the finals, and that this is the revenge you have planned for your sister beating you many years ago?'

Rupi Masi looked positively hurt. 'Yes, it's true that she beat me many years ago, but isn't it a competition? Someone has to win, someone has to lose! Senior Mrs Ludhiana is a contest to get the ladies out of the house, to show their skills and beauty and grace—it's an excuse to come together and celebrate the senior ladies, not to pit them against each other for gossip!'

'But this obviously is a rivalry the entire city is waiting to watch.'

Rupi Masi's mouth fell open as she stared at him first, and then at me, as if I could offer some logic for what he had said. I had nothing though and Rupi Masi walked away. I didn't think that what she had done was the best tactic to change the impression people had about her, but I followed her nonetheless and asked what the problem was.

'The problem? Come on, Tara, why should people be allowed to think that I am doing this to take revenge from Kanu?'

'But aren't you?'

She let out a sigh of disdain. 'A little bit, yes, but she is my sister! How can I allow people to make a mockery of our relationship and make us look like villains? This was crossing the line. I might be here because I didn't win Mrs Ludhiana and Kanu did, but most of all, I am here for myself, like everyone else.'

I nodded and sympathized, and then accompanied her to the dressing room, kissing her good luck.

'I will look out for you in the audience, Tara. I don't know why, but I am feeling very nervous.' I assured her that she would be all right. I would be allowed to see her next during the tea break after the first two rounds. That easily gave me more than two hours to head back home, search for the magic ingredient and be back before Rupi Masi realized that I was gone. I ditched Uncle and told him I was sitting in the front. Instead, I went to the very back, near the exit. Once the dance performances started, I rushed out, hailed an auto and left for the house, the keys safely in my bag.

I had a map of the kitchen in my head, planning which shelves I would check first. The only thought that nagged at me was that I might miss Rupi Masi's performance. I was sure that she would look for me in the audience. I knew I could easily say that I was in the bathroom, but the thought continued to gnaw at me. What if she stumbled and I was not there to cheer her on? She would lose again, after months of preparation, and the relationship between Rupi Masi and Kanu Masi would be irreparably destroyed. Then, I was sure, Rupi Masi would not mind giving an interview like the one today. I decided to hurry up and head back to the banquet hall as soon as possible.

I unlocked the gate quietly, crossed the verandah, past the charpoys, and pushed open the door to the drawing room, which had been converted into the dance room. It was completely bare except for the little mattress in the centre, on which lay two tablas and some *ghungroo*s. I smiled as Rupi Masi's '*Ta Thai, Thai Tat*' came to my mind.

I hurried to the kitchen and reached for the shelf that had little steel boxes containing the spices used each day. I opened each one, smelling them uncertainly. I couldn't tell if there was anything different about any of them and continued, pushing away thoughts of Rupi Masi waiting nervously for her turn to perform. I wondered how her dance would compare to Kanu Masi's. Minutes later, I felt completely ridiculous looking at the chilli powder and garam masala. But it could be *anything*. Hadn't Lalaji once said that the best sweet had a pinch of salt in it?

I opened more cupboards and shelves, wondering how in the world I would recognize the magic ingredient. Lalaji had said it would reveal itself, but there was nothing being revealed there, not to mention the risk.

I hurried to the garden, taking a quick look around, but there was nothing there either: a neem tree, tulsi, pudina, mogra. Was Lalaji's suspicion unfounded? Whatever it was, it wasn't in this house. I kept thinking about Rupi Masi as I locked the gate and hailed an autorickshaw.

I entered the banquet hall just in time; Rupi Masi was up next. The woman on stage was trying some version of *gidda* and it didn't seem to be working in her favour. I smiled. This would be a great act to follow for Rupi Masi. She would absolutely kill it.

When Masi came on stage and the beats of 'Gur Naal Ishq Mitha' filled the hall, the crowd yelled 'oho' and 'aye haye'. I knew that her performance would be a hit, no matter what. It hit all the right notes with the crowd—a new-age song with an old woman dancing to it, a woman known for her Kathak training. Rupi Masi was so graceful! Her hands and feet moved with the precision and *ada* of a classical dancer, yet she danced to Punjabi beats, to a song loved by everyone in the hall. I began clapping and hooting from the back, and the crowd followed.

The Bally Sagoo remix had been a fabulous choice, as Rupi Masi mixed some of her mudras into the dance. When the chorus came on for the final time, almost everyone in the crowd got up, raising their fingers to do 'balle balle' step. It might easily have been the most exciting performance Vatika had ever seen. When she finally stopped and the song ended, the crowd burst into thunderous applause. I knew the crown was ours—until Kanu Masi came on stage.

I always underestimated Rohit and Mohit in matters of strategy, and that was my Achilles heel. So when it was Kanu Masi's time on stage, I was certain that nothing could match Rupi Masi's performance. Then her song came on and I felt something tugging at my heart. I could see the same happening to everyone else, as it was not just Kanu Masi on stage, but also her husband.

The beats of 'Aajkal Tere Mere Pyaar Ke Charche', in Mohammed Rafi's mellifluous voice flowed from the speakers. Both Kanu Masi and Uncle fell into a well-rehearsed routine. They moved with confidence and Uncle even went down on his knees to serenade Kanu Masi. She was wearing a pink sari exactly like Mumtaz's. Hell! Uncle even had a trumpet like Shammi Kapoor. They were cute, they were vulnerable and they were old. Their dance was not as fantastic as Rupi Masi's, but I saw a smile on the face of every member of the audience, a wistful look that seemed to wonder if they too could dance the same way with their partner. That's when I knew that they had not just given us a performance to compete with, they had won the round. Because a good love story always wins.

Rupi Masi had been the epitome of grace and beauty, but her performance fell slightly short of Kanu Masi's. I clapped along with everyone else as their performance ended. I was, of course, tense.

The next round was pretty ordinary and didn't offer Rupi Masi much scope to gain an advantage. It was a basic sari-tying competition that went without any hitches. I chewed on my nails, wondering what would happen. The final round would decide everything. During the tea break, Rupi Masi didn't emerge from the dressing room. I went inside, straight to the bathrooms, and found one locked.

'Rupi Masi, I know you are inside. Come on, let me in!'

She did let me in. She seemed to be in shock, her eyebrows furrowed. She sat on the toilet seat, her head in her hands. It was evident that she was tense. I balanced myself on the floor, placing my hand on her shoulder.

'Come on, Masi, you can't give up. Not now . . .'

She finally looked up, straight at me. 'I did everything, practised so much . . . and I am going to lose again.'

I gripped her hand tightly as she kept repeating she would lose. I was at a loss for words for a few minutes, but then managed to pull myself together.

'Masi,' I held her by the shoulders, 'so what if you lose? So what?'

She looked at me like I had forgotten what was at stake. 'Then I am a loser. A woman who tries so hard but still loses. A woman who has been painted a villain in the entire city because she wants to beat her innocent sister in a harmless, fun-filled contest. Who is so vengeful apparently!'

'Masi, if you lose, the only thing you stand to gain is winning something else! Tell me, what happened when you lost Mrs Ludhiana?'

'I lost a relationship? A sister, lost my self-respect—'

'Masi, no! What did you gain? You threw yourself into learning Kathak. Look what happened after that! You became the most accomplished, the most popular Kathak teacher across the city! When someone thinks of Kathak here, they think of you! So tell me, how does it matter that you lost, if the loss led you to winning so much else? Doesn't the best win emerge from a loss? Losing Mrs Ludhiana might have been the best thing that ever happened to you, don't you think?'

She took a deep breath, got up, straightened her sari and pursed her lips. 'Let's go for tea,' she said. I followed her uncertainly, but she seemed all right, greeting everyone as if she hadn't just had a meltdown in the bathroom.

Before the tea break, the three final contestants had been announced—Rupi Masi, Kanu Masi and another lady who, in my opinion, didn't stand much of a chance. It was her turn as soon as the third round began. She had to answer a question about who her role model was. Kanu Masi did better when she was asked if she believed in friendship. Everyone *wanted* this rivalry to play out on stage.

When Rupi Masi came on stage, I was waiting with bated breath. The question for her was: If you could go back in time and tell a younger you something, what would that be?

Rupi Masi smiled widely, as if the answer was at the tip of her tongue. 'I would tell a younger me, "Rupi, stay calm, look around. What does it matter, this or that, these little material things, these irrelevant validations you hold so close to your heart? What does it matter? I would tell the younger Rupi that life is a traitor, that things go to dust and that the tide of luck changes in a matter of seconds. There is only one thing that stays: your family. There is only one thing that matters: your family. Only one thing that will stay through all the dust and glitter: your family."'

I held my breath as Kanu Masi came running on to the stage and hugged her sister. The crowd erupted in wild cheer.

The judges tallied their scores after the round. They praised all the contestants and spoke a little about the competition. Finally, they announced the winner. It was Rupi Masi! She went on stage to receive the crown but didn't wear it. Instead, she shared it with Kanu Masi. I clapped my hands and looked at Rohit and Mohit, who seemed shocked. Was this done on purpose, to hold a mirror up to us, to show us what we were doing wrong? Was this the message of our journey, that we mustn't spend years fighting with each other? I couldn't imagine a better plan to teach us this lesson.

But I was still very confused. Lalaji pit us against each other and asked us to compete. It's true that we had our share of troubles, but couldn't he just tell us to sort it out instead of putting us through this complicated plan?

When Rupi Masi finally stepped off the stage, I rushed to her, as people swarmed around her to offer congratulations.

'What was that?' I muttered.

'Oh, you were right, Tara,' she whispered with tears in her eyes. 'So what if I had lost? The only thing I had truly lost was my sister! I have won so much now, and I only have you to thank!' I stared at her, more confused than ever, as she walked towards Uncle. It's a good thing that Rohit and Mohit looked as confused as me, or I would have assumed it was one of their clever plans to derail me.

All members of the audience wanted to meet Rupi Masi and Kanu Masi separately too and congratulate them. The *Ludhiana Times* journalist conducted a half-an-hour interview with both of them together, while Rohit, Mohit and I waited in silence, sneakily looking at each other. None of us knew what this meant for us. I knew that they too hadn't managed to find the magic ingredient.

'What the hell happened?' I asked them, breaking the silence. They shook their heads.

When we saw both the uncles smiling and talking to each other, I was convinced that what we had seen wasn't a ruse—Rupi Masi had realized the futility of the silly rivalry and let it go. Once the journalist left, we flanked both masis and kept other people at bay.

'Will you forgive me, dear sister? Because if you don't, I wouldn't know how to live with the guilt,' Kanu Masi asked Rupi Masi. Both of them burst into tears and hugged. I felt very embarrassed and turned to Rohit and Mohit. They too seemed uncertain.

'Don't worry,' Rupi Masi said, looking at us. 'Everyone takes their own time. But honestly, now is not the time to preach. We must go and eat something. Oh, stop looking so disappointed, you three. No one conquered the world on an empty stomach!'

Tired, but full of food, we returned home. Rupi Masi and Uncle retired to their room, while I sat in the kitchen, staring at the cupboards. The kitchen had way too many spices, I realized, twice the number in the kitchen at home. Was it because they were trying to hide the magic ingredient, maybe using this method to camouflage it? I went back to staring at the kitchen as if doing that would make the magic ingredient pop out from wherever it was hiding. I suddenly felt empty and lost, wondering what I was doing with my life. Here I was, on this random cat-and-mouse chase for an ingredient that showed no signs of revealing itself. But I had been constantly thwarted in my chase, made to work hard for something, only to realize that all the work I had put in didn't amount to much.

And then my thoughts went back to Nikku again, to the start of the journey when we were together. How different it had been then, a true sense of adventure. I remembered drinking the terrible whisky in that bar with him, the crazy woman at the highway dhaba and the way we ran from there to our Fiat.

At least an hour must have passed with me staring at the kitchen in frustration, unable to move, when I heard someone behind me. 'I don't have the magic ingredient,' Rupi Masi said and pulled up a chair. She looked nothing like the woman who had broken down in the bathroom at Vatika. Instead, a calm serenity enveloped her face.

'And that's the truth?' I asked bluntly.

Rupi Masi nodded. 'We came to this side from Pakistan a few days after your Lalaji and his family left. I was very young at that time, must have been eight or nine. But there is a big difference between a girl of eight years now and eight years then! Your Lalaji was much older, of course, but he had already told me that there was a magic ingredient. He suspected that I went back to find it from Bibi; I was close to her as well, you know, and I was really interested too. All these years he has been thinking that Kanu and I conspired against him, and we let him think that. We said we know it, but we don't. We never did.'

'But why do you have so many boxes and spices?'

She sighed. 'My husband stocks these in the shop, so I always have variety!'

I put my head in my hands.

'But I do know where you might find the magic ingredient,' she said.

I looked up at her in shock, as she smiled wryly.

'You know where?'

'I might.'

'Where?'

'The ashram. Your Lalaji always hinted that it grew there, but he never entered that place. It was always full of foreigners wearing these malas. But I wonder—didn't your father go there?'

The secret gardens. *Of course*! I should have headed there when Nikku told me about them. It made absolute sense—my father's visits to the ashram, its proximity to Siyaka. A journey only makes sense if the answer lies at home, as Murti Devi had said. With a pang, I thought of Nikku again. I didn't feel like going any further yet and asked Rupi Masi if I could stay with her for a couple more days. She said yes. It turned out that she and Kanu Masi had talked to Lalaji a couple of days ago, and he had told them about the task. And since both of them had won, Rohit and Mohit also knew at the same time as me, about going to the ashram, and I was sure they'd be on their way already.

I didn't sleep well that night; my disturbed state of mind didn't allow me. The next day, with no more preparation to do for the pageant, I hung around aimlessly. The day after that, I was restless but unable to move. It was then that I heard it—a very familiar voice yelling my name outside the house.

Chapter 18

'Wha—how—why in the . . .'

Nikku stood in front of me, on the steps outside the gate, staring at me with an expressionless face. I had forced myself so much to not think of him that it felt like I had forgotten bits of him: how he stood tall, towering over the gate, how I would try and flatten his stupid hair when it stood up. How his floppy ears stood out, how his eyes were wide and unassuming, and how he gripped the strap of his bag in one hand, as though ready to run.

To be honest, once I got over my spluttering and after we had stared at each other for a couple of minutes, I did feel like giving him a shove. But I held back and crossed my arms against my chest, raising my eyebrows high.

He said nothing and kept looking at me. I could see a bit of terror in his eyes now. Maybe he really was scared I'd hit him. I wasn't going to be the one to break the silence, so I stared back fiercely. Slowly, a question mark seemed to loom over his head. 'Taru?'

Just him saying my name out loud, for some reason, brought tears to my eyes. I clenched my teeth and swallowed, refusing to show him my weakness.

'What?' I asked brusquely. If he couldn't tell how my voice shook beneath it, he didn't know me at all. His face grew sad at my response and he hung his head, muttering a sorry.

That took me aback. 'Wh—why are you here?'

It was his turn to frown. 'I told you, I'll be with you on this trip, all through. You left me, so I came to find you.'

'How did you find me?'

'Well, once you left without a single word or goodbye, I looked for you everywhere. I didn't want to call Lalaji, as I was too afraid what he might think of me, abandoning his granddaughter in a big city. So I went back to Siyaka to explain the situation to him, so that he might hear me out better, but he was never home! Your mother said he was barely ever around and that she suspected he might be up to something secret regarding the magic ingredient. Finally, I caught him early one day and he told me that you would be here. But he also asked me to wait a couple of days. So here I am, by your side. Speaking of that, what happened to your face?'

I touched my wound, which still hadn't healed completely. 'I don't want you around, Nikku. Not if you're going to run off at the first chance you get, or judge me for wanting to remain in Siyaka, or simply declare that you are off to do your big things, whatever they are, and that if I'm left behind, I just am. I don't want that kind of . . .'

That kind of what? He had never committed to anything, so why was I even mad at him? Except that he had, through everything he did, and it infuriated me that he never accepted it, never lived up to it. He had committed the day he sat with me for lunch at school, uncaring of what the other kids would say. It was such a big deal for boys and girls to sit together. He would be teased for it forever, but he sat by me. Then he left and drifted further and further away, his letters short and curt, and only a handful of phone calls in seven years.

'Tara, I'm back,' he said seriously. I looked up because he had said my name properly. 'Because I love you. I've always been too stupid to say it or even admit it to myself, but I am done being stupid. What I said in Delhi, I don't really mean it. I think about it sometimes, but who doesn't—I mean, there is more to this than Siyaka and I want to venture out sometimes, but if there's one thing that the past few weeks have taught me, it's that it doesn't matter where you are. What matters is who you're with, and I want to be only with you, Tara Taneja. It doesn't matter if it's Siyaka or Delhi or Durban.'

My first thought was to ask him where Durban was, but this wasn't the moment. Seeing me smile, he stepped forward. I held my arm out. 'What about Meenakshi?' I asked sharply and he looked away embarrassed.

'It was nothing. It happened at the start of our trip. I have never felt so terrible as when you got up and left me in Delhi.'

Had I not revelled in Aman's attention too? Delighted to be kissed and made to feel special? I jumped up to hug Nikku and he put his arms around me. It was at that moment that Masi walked up behind us.

'What are you staring at, Masi?' I asked without even looking in her direction. 'He had gone away for some time. Now he's back.'

We caught the bus back to Siyaka the next day. Nikku and I held hands, and his head rested on my shoulders. Going by his breathing, it sounded like he was comfortably asleep. I tried not to move. We were finally going home! Well, after we made a stop at the ashram. After all this roaming around, we were right back where we had started. I wondered if this was the message Lalaji was trying to send to us. That it all begins at home? That there's no place like home? But I already knew that and was living it every day. Why would he send me on this chor–police chase to make me realize something I already 100 per cent agreed with?

As I thought of the ashram, my mind threw at me the few memories I had of my father: playing with a ball in the park, the three of us in a boat in the lake and me constantly being afraid that it would topple. Memories of me extending a protective hand towards my parents and them laughing in adoration, leaving me confused. I had imagined some memories from my mother's stories too, but I realized with sadness that my father had never really been a part of my life. It was like trying to miss something I never had.

What would we find at the ashram? Was I about to discover more than one secret? Murti Devi's words came back to me. Hadn't she said that the answer lay at home? A search, a quest, only made sense if the final destination was home. So much had happened since then that I had completely forgotten about her.

Nikku stirred. I stroked his hair lightly.

What if Bauji was right and the magic ingredient was gulkand? I had never smelt any rose in the laddoo, but it could easily be so. And hadn't Bauji said it would be the simplest of things? But why would gulkand take me to the ashram? It didn't make any sense, unless there grew some special kind of gulkand.

I had never really imagined the secret ingredient, not as a literal ingredient, a simple little ingredient that maybe added a little something to our laddoos. What if after all this drama the magic ingredient turned out to be underwhelming?

The thought made me uneasy. I tried to sleep, but with no luck. I could smell the familiarity, the smell of rain as we got closer. Nikku woke up and bought some channa when the bus stopped. Later, we told the bus conductor to drop us off at the ashram. He laughed at us.

'We want to see the swami,' I said.

The conductor laughed some more and told us jovially, 'Madam, he's a *harami*, not a swami!'

Nikku chuckled, amused. I felt a wave of indignation on behalf of my father. 'Why do you say that?'

'Girls to wake him up, girls to put him to sleep! Parties here and there . . . no wonder the ashram is so *badnaam*!'

When we got off the bus, we still had some distance to cover till the entrance of the ashram, but we did so with a spring in our step. This was it, the place where we would finally find the magic ingredient. It had eluded us all this while, but now I knew that it was all preparation for what was to come. The road ahead was deserted, a lone bike or scooter sometimes passing us by. We must have walked for about forty minutes before we reached the entrance and saw food stalls lined up in a row. Pickled raw mango, sugarcane, cucumber with chaat masala and even fried patasha. We had our fill first and then entered.

All the while I was thinking of my father who would come here often. Had he also started serving the ashram like one of the solemn-faced volunteers?

At the reception, we told them that we were there to stay, to experience the ashram for some time. The people seemed beyond pleased. They told us that either we must pay or work. We chose to work as it would save money. I hoped it would also help us learn the secrets of the place quickly. All I wanted was to find the magic ingredient and leave.

For the first couple of days, we were given basic training. We were staying at the temporary housing and were assigned tasks and jobs. Soon, we were familiar with the layout of the ashram and were even warned of trespassing.

'The paths around the ashram are designed to make you lose your way,' we were told. 'If you deviate from your designated path, it is quite likely that you will get lost and it might be days before someone finds you. Ashram volunteers will be keeping an eye on you at spots where you least expect it. Here, someone is always watching you—we know what's going on all the time. If found violating the rules, you will be expelled without any explanation.'

While we were told only about areas that we needed to know in the beginning, after a few days we observed and pieced together information from both reliable and unreliable sources. We learnt just how big the ashram was, with areas accessible based on which stage people were at in their journey in the ashram. There were three stages in all, the final one granting permanent member status and allowing access to the prayer room. To go inside, one had to be at the final stage. Those who had been inside never revealed what they saw. In one corner was the permanent housing block, for those who had graduated from temporary housing.

A little way off from the permanent housing block was the forest. While a wild animal hadn't been spotted in months, only an idiot would venture inside alone, they said. Collaborated expeditions took people into the forest, and that was the only way to go. Behind the forest was a stream that led right into Dima Lake. This surprised me the most, but Nikku said it was definitely artificially created. Next to the stream were the factories, and that is where they manufactured jute and cotton products.

Some way off from the factories, at the opposite end of the forest, was where the Secret Gardens were supposed to be. One was allowed access to them, to tend to the gardens, once they got to the second stage. I told Nikku that was where they had to reach. I was sure we would find out more about the secret ingredient inside the Secret Gardens. Then, we could get out of here—we were not permanent members yet and could leave anytime. Ahead of the Secret Gardens, closer to the reception, was a big auditorium and theatre where they often screened shows and art displays, to show the world what they were doing.

I found Rohit and Mohit there on the second day, as temporary members. If they reached the Secret Gardens first, I would definitely lose.

Every day, we would be given different tasks like simple gardening, sweeping, cooking, dusting, cleaning the toilets, or even managing the visiting crowds. We were instructed to maintain solemn, serious expressions in front of outsiders.

Nikku and I had made friends with some people who were with us in the temporary housing—some were enthusiastic and fully devoted to the ashram, taking their journey extremely seriously. Others were sceptical and had come to see how things were; they hesitated to commit. We fell into that group. Nikku and I didn't talk that much, but listened more, hoping to pick up some clues.

Rumours circulated galore: there was talk of parties that started much after people went to bed and lasted into the mornings, involving every kind of drug. People said one was taught to follow their most primal instinct at these parties. They said these parties happened in the warehouses of the factories, in the abandoned corners of the permanent blocks and deep inside the forest. When I asked how the ashram people allowed these parties, they laughed at me. 'They are the ones who organize it, silly,' I would be told.

It took a while before we began hearing the rumours we wanted to hear—about the Secret Gardens. They said there grew plants, weeds, flowers and fruits that were found in the remotest corners of India, by recreating the conditions in little houses of sun and heat. Apparently, there were varieties of flowers that bloomed only once every few years and fruits with nectar not found anywhere else in the world. The Secret Gardens were tended to with care and nurture reserved for the most beloved of infants.

To verify all this, I needed to get to the second stage, but that was completely at the discretion of the ashram people. Who knew how long that would take? It could be weeks, months even, before they were convinced that I had made progress. In any case, it was vague what it was all supposed to mean. Maybe they noted down how seriously you took all the tasks and meditation tasks.

Nikku and I decided it was time to take some drastic action: to befriend the gardeners.

It wasn't easy though.

We tried to approach the different gardeners, those who maintained the other parks and gardens around the ashram. But every time we tried to speak to one of them, they either gave us a look of disdain and walked away, as if we didn't know the rules, or shook their heads imperceptibly, as if to say, 'You will learn.' But our efforts finally paid off. One of the gardeners extended a hand of friendship in exchange for a supply of cigarettes and friendly chats.

His name was Ramakant. He had come to the ashram when he was much younger and unable to support himself. His rickshaw had met with an accident, his paan business never picked up and he didn't have a single paisa in his pocket. Without a wife or children, he was able to wander, and in his wanderings he had reached the ashram, where they agreed to clothe him, keep him and feed him—all in exchange for his time and energy to help the ashram grow.

'That time it was nothing, just acres of wild land,' he said, 'and now look at it. If they weren't so secretive, it could be a bigger tourist spot than Taj Mahal!'

Nikku and I agreed. 'But why are they so secretive?' Nikku asked him.

'Stuff goes on here. Stuff the general public should not know.'

'But what kind of stuff? You have been here for so long, you must know.'

'I know some things, boy, but it's not my information to pass on. It's one of the rules at the ashram and I respect it.

I have seen things in my time here, things no one would believe are happening.'

'But what—'

I held Nikku's arm. We were not there to know the ashram's secrets. For all I cared, they could be exploring the multiple planes of spirituality or proving that zero didn't exist, all while having their hippie parties. It didn't matter to me. It was more important to get information about the Secret Gardens.

'But you don't care about any of that, do you?' I asked Ramakant. 'You are happy in the Secret Gardens.'

He nodded. 'Precisely. I have been here for years, and only for my special gardens. They are like my children. I have planted them, taken care of them and seen them as they grow. I'll be with them till the end of my days. Plants, unlike children, don't grow up to leave, you see. Ha ha!'

Nikku smiled. 'So . . . what do you grow in the gardens? Magic plants?'

'Plants *are* magic, boy! You won't believe the things they can do—'

'I am looking for something like that,' I interrupted. 'Something that is magic. An ingredient that is magic, which contains the light of the sun and the twinkle of the stars. One that is very rare and used to grow in what is now Pakistan. Do you have something like that here?'

He didn't reply for a while and I doubted my bluntness. Maybe I shouldn't have revealed our reason for being here so quickly. After all, he seemed completely loyal to the ashram. But I couldn't go back then and so decided to press my point harder. 'We are on this journey to discover this magic ingredient. We think that it is grown in the Secret Gardens.'

Some birds cooed in the distance and I looked around fearfully. What if someone was listening to this conversation? I gripped Nikku's hand. Ramakant seemed unafraid though.

'There are many things in the gardens that are magic, but in the end, they are pure science and botany, of course. The one you said, there are some that might fit the bill . . .'

With a pause, he continued. 'Let's see. It could be . . . no, that wouldn't be special enough. We have this variety of aparajita that is really . . . no, I suppose if there is an ingredient full of magic, it would be lalkusum. But we were just talking about this one a couple of days ago, two boys were asking about it. What, is it very valuable outside?'

Rohit and Mohit had got to it. There was no time to waste.

'No. But what's this flower?' I asked, leaning forward, excited.

'Oh yes, it is one rare flower. It's the red flower, and I haven't seen it anywhere else. If you crush the petals, the juice that comes out is so red that it puts paan masala spots to shame. And it is heavenly sweet, so much so that at first go, you will mistrust it. How can something so red and so sweet be so real? It's not your typical cherries or apples. It's a flower! It's soft and smooth, as light as a feather. It must be the lalkusum, difficult to grow, but when it does, it's in large bunches. Anyway, a few drops are enough to sweeten anything. It is visible though. If you use it, it will give your food a very light tinge.'

I was so grateful for the information that I hugged him. When we walked back, Nikku expressed his doubts. 'So Rohit and Mohit also know about this.'

'But it adds up, Nikku,' I said excitedly. 'It grows right here in the ashram, in abundance, if I may add. I'm sure they must sell it outside, but only illegally and to locals. That's why Lalaji is able to get it, but we haven't heard of it commercially. You only need a couple of drops, or maybe a bit more when we make large batches. Lalaji must store the nectar in the small bottle that he carries with him and add it to the mithai every morning. What else can it be, tell me?'

'I don't know. I'm not an expert on all this laddoo stuff, but is this really it? The flower, lalkusum?'

I was barely even listening any more, thinking about my father instead. Was this why my father had started visiting the ashram, to ensure a continued supply of lalkusum? He must have made some contacts, must have had his reasons for coming here. Now that I knew Rohit and Mohit knew about this, I had no time. I had to make sure I got my hands on the flower before they did.

I went to sleep thinking about it and even dreamt of it. I kept chasing it, but it always slipped out of my reach. I kept calling out to Nikku, but he played hide-and-seek with me...

The next day we heard that Rohit and Mohit had graduated to the next stage. Nikku and I furiously went to the ashram authorities and requested that we be promoted too. The man in charge, rumoured to be close to the swami, was the one who took such decisions. He wore a neat, half-sleeved shirt and glasses, his hair neatly combed back. He laughed at our request before he realized we were serious.

'You do know what you're asking is impossible, right?' he said, his voice strict.

'But why?' I asked, trying to hide the impatience in my voice. 'We are fully devoted to the cause here and would like to graduate so we are able to contribute more. Why is that such a bad thing?'

'If you're fully devoted, then you must show that by doing well the tasks assigned to you. We cannot entertain requests based on random whims and fancies, or worse, moods that might change the next day, unable to handle the commitment. The ashram has some rules and they have been made to measure the spiritual journey of a person, and then assign them a stage. You cannot just come waltzing in here to demand a graduation!'

'But, Sir,' Nikku spoke up, 'if you could just consider it. I know it's not the norm, but we are really enthusiastic. Also, I have a disease, so I never know when I may have to, umm, leave and go to the hospital. It affects the blood directly, so . . .'

The man narrowed his eyes at us. 'We do not take kindly to lies. Now please return to your assigned places.'

'You let the other two boys graduate to the second stage!'

'But they had a reference,' the man said. 'Their uncle was a permanent member.'

My mouth fell open. 'That was my father!'

He looked sceptical. 'Listen, Miss. I already told you, we do not take kindly to lies. However, if you do have a reference, you can submit an application with proof. After verification, we can try to do the same for you.'

Both of us walked back to our quarters. It was too late, yet we agreed that we couldn't give up after all that we had been through. This was the final hurdle and we had beaten greater odds than this. We came up with a plan to sneak into the Secret Gardens at night. Nikku suggested that we mark our path, so we could return easily. We arranged for a flashlight and little bottles to store the nectar. We were ready. If from Mathura to Ludhiana, the police and criminals could not stop us, neither could the ashram people.

But our plan was of no use because early in the evening I saw Rohit and Mohit pass me coolly, stains of the lalkusum on the outside of their cloth bags, as they smugly told me, 'Game over. We are headed home to Lalaji. You keep trying.'

I stared at them. Nikku said we could still sneak inside and get some lalkusum. Maybe Lalaji would still consider it.

I shook my head. 'No.'

'But why! Don't give up, Taru!'

'No. I just realized. Lalkusum is not the magic ingredient.'

Chapter 19

I mixed the besan and kesar, adding water in measured pours, putting in that pinch of salt that Lalaji loved so much, mixing it all into the batter. The sugar boiled in the water on the stove, and I kept an eye on it, heating up the ghee in the kadai, my mind focused. I put my finger in the batter to feel the consistency. Satisfied, I took out the perforated boondi ladle.

It was like everything was clear now. My answer started to make sense. I spread the batter over the ladle as it fell into the kadai in drops, frying up to be little boondis: the pride of Lallan Sweets. The boondis, meanwhile, sizzled and glistened in the oil, frying to a warm and delicious yellowish-orange. I removed them from the kadai in bunches and placed them in the sugar syrup.

For two hours I was busy preparing the laddoos, putting everything together with care and detail. This was it—the final competition. Everything that we had been working on for the past few weeks, even our lives, came down to this. Rohit and Mohit were in their own kitchen across the verandah, making laddoos. I had told my mother not to help me. This was my job. At the core of it all, of Lallan Sweets and our traditional business, it was all about making laddoos, wasn't it? And if I couldn't do this on my own, who was I and what was I even fighting for?

I was bathed in sweat when I left the laddoos to set. I crossed the verandah and went to Lalaji's room. I waved away the hookah smoke.

'I'm ready Lalaji,' I told him. He nodded.

On one side of the table stood Rohit and Mohit behind their thali of laddoos. When I didn't see the reddish tinge on their laddoos, I doubted myself. But when I saw the newspaper beneath their thali, stained as red as their hands, I knew they had used lalkusum. Aunty and Pappu Uncle stood behind their sons. My mother, standing behind me, looked tense and worried. Did she think I was going to lose?

Lalaji sat in the centre of the room on a chair and said, 'Present your laddoos.'

Rohit and I put our laddoos in front of him and waited, hardly daring to breathe. Whatever the case, I was sure that they had the wrong ingredient. There was no way that lalkusum could be the magic ingredient. I had known as soon as I saw the stains on their cloth bag in the ashram. There was no way that ingredient had been in use for years without those red stains escaping our eyes. No matter how careful Lalaji had been, lalkusum was bound to leave some trace. I was sure, but I waited for Lalaji to confirm it.

He took a bite of their laddoo first and chewed for a long time until every last boondi was swallowed. I couldn't read his face at all. He then picked up one of my laddoos and ate it in the exact same manner. He nodded once he had eaten the last bit and then said, 'Present your magic ingredient.'

My heart beat faster as I looked at Rohit and Mohit, taking out the lalkusum from their bag excitedly. I gripped the side of my thali and could feel my mother's eyes on me. Lalaji held the lalkusum in his hand, examining it carefully and sniffing it. I saw realization dawn upon Pappu Uncle's face. If it really had been the magic ingredient, Lalaji's face would have betrayed some sense of familiarity.

Nevertheless, Lalaji turned to me. 'Taru, your ingredient?'

I shook my head. 'I can't say it.'

'But you have to.'

'Not in front of everyone, I won't. The secret of the magic ingredient has been protected for years. It should remain that way.'

He nodded and signalled to the others to leave, but Rohit and Mohit stayed. They deserved to. Pappu Uncle protested, but under Lalaji's warning look, he paled and shut the door behind himself. Now that the others were gone, I turned to look at Lalaji.

'There is no magic ingredient, is there?' I asked him.

There was absolute silence as both of us stared at each other, unblinking. I wasn't going to be the one to give up, to accept defeat. Not even the fan dared to make a noise. Finally, Lalaji averted his face. I yelled, 'I knew it! I was right!'

Rohit and Mohit howled in protest, insisting that was not true, that they had found the lalkusum, that it met all the criteria Lalaji had laid out. But Lalaji shook his head in resignation.

'So this is it, huh?' I asked. 'This is it, the magic ingredient—the lie.'

It made me quite mad when I said it out loud. Because it wasn't just *a* lie—it was a series of lies. Years and years of lies, not only to the world, but also to us, to his own family.

Who else was involved? Who else knew about this fraud? I was scared to ask.

'No, Taru,' Lalaji said, 'before you declare it a lie, you must know the entire story. Right from the beginning. And then you pass a judgement. Tell me, is that acceptable to you?'

I nodded. Rohit and Mohit looked shocked beyond measure as they sat down on the chairs around the table. I tasted a lalkusum laddoo and had to accept that it didn't taste half bad, that it had a distinct taste from the usual Lallan Sweets laddoo. I sat down at the table too, and somehow felt closer to them than I had in years. We had all been played for fools.

Lalaji took a sip of water and began with his characteristic cough.

'Rewind to many years ago. Remember I told you that we finally had that coveted corner in Anarkali Bazaar, the pride of Lahore?'

'Corner?' I interrupted. 'I thought you said a shop.'

'Taru, come on.'

I nodded but couldn't help be sceptical. Lalaji had so many stories about the past and half of them contradicted each other.

'We had a corner. Preparations were in full swing to set everything up. Every day we made new varieties of mithai, trying and testing. For a child, what could be better than that? The streets would be abuzz, rickshaws and tongas dodging the beggars on the ground, a buffalo running wild here and there. But inside the shops was the fun: jewellery, spices, earthenware, dupattas, mithais . . . everything you can think of. It was the Chandni Chowk of Lahore back then. People used to go there on a day off. It was going to bring us good fortune. You see, when we were trying the mithais, the entire mohalla in Dera Gazi Khan was involved. Not many in their neighbourhood had managed to buy a shop in Anarkali Bazaar!'

'A corner,' I reminded him.

He laughed. 'A corner it may be, we put all our energy into it. And that's how I got to know Mensur Bibi, from a few gullies down. The Hindus in our lane would call her a witch, and oh they weren't all wrong. You see, she was a magician: a magician with her words and a magician with her food. She could cure illnesses, make you wish for things you never knew you could have and concoct *kaadha*s for every occasion—childbirth to funeral. People would come to her because they believed she would bring them luck. And many times, it would happen that wishes would be fulfilled after drinking one of her kaadhas. One day, I tasted her halva. It was not like the Karachi halwa they sell these days. No. It was pure. The milk and the ghee we had back then would be like magic to you now. I had the halva, children, and I knew that was it. It was magic. This was what we needed to sell.'

The three of us were listening closely.

'After that, I tried to stick by her side at all times, hoping to catch a glimpse of what she put in the halva. But I never found out. "I can't tell you, little lallu," she would say to me and laugh, "because if I tell you it won't be magic any more." But I didn't give up. I kept asking her and finally she told me it grew only in select places. Bibi pointed out to me on a map where all it grew.'

'But what was magical about it?' I asked him.

Lalaji looked up in frustration. 'You see, that's what the toughest question is. You wouldn't know magic until you see it, but once you do, that's all you dream about. Once I tasted that halva, I knew that I would never have anything else like that. I told you: it has the light of the sun and the twinkle of the stars. It's like the softest touch and the most memorable song. My grandfather used to say that good food is like music. It may be out of your mind for some time, but you will remember it forever, as someone remembers a song forever. You may not sing it all the time, but in some part of your mind, it has already made a home. "This mithai you make, Lallu," Bibi used to say, "should taste like your best kiss." But I had never kissed anyone, so I never knew.'

I put my head in my hands. I did not need to hear about my grandfather's best kiss.

'As I grew closer to her, Bibi promised me that she would one day tell me the magic ingredient. She had a soft spot for me, you know. But then everything was destroyed. Of course, there had been word on the street for some time, but in a matter of days, hours even, everything changed. We had to give up our shop and make the long journey here. We lost it all. We reached Ludhiana broken, battered and bruised, in shock over what had just happened. We were evicted from what we had called home all our lives. We had to leave everything behind. There were no banks that held our money—we had stored all that we earned in gold, cattle and grains. Before leaving, I said goodbye to Bibi. She was as much in shock, but she didn't have to leave.'

'So you never found out about the magic ingredient?'

He shook his head sadly. 'Never. I knew what it tasted like and tried to describe it as best as I could, but of course words are not enough. I only remembered the areas Bibi had told me it might be found in India. And these are the cities where you all have been.'

'What do you mean?' Rohit asked.

Lalaji sighed. 'When we reached India, we had a lot to set up. From Ludhiana, we relocated to Siyaka and were given this small shop. We had a lot to rebuild. But I never forgot the magic ingredient and the thought of it took over my mind like a parasite. Remember I told you I was in Mathura when I met your grandmother? I was there looking for the magic ingredient. All the places you have been, I went there too, trying to look for it. And when we finally set up Lallan Sweets years on, I didn't have the magic ingredient.

'The market was just coming up and people didn't have money. If someone wanted to have sweets, they would just make them at home. I didn't see Lallan Sweets doing very well, except on Holi and Diwali. So I did the only thing that seemed clever to me at the time.'

'You pretended you had a magic ingredient,' I completed his sentence for him.

Lalaji nodded. 'Business was business. When I heard Natwar, your Bauji, Tara, speak of a secret ingredient, I was reminded of my own quest. We had a house to run, so I spread the rumour that a magic ingredient we had brought from Pakistan was used in our sweets. I made this elaborate show of going into the room each morning and putting something into the thali. Back then, this was the entertainment of the day. People would wait outside the shop to see me go in and put the magic ingredient. It became an elaborate show. And it worked—the popularity of the laddoos soared and we couldn't make as many as we had to sell. Soon, Lallan's magic ingredient was as famous as Siyaka's Victorian town.'

'But there was no magic ingredient,' I said. I don't know why, but it broke my heart.

'Tara, yes, you're right. There was no magic ingredient. But there was one out there, and I knew it because I had tasted it. And the thought was like an obsession in my head. I never forgot about it.'

'But why?' Mohit asked, genuinely confused. 'Now you have Lallan Sweets, people are buying sweets from there thinking you are using the magic ingredient. Everything is going well, even without it . . . why do you still want it?'

'I cannot explain it. Just knowing that there is a magic ingredient out there makes me want it. Imagine, if people already love our laddoos, what we can do if we do have the ingredient. How can I forget about it and simply move on? Call it human greed, temperament. Haven't men gone in search for riches that they didn't need? At least our intentions were noble—to find a magic ingredient, instead of gold and treasure!'

'Our intentions?' I asked.

Lalaji walked around, looking troubled and sighing. 'Yes . . . ours. At some point, Tara, your father also went to look for the magic ingredient. You see, I hadn't told anyone that I had no magic ingredient, not even my family. So one day I said to my son, like I did to you all, "Lallan Sweets will not be inherited, it must be earned." I gave him some tasks, at these very places, hoping he would come across the magic ingredient in some way. I told him to find it but never told him that I never had it. Pappu was not in Siyaka then. He was studying in Patiala, and your father, brave and curious as he was, left in search for it.'

My heart beat faster as I looked at Rohit and Mohit. Why had no one ever told me this? Did my mother know? Were they even married back then?

'And?' I asked Lalaji.

'Like me, he couldn't find it either. He returned months later, tired and barely alive. He told me that he had failed me. I was overcome with guilt at what I had put my son through and told him the secret. I made him take the sacred oath to never reveal that we didn't have a magic ingredient. Life went on as it was.'

This was absolutely bizarre. None of it made any sense. Yet Lalaji was here, narrating this crazy story that he had actually lived, and made us a part of as well. I imagined my father returning home, wrecked with guilt at not having found the magic ingredient, thinking he didn't deserve to be at Lallan Sweets—the thought made me mad. Lalaji had deceived him, and continued to deceive all of us, sending us on this useless chase at the end of which was nothing.

'How could you do this to your own son, to us?' I asked him, furious. 'You went on the quest and you couldn't find the ingredient. Yet you sent all of us there, even though things had not worked out for you! What was the point of all this?'

'But it's somewhere out there—'

'I don't care!' I yelled. It felt like a part of me had died when Lalaji said that all these years there had been no magic ingredient. 'And what about all the stupid tasks you made us do? A picture at the Taj Mahal, the pots on my head, working at Bombay Halwai, how in the world would those help us find the magic ingredient? I mean, if it exists, I probably saw it and missed it because I was too busy getting the damn picture! Why didn't you tell us to ask around for an unusual plant or flower or cooking technique?'

Lalaji shook his head, also agitated, and started walking around. 'I have a reason, Taru. Firstly, of course I didn't want you to know that I had no magic ingredient. You would never go looking for it otherwise. So I needed to make up some tasks, so you would think it all leads somewhere. Secondly, you're forgetting it's a magic ingredient. It is, literally, magic. I am positive that those who go looking for it, at the right place and right moment, will know it when they see it. Or rather, the magic ingredient will reveal itself to them.'

'But why?' I asked.

'I've always known it. Even when I had tasted the halva, I just *knew* there was something in it. It's like knowing all of life's secrets, or the first time you realize that this is it, that this is love, or the first time you hold your baby in your arms and think there is nothing greater in the world. That's how you just know magic. And that's how I felt when I looked up at Bibi after tasting the halva. She knew that I knew there was a magic ingredient.'

'So you just made up these random tasks?' Mohit asked him.

'Well, partly,' Lalaji replied, sitting down again, 'but there's another reason as well. The Rasiya group has been known to add secret concoctions to their food that they refuse to share with the rest of the world. I was hoping at least one of you might stumble upon something there. There was a rumour that some special plants grow under the moonlight when it is reflected by the whitest marble, so you went to the Taj Mahal. And there was a very good chance that Bombay Halwai would have a secret ingredient. Natwar comes from the same town as us and has a mithai shop. And Rupi and Kanu, well, I believe they have hidden stuff from me. They knew about my obsession with the magic ingredient, and they used to visit Bibi too. But I realized that anybody who has the magic ingredient wouldn't care about Mrs Ludhiana or whatever. They would open the greatest mithai shop in the world . . . I've started to think they're right old frauds.'

I couldn't help but laugh a little. 'Right old frauds. Like us.'

I could feel Rohit and Mohit staring at me. Lalaji wasn't laughing either. 'We are not frauds, Tara,' he said quietly.

'Are we not?' I asked him, my anger getting the better of me. 'For years we have been telling the entire town, people who have grown up with us, helped us, our neighbours, those who regularly come to our shop to buy sweets for their happiest days, who have trusted us while they ate blindly that there's a magic ingredient in here! We have broken their faith, lied to them and deceived them, not once but over and over again, throughout all these years. And not just you, my father as well! These people who have helped run our house, we have cheated them.'

'That's not true, Taru,' Lalaji said.

'What else do you call lying, Lalaji?'

'The magic ingredient is not just why people buy Lallan Sweets.'

'That's not true! You just said that is the selling point. The reason why people come here, because they all want the magic ingredient!'

Lalaji banged his hand on the table but then immediately gathered himself and spoke calmly. 'Tara, try and understand. You too, Rohit and Mohit, all of you have done a great job with the quest. It doesn't matter that you didn't find the ingredient. Think about your journey of the past few weeks, all your adventures, all the people you met and the things you learnt, what was it about? You think it was merely about finding the magic ingredient? An action inspired by greed? Think about it, go on!'

I shut my eyes and went back to the beginning of our journey and all that had happened to us. I remembered Nikku's words—it doesn't matter where you are, it matters who you are with. It's true that I hadn't obsessed over the magic ingredient the whole time. I was so involved with dealing with the many problems and people that came our way every day that it really hadn't been that much about the magic ingredient.

'It was about your journey, Children, the time spent on the road, the relationships you formed, the people you met, and the lessons you learnt—not about some silly magic ingredient! Granted, it is still out there and is like a little slice of heaven—but it's the quest that counts! The quest has proven that you are smart, mature and responsible adults who will run Lallan Sweets better than their fathers ever did. Of course, sometimes you will make mistakes and end up breaking some rules, but I want you to remember that Lallan Sweets, these laddoos that we make, are not all about the magic ingredient. It may make people come to you once, or maybe twice, but people in this town have been buying laddoos from us for decades. And that is because what we do here, we do it with love and care. Every single day that this shop has existed, I have been there to oversee the sweets being made, to get them displayed and packed. The effort and love of this family goes into the running of this shop and that's why we are not frauds, Taru. We don't mix water into our milk, we don't dilute our ghee, we don't add processed sugar.'

There was a knock on the door then and Lalaji went to open it. It was Pappu Uncle, demanding to know what was happening. He called for his sons, who replied that they needed some more time. Pappu Uncle backed off after a couple of minutes and Lalaji shut the door again. None of us spoke for a while and I finally understood what Lalaji was saying. *Our love and care*—the magic ingredient. I remembered all those mornings I had seen Lalaji rushing to the shop, making plans with everyone to beat competition, making sure our sweets were the most delicious, encouraging and inspiring us with everything that he did . . .

'You do add some magic to it, Lalaji,' Rohit spoke up.

Lalaji folded his arms across his chest. 'I do, it's just not anything tangible. But I still have hopes that we will one day find the magic ingredient.'

'No,' Rohit said. 'That's not what I meant. The mithai we make, everyone has their own unique quirk. You add this pinch of salt, you told us. I always see you do it. That's what makes our laddoos magical.'

'That's an old trick in the book, Son,' Lalaji said laughing. 'People do it. Who *really* knows how to make mithai.'

'That's you,' Mohit said. I could see Lalaji was touched.

'Lalaji,' I asked suddenly, 'what about the sari? And the necklace? What did Chandigarh have to do with the magic ingredient?'

'Oh,' he said and suddenly seemed nervous, rubbing his forehead, 'well, that was an errand I made you run.'

I looked at Rohit and Mohit, confused. They seemed equally perplexed. 'But why would you need a sari and a necklace?'

'Not me,' he said. And then, with a resigned expression, he said, 'Someone else does. Kalawati.'

'Who's that?' Rohit asked.

Lalaji sighed, but it was a long, relieved, happy sigh. 'My to-be wife.'

Chapter 20

In a small town like ours, it was the scandal of the century—seventy-five-year-old Lalaji getting married to his childhood love, Kalawati, after both their spouses had died. Some people even suggested that the two had waited all their lives for their husband and wife to pass away. But it was the kind of gossip that contributed to a lot of jealousy. Most people were aghast on the outside, but wistfully thought to themselves, 'What a lucky bastard.'

And since Lalaji was loved by all in Siyaka, I knew that this really wouldn't last long. Sure enough, a couple of days after the news spread, people started coming to the house to offer their wishes and congratulations. Where the going got tough was with Lalaji's own children. When he told Rohit, Mohit and me, we were shocked initially but, of course, delighted that he was going to live the rest of his years in love with someone. What could be more beautiful than that? But it was Pappu Uncle and Aunty, as well as my own mother, who found his decision audacious and inappropriate.

They argued with Lalaji saying, 'It's your grandchildren's age to get married! You had a good, long run! Now is your time to settle in an ashram, and you want to settle in the marital bed instead! What about the memories of our Amma?'

Lalaji, however, still had enough authority to shut them up. 'Your Amma died many years ago, Pappu. Don't pretend that you think about her every day. I loved that woman and will think about her each day, but I deserve some companionship after all these years! Kalawati will be like your mother, and if you don't want to think of her like that—then don't. It doesn't matter. My grandchildren are better raised clearly and know what's important.'

Pappu Uncle calmed down after a while, after he was mentioned glowingly in an article headlined 'Beloved Sweet Seller Finds Love Second Time at 75'. Business, of course, soared beyond measure as people came to hear Lalaji's stories, as well as taste the famous sweets at his shop.

Since none of us had actually found the magic ingredient, but all of us had done well, it was decided that Rohit, Mohit and I would be equally responsible for the shop.

'After my wedding, I will no longer put in the magic ingredient or oversee the production of the laddoos. Taru will be in charge of that,' Lalaji told us. I looked at him with narrowed eyes. Was I to put in the magic ingredient!

'She will also be in charge of marketing the laddoos, and expansion,' he said. 'So all decisions about expansion: whether Lallan Sweets will become a bigger shop or a restaurant, or whatever, she will take the final call. In consultation with me, of course, as long as I am there, huh?'

'And my sons?' Pappu Uncle asked fiercely.

'Rohit,' Lalaji continued, 'will oversee sourcing and quality checks, as well as production, apart from the magic ingredient. Mohit will look at packaging, display, maintenance of the shop and accounts, with Tara's help.' None of us wanted to argue with that.

Now that the magic ingredient was known, or should I say left unknown, Rohit, Mohit and I had to take the sacred oath to never, ever reveal its secret. We performed an elaborate ceremony, complete with a havan and chants, and *samagri* being thrown into the fire. Then we went into another room, the four of us, where the priest waved peacock feathers over our heads, sprinkled holy water on us, gave us a sacred coconut to swear on, and asked us to repeat some words after Lalaji. When I saw him close his eyes and say the prayers with dedication, the nagging doubts in my head took a backseat.

I wanted to believe Lalaji when he said there was a magic ingredient. Just because you don't see something doesn't mean it ceases to exist. My mind went back to when we were in Bareilly and Nikku insisted that he had seen the ghosts: *I saw what I saw, Taru.* I also remembered Murti Devi's words: *you think everything there is to know is already known? There are worlds and knowledge . . . passed down from generation to generation . . . there are crafts well-hidden . . . you will never know what happens there because there are some things you will never know . . .*

Was that it then? Were we trying to acquire knowledge that wasn't meant for us? I thought about Lalaji and how he had tried all his life. At the same time, I couldn't help but think that Lalaji, perhaps, wasn't the deceiver, but rather the deceived: what if his Bibi didn't use a magic ingredient either? But Lalaji had said that as soon as he tasted it, he knew. What if it was what he wanted to believe? If he was right about something, it was this: the value lies in the pursuit, the quest of it, rather than the answer itself. After all, hadn't the quest brought me and Nikku together?

Lalaji was most happy about Nikku. Well, okay, maybe that was the second most-happy thing for him because he was the happiest about marrying Kalawati. She was sweet, quiet and looked adoringly at Lalaji. She would blush every time someone congratulated them. I couldn't believe that she had ever smuggled away a steel almirah from under Sharma Aunty's nose. She took an instant liking to Rohit, Mohit and me when we presented her with the sari and necklace. Perhaps that was Lalaji's plan all along, to build the bridge of friendship between us.

'I really am the luckiest man on earth,' Lalaji had remarked. 'I loved two women in my life and got to marry both of them. How many people can say that, huh?'

Speaking of two loves, I finally had to face Sahil. The niggling thought of him had stayed with me the entire time. I wondered how I would break it to him, how I would tell him that I couldn't continue whatever we had any longer, that I had always loved Nikku. I wanted to tell him I was truly very sorry about how everything had gone down, that I truly valued his company and wished the best for his musical career. Except these words died in my throat when I met him, because he apologized to me. He was moving to Delhi to be a DJ, he said. A hotel had liked his music and invited him to play at their club, and if he didn't take this up he would always regret it. I told him I understood and asked him excitedly if he would play at Ghungroo. He said no but added that, one day, he would. Somehow, I believed him. I think

I had learnt to have a little more faith. How could I not learn from Sahil to keep believing in something? That was perhaps the only way to live.

Talking to our mechanic turned out to be more difficult. Nikku and I went to him together. He had been visiting both our houses every day in our absence, asking about his car. When we told him that it had been stolen from us, he lost his mind and started shouting, telling us he would take revenge, that we had stolen the car from him and were now refusing to return it.

'Shambuji, come on. How in the world will we drive a sky-blue Fiat in this town without you knowing about it? We really didn't steal it!' I tried to explain.

'Maybe not here, but I know you will drive it someplace else!'

'We are not going anywhere else, Shambu,' Nikku said. 'We are staying here, in Siyaka.'

I looked at Nikku when he said that, even as he went on staring at Shambu. 'Besides, you lied to us. It wasn't a Siyaka car. It was stolen from Bareilly, wasn't it? You stole it from someone who had already stolen it! So really, you didn't lose that much.'

'Achcha, who told you it's stolen from Bareilly?'

Nikku and I stared at each other and laughed. Then Nikku fished out the newspaper from his bag. 'Oh, the things we have heard, Shambu . . . tell me, isn't this your car? It's in the newspaper! Can you read it?'

Shambu shook his head, staring at the newspaper. Nikku guessed he couldn't read. 'It says that they will find who last stole this car and put him in jail. Because someone was murdered in this car. Do you understand what that means, Shambu? You will be blamed for the murder.'

Shambu calmed down a bit at that and we finally settled at giving him a box of mithai every week for the next six months. It was a lot, I had to admit, but I did feel bad that we had lost his car. After all, I was the in charge now and could afford this much.

'You said that we'll be here in Siyaka and that we're not going anywhere,' I said to Nikku as we walked back home.

He looked at me and smiled that stupid grin of his. 'I meant it.'

'But, Nikku, you don't have to. I mean, what will you do here? Because I seriously mean it. I will come to wherever you are, visit you, whatever it takes. After all this, you know we can do anything, huh? I won't be the one to kill your dreams.'

'I won't be killing my dreams. We will see; we'll face it the next few days. I want us to be together.'

'We will be together.'

He looked at me, his expression sombre, and said, 'Yes, but I mean *together*.'

'I know what together means,' I said, confused.

'I don't think you do.' And then, after a pause, suddenly embarrassed, I saw him brace himself. 'I want us to get married.'

My heart seemed to have stopped right where it was. I found it difficult to look at him. Yet I could feel his anxious gaze upon me. I burst into laughter eventually. 'Really? It took you so much effort to say it though.'

'It was not a lot of effort. I just wondered whether you might have second thoughts about me and think that I am not reliable or something. But it's all I want, Tara Taneja, if it isn't obvious already.'

'You waited all these years until I get my inheritance, right?'

'Oh no, you saw right through me!'

We walked hand in hand by Dima Lake and I tried to remember the last time I had felt so much at peace. My heart was dancing, but we sat together quietly and watched the gentle swoosh of the wind against the lake, a lone boat in the distance and a few people down the path who were making stones skip on the water. I remembered my time at Sukhna Lake with Aman and the other thieves, and realized that I still hadn't told Nikku what had happened there. I dreaded telling him about the kiss with Aman, but I knew I had to. So I told him everything, from the time I got down from the bus in Chandigarh. He listened quietly and, at the end, I felt better for it. He wasn't happy about Aman, but he chose not to dwell on it. He was mad at how they had thrown me out of the car and handed me the drugs, but he also laughed at the entire situation, especially at how I had walked out of the police station. It felt as if that conversation had brought us closer.

When it was dark, I drove the Kinetic back, with him sitting behind me.

'These days with you, they were some of the best in the last few years,' he said to me, hugging me around the waist. 'Just like when we were younger.'

I parked the Kinetic and we walked around on our road, the same one where Nikku had first extended his hand of friendship by frailly committing to protecting me from stray dogs.

I held his hand. 'Now all our days will be together.'

Nikku chuckled. 'Well then, maybe I'll have a go at Sabharwal Stationers here in Siyaka. How bad can it be?'

'Really?'

'Of course not. I was joking! I can't possibly do Sabharwal Stationers.'

I squeezed his hand and was about to reply when I heard my name.

'Tara Taneja!' I heard a voice call out and turned around.

I couldn't believe it. It was *him*. All the way from Mathura. Vijay Mathur.

'Oh my God! What the hell are you doing here?'

He wasn't alone. There were at least five of his friends behind him, and one of them actually held a dhol. I looked at Nikku who was flabbergasted. He held on to me, but not protectively, rather as if he needed support. Neither of us could believe our eyes.

'Tara Taneja,' Vijay Mathur said walking forward. I clutched Nikku's arm in slight fear. 'I promised I would come for you, to ask for your hand in marriage, from your grandfather. And here I am. See? I always do what I promise.'

I yelled so loudly that he was startled. 'What is wrong with you? I told you I am with Nikku and I love him! I am going to marry him, not you. Do you understand?'

Vijay Mathur placed a hand on his heart, as if I had just shot him with an arrow. We stood in silence for some time. When I opened my mouth again, he held up his hand.

'No, don't say anything,' he said. 'I know you are saying that now. But you haven't heard my offer. Your grandfather hasn't heard my offer. I will go tell him. Sukhi, hit it!'

The guy with the dhol started playing it as I put my hands on my face in embarrassment. Nikku finally unfroze and fell to the ground, laughing. Throwing a look of disgust his way, I quickly followed the guys who had just walked into my house, led by Vijay Mathur. The dhol only grew louder as our neighbours popped their heads out, wondering what the celebration was about.

'Aye, Tara, are you getting married?' A woman called out from across the road. I ignored her. My own mother rushed out to see what was going on and obviously didn't know what to make of the scene—Nikku on the ground laughing, me running behind five men carrying a dhol and Vijay Mathur leading the march.

Inside the drawing room, Rohit and Mohit looked confused as Vijay Mathur removed his shoes and folded his hands in namaste and took a seat on the sofa, uninvited. The dhol guy kept on playing until Vijay Mathur held up a hand again.

'I would like to speak to Lalaji, please,' Vijay Mathur said professionally. Rohit and Mohit looked more confused than ever, glancing at me for answers.

'Listen, Vijay Mathur,' I said, 'I appreciate your determination but I already told you—I am not interested!'

'Lalaji, please,' he responded, talking directly to Rohit and Mohit.

'Who are you and why are you here?' Mohit asked.

'Myself Vijay Mathur,' he said. 'I was Tara's classmate in school. You don't remember me? We have met a few times. Anyway, I am here to ask for Tara's hand in marriage. Let me tell you what I own. We have four acres of land in UP and a shop in a prime location in Mathura. We have twelve cows and a house with five bedrooms. Tara will need nothing if she is with us. Moreover, let me tell you, I ask for no dowry.'

I was aghast. The nerve of this man. I decided that enough was enough and decided to tell him that if he didn't shut up and leave, I would call the police. To my complete and utter surprise, Rohit spoke up first. 'But can you not hear her? She said no. What the hell do you want to talk to Lalaji about?'

Vijay Mathur was shocked, but not more than me. I had never seen Rohit come to my defence.

'I was just hoping to talk to Lalaji. As the elder, I am sure he takes the decision—'

'We all take our own decisions,' Mohit said flatly, 'especially Tara.'

I could have cried with joy then, but the dhol guy decided that this was the moment to salvage a bad situation and started playing again. I had to shut my ears to block out the loud beats. Nikku entered, still grinning, and sat next to Vijay Mathur, crossing his arms and watching the whole tamasha unfold. The dhol guy kept on playing until Lalaji emerged, a dazed look on his face.

Vijay Mathur raised a hand to make the dhol guy stop and got up to touch Lalaji's feet. Instead of blessing him, Lalaji shot me a look of disdain. I stifled a giggle.

'Who the hell are you?' he asked Vijay Mathur.

'Myself Vijay Mathur, Lalaji. I used to live here with my mamaji. Guptaji? You know him. Tara and I were in the same school.'

Now Lalaji looked at Nikku, who tried to look serious but was clearly failing.

When Lalaji didn't say anything, obviously aggrieved by this uninvited gang entering his house, especially the dhol guy, Vijay Mathur went on.

'I am here with a marriage proposal.'

Lalaji stared at him blankly. 'I am sorry, but I have already chosen my bride.'

I laughed as Vijay Mathur shook his head frantically. 'No, I am here for Tara.'

Lalaji looked at me. 'Seriously, who is this joker? Did you already speak to him?'

'I did, but he said that he would only listen to you!'

Lalaji simply turned around and started walking away, Vijay Mathur yelling behind him. 'But I have twelve cows!'

'What about you, Nikhil?' Lalaji said. 'Don't you want to speak up at this point?'

Nikku got up, serious, and then started singing:

'Tamaatar jaisa laal,
bhediye ke baal,
He just wants a kiss
But he's a tai-tai phis!'

I could see Lalaji shaking with laughter.

Three Months Later

The wedding was supposed to be a small affair, but it turned out that nothing piqued the curiosity of the city more than the marriage of two people in their mid-seventies. We even had people coming from across the city to congratulate the couple. At Lallan Sweets, we worked doubly hard, a box of our special magic laddoos prepared for all the guests. I avoided addressing Kalawati because I didn't know what to call her. When I saw Lalaji so happy and radiant, nothing else mattered. Bauji too came all the way from Delhi and there was a joyous reunion. When he finally met Nikku, he surveyed him with the greatest strictness and asked him questions about his future.

My mother constantly wished for my father to have been around to see this happy day. I missed him too and hoped he was happy wherever he was.

Rohit, Mohit and I had bonded under the sacred oath. We didn't exactly see eye to eye on everything, but we had Lalaji as our mediator and consultant. Each day, we worked better with each other, laughing about our adventures on the road.

I noticed Mohit and Rohit too come into their own. They had refused to reveal the magic ingredient to Pappu Uncle. While he was hurt and felt betrayed, he finally understood: it wasn't theirs to tell. He hadn't shared the journey.

Nikku demanded that since he had been part of the journey, he should know the magic ingredient. I explained to him that it didn't work like that and that I had taken a sacred oath. So he kept trying to get the magic ingredient out of me by asking me the most unexpected of questions, hoping to catch me off guard.

'Taru, who was your favourite *Hum Paanch* sister?'

'Sweety.'

'She's the elder one?'

'The middle one.'

'And what's the magic ingredient?'

I looked at him, smiling and shaking my head. 'You try. I appreciate that.'

Nikku sighed in disappointment and then tried another way—to instigate me. 'Maybe you don't know the magic ingredient, that's why you can't tell me. Where's your Lalaji?

Let's go find him. It'll be nice to be around somebody who actually knows things.'

But I didn't give in, even though I was dying to let him know how warm he had gotten to the answer. He never fully gave up though.

The day we went to watch *Dilwale Dulhaniya Le Jayenge*, he said, 'As your future husband, I command you to tell me the magic ingredient.' Nikku said while we waited outside the theatre for the movie to begin.

'Oh shut up, Nikku.'

'What? I will be your husband, and they say I am allowed to command.'

'The only thing you'll be commanding is your tongue to mind itself.'

'Why? Are you planning to go back to Vijay Mathur?'

'It's an option I'd do well to consider . . .'

'I'm sure it'd be great fun to take care of the twelve cows . . .'

Later, all his cockiness vanished when I saw him almost-crying at the point when Amrish Puri let go of Kajol's hand and said, '*Ja, Simran, ja, jeele apni zindagi.*' He tried to wipe off his eyes when the credits rolled and the lights came on, but it was too late. I laughed uproariously. Contentment shone on his face as we exited; he was massively relived to see Raj and Simran together in the end.

'I win the bet then,' I told him. All around us were people who had just come out of the movie and couldn't stop talking about it. The vendors selling bhutta and budiya ke baal were clearly having a field day.

Nikku bowed. 'Hands down. Shah Rukh Khan is a superstar. You were absolutely right.'

I punched the air, delighted. 'But we never decided on the outcome of the bet!'

'Maybe we can take another trip,' he said, linking his arm with mine, 'but this time, the quest will be for Shah Rukh Khan. Siyaka to Bombay in a stolen car, a ditzy couple encountering a crazy dhaba-owner, a mysterious psychic and thugs from the moonshine mafia . . .'

'Don't forget the ghosts in the haveli,' I added.

'The ghosts were real, Taru.'

'Of course, they were . . .'

'Say it like you mean it.'

'I mean it!'

'I'll show you next time.'

'I am so excited about Bombay. How far is it anyway? We have to take some of our laddoos for Shah Rukh . . .'

Acknowledgements

This book is the result of my extremely Siyaka-like childhood—the long, summer evenings spent playing kho-kho, fighting about Gallery strategies and planning ultimate Holi battles—that I recall with intense vividness, large parts of which I have used in *Lallan Sweets*. So many years of my life were spent looking forward to the evenings when I could go out and play, and reading too. I have only Mum and Dad to thank for this.

Ever since I was a little girl, I wanted to go on an adventure, and so this story came easy to me: it's very likely that two people who grew up in this fantastic manner would go on an adventure like this. Make no mistake, this is me living vicariously through Tara.

I'd like to tell my sister, Rose, who helped me plot the most important bits but still hasn't read *Lallan Sweets* ('I only read *good* books, yaar'), I love you.

I also want to thank Roshini Dadlani, my fabulous editor, who not only has unwavering faith in my work but also great vision for what it can be. You are awesome!

A big thanks also to Aslesha Kadian for her detailed edits on the text, and to Khyati Behl for working so hard on my books.

The entire team at Penguin Random House India, thanks for making this book what it is!

A big hug to Mallika and Aarushi for their initial feedback, and to Sajili and cool mummy Mini for her '90s partying stories. Also, thank you, Shriti Tyagi, for your Bareilly stories, and Vielen Dank to Leon for being such a Nikku in Munich—it was a blast!

All my love to Sharan for his supportive attitude ('Taru and Nikku? Seriously? You couldn't find stupider names?'). If I could somehow thank you in all the books in the world, I'd do that. If only you could do me the giant favour of actually reading what I write . . .

My lovely readers, all my gratitude to you, for knowing that there is always a magic ingredient out there, but which we will never need because it's only how we perceive things that matters in the end, doesn't it?